Praise for

IN THE BLINK OF AN EYE

"Quite simply a masterpiece."   —Kate Forsyth, author of
                      Beauty in Thorns, Bitter Greens, and *The Wild Girl*

"A heart-wrenching, beautifully told story about tragedy and the slow journey toward hope. As Finn, Bridget, and Jarrah wade through their grief, readers will find themselves surprised by moments of grace. This story will linger long after the last page is turned."
                              —Nicole Baart, author of
                      Little Broken Things and *You Were Always Mine*

"This achingly beautiful novel broke my heart. And then put it back together."   —Wendy James, author of *The Golden Child*

"A beautiful work. One of the most moving and artistically satisfying endings I've read in a long while."
                        —Susan Johnson, author of *The Landing*

"A novel that will get into your bones—captivating, heartbreaking, and immensely beautiful."
                    —Eliza Henry-Jones, author of *In the Quiet* and *Ache*

"A poignant triptych of family grief and redemption that sees the author's prose leap to a new level of magnificence."
                    — Ashley Hay, author of *A Hundred Small Lessons*

ALSO BY JESSE BLACKADDER

The Raven's Heart
Chasing the Light

IN THE BLINK OF AN EYE

JESSE BLACKADDER

St. Martin's Press
New York

This is a work of fiction. All of the characters, organizations, and events portrayed in this novel are either products of the author's imagination or are used fictitiously.

IN THE BLINK OF AN EYE. Copyright © 2017 by Jesse Blackadder. All rights reserved. Printed in the United States of America. For information, address St. Martin's Press, 175 Fifth Avenue, New York, N.Y. 10010.

www.stmartins.com

Library of Congress Cataloging-in-Publication Data

Names: Blackadder, Jesse, author.
Title: In the blink of an eye / Jesse Blackadder.
Description: First U.S. edition. | New York : St. Martin's Press, 2019.
Identifiers: LCCN 2018041170 | ISBN 9781250199959 (hardcover) | ISBN 9781250199966 (ebook)
Classification: LCC PR9619.4.B559 I5 2019 | DDC 823/.92—dc23
LC record available at https://lccn.loc.gov/2018041170

Our books may be purchased in bulk for promotional, educational, or business use. Please contact your local bookseller or the Macmillan Corporate and Premium Sales Department at 1-800-221-7945, extension 5442, or by email at MacmillanSpecialMarkets@macmillan.com.

First published in Australia under the title *Sixty Seconds* by HarperCollins*Publishers* Australia Pty Limited

First U.S. Edition: March 2019

10 9 8 7 6 5 4 3 2 1

To help understand how a swimming pool functions, one should consider how the human body works. The heart circulates blood in the body much the same way that a centrifugal pump recirculates swimming pool water. The kidneys remove toxic wastes from the blood just as filters remove debris from the pool water. Just as the veins and arteries carry blood to and from the heart, so do a series of influent and effluent pool pipes.

Tom Griffiths, *The Complete Swimming Pool Reference,*
second edition

PROLOGUE

The boy steps into the day like he owns it – like he is, in fact, God and has conjured this up with a sweep of his hand before breakfast: this achingly blue sky, this currawong sending out a ringing call from the verandah post, this water dragon sunning on a warm rock to loosen her scales, cocking her head and blinking a yellow eye in his direction.

He breathes, a fast in-breath, sucking the day into his lungs like nourishment, and considers his kingdom. Today, where and what? Beneath his bare foot the ground is damp and alive, the worms reaching for the surface with its promise of moisture. It stormed in the night, and from everywhere rises the scent of soil opening, of grass reaching down its roots, of frogs waking from enchanted sleep, their dried skins cracking. He smells the formic pinch of the ants' relief at having survived the deluge, and the sticky sweet of the white flowers.

Another footfall, the ground pushing back up as though it delights in the press of him.

The limitless possibility of the moment shifts focus to something that ripples and dances, hurting his eyes with its intensity, beckoning. He steps out with a calm assurance, and as he approaches, the object of his desire fills his vision, calling him.

The fence rears up in front of him, blocking the way. He wraps his fingers around the bars and shakes. It rattles, but doesn't yield. He presses his face into the gap, trying to push through. On the other side, the water splits into dazzling prisms. It wants him. He feels it as a sure certainty in his belly, a tug on his navel with a promise of everything he could ever desire. He remembers the feeling of weightlessness, the delight of floating in the universe. The water promises to give it all to him again, putting him at the centre, the floating god of creation with the pulse of moving liquid in his ears.

From beyond the pool, a hissing sound and an acrid stink. He knows that smell and he wants it too.

'Dadda,' he calls, reaching up. 'Dadda!'

PART ONE

FINN

Later, Finn could trace the seismic shift back to the afternoon he stood in the fading light and slid the fine sandpaper over the curve of Huon pine. The initial scrape of grit had smoothed out to a soft glide, the grain of the wood revealing its hidden whorls. He lifted the sandpaper, puffed the fine dust away and ran his hand over the wood's surface. It rose under his fingers like something alive.

The light was nearly gone and the air, at last, felt slightly cooler. Finn's sweat had dried and crusted into a hard mix of salt and sawdust on his skin. Invisible creatures – frogs, crickets, he never knew what they were – burst into a racket outside his window, ushering in the evening.

He smoothed an oiled cloth over the haunch of wood, which rewarded him by glowing in the last of the light. He placed it on the ground, shoving aside the jumble of scrap metal with a twinge of guilt. *That's* what he was meant to be working on; his agent was convinced his clockwork constructions were the way to a breakthrough. But it didn't feel like real sculpture, not like his carving.

The piece Edmund had spotted during a Skype was a machine born out of Finn's frustration with getting from the kitchen to his studio, a clumsy two-handed operation with gates and latches and sliding doors in and out of the pool area. He'd put his mind to solving the problem, taking due account of the safety principles involved in pool fencing, and adding clockwork characterisations to amuse Toby. A wall-mounted system of pulleys and gears, styled as an owl, elegantly opened and automatically closed the gate between the verandah and the pool when Finn pulled the high brass lever. A second apparatus, with a dragon's head and outspread wings, operated the sliding doors linking the studio to the pool. Yes, he'd created them to look good – clunky, evocative creatures made of oversized cogs and gears, burnished metal and chains that fascinated Toby when they cranked into life. But before Edmund declared them art and named them – *Owl Sentry* and *Dragon Sentry* – Finn considered them simply functional.

Edmund had demanded a spec piece – he was sure he could sell one. Just like *Owl* or *Dragon*, he'd urged. But Finn had got only as far as gathering scrap metal, old machinery parts and gears and stacking them on the bench.

The sound of voices drifted over from the house and he looked out into the indigo-orange sky of a subtropical dusk. Bridget must have come home. When the wood had him, he didn't hear a thing. He never kept a clock in the workshop lest its hard little hands yank him back from his thrall. And so, not for the first time, he was late. He'd left the kids to their own devices and now she was home, and it was Friday. That meant a bottle of wine with dinner, and probably she'd want to fuck to throw off the week and he'd want to fuck because of the sensuality of the wood under his hands all day, and they'd mark the passage from the working week to the weekend and the relief that their marriage was still intact. Their sex life had been revitalised by what happened, at any rate, and thank God it turned out they still desired each other's bodies, no matter his convex belly and balding head and her bunions.

He should have started dinner, but he needed a swim. A quick plunge, no lights on, to sluice the dust and sweat from him; more satisfying than a shower. He pulled *Dragon Sentry's* heavy lever, and with a clanking of gears the thing opened the sliding doors of the studio and admitted him to the pool area.

After ten months he could still hardly believe Bridget had agreed to buy this purple weatherboard home, with its red trim, wonky doors that didn't lock, crooked corners and overgrown garden of bold tropical plants – mauve jacaranda, red poinciana, pink frangipani, yellow trumpet flowers. So different from their old brick bungalow in Hobart – and from the airy beach house Bridget had had in mind when making this sea change.

He shucked off his overalls and underpants at the pool's edge, leaned over the water and tilted, making a hole in the surface with his hands and pouring his body into it. Underwater, he rubbed at his arms, face, hair, loosening the dust so it detached and floated in little whorls and bubbles.

JARRAH

'Jawwah, weed it.'

'I'm busy.'

'*Weed it.*'

'Dad can read it. I've got homework.'

'WEED IT!'

'ALL RIGHT!'

I slapped my maths book shut, glad of the excuse, though I sighed and pushed myself up like it was a big effort. This was usually how it panned out in the afternoons. Dad distracted with his art, Mum busy and important and not home from work, me trying to do homework, and Toby trying to stop me. Changing towns hadn't changed that.

I flopped down on my bed. Toby clambered up, threw himself on my chest, and started to bounce up and down. 'Horsey!'

'Hey, we're meant to be reading.' I let him do it a few times and then reached over and picked up the tattered copy of his favourite book from the bedside table. '*The Monster King?*'

He gave a whoop of excitement. He never got sick of it. I took a deep breath, adjusted my voice and began.

Toby wriggled around and cuddled up next to me, waiting while I tucked my arm under his head. His blue eyes fixed on the pages as I read, putting on my best deep, gruff voice for the monsters so he shivered and squealed.

If it scared him so much, how come he still liked it?

I turned the final page.

'Gain!'

Toby would be happy if I read that book to him twenty times in a row. I heaved another dramatic, weary sigh and dragged out the words to make him laugh. 'Aaall right.'

The thing is, I didn't get bored. The feel of his small body against my side, his attention, the smell of his hair, kind of sweet and salty together. When it was just him and me, something churned in me so I could hardly stand it.

During the third reading the light changed. Mum was running late and Dad must have forgotten the time. I felt Toby's body soften and his breath deepen. His leg twitched, and I paused and looked down at him. He was asleep, way out of his naptime, one hand splayed on my chest, the other clutching a stray piece of my hair.

Two reasons he was my best friend. First, the obvious. He was the only one who never judged me. Never looked at me weirdly, never thought something was wrong with me.

I heard the engine in the driveway and closed my eyes. I could count the moments of peace left. I heard Mum pull on the handbrake, switch off the ignition, unclack the seatbelt, open the car door, scrabble for her handbag on the floor of the front seat. Her shoes crunched on the gravel. Five moments more of Toby and me. Four moments as she reached the verandah and slid the screen door open. Three as she stepped inside. Two as she started up the stairs. One as she called out.

'Yoo-hoo? Boys? Marital companion?'

Our mother's voice could reach Toby even in sleep. He jerked and his eyes flew open. In a single move he was upright.

'Mumma!' He squirmed off the bed and bolted for the door. I heard the rhythmic thud of his bare feet, the squeal as he caught sight of her at the top of the stairs, his leap into her arms. I heard snuggling, kissing, nonsense words. Felt that dig of jealousy.

No one would have blamed me for being jealous of Toby. Thirteen years younger than me, he'd turned up from nowhere. Before that I'd been the only sun in our little universe.

'Hey, Jarrah.' Mum stood at the door of my room, balancing Toby on her hip as she kicked off her shoes. 'Your dad's in the pool. I take it he's forgotten the time again?'

I sat up and scratched my hair. 'Looks like it.'

She smiled. 'At least it's Friday. Thai?'

'Pizza?' I countered.

'Pissa?' Toby chimed in, patting Mum's face with his small hands as he doubled my vote. 'Swim?'

She rolled her eyes. 'You guys win. But I choose next time, right? Jarrah – homework?'

I rolled my eyes right back at her and she laughed.

'Yeah, bugger homework. Let's swim.'

'Sure.'

She came over to the bed, Toby still clamped to her hip, and smiled down at me. She had a nice face. I didn't just think it because she was my mother. Curly dark hair, pale skin, blue eyes. She reached out and ruffled my hair. Curly and dark, same as hers.

'How was your day, boyo?'

I pulled a stupid face. 'Fine.'

Toby poked Mum's cheek and she laughed. 'Got to get out of these clothes. Thank God it's the weekend.'

She spun and strode out of the room, taking Toby with her. He glanced at me for a second over her shoulder before they disappeared.

That was us. Mum in her new dream job researching koala habitat. Dad looking after us and doing his carvings. Me getting through year ten.

No, I wasn't jealous of Toby. There was plenty to go around in our household. It wasn't that.

It was this – the second reason, the one I kept secret: I wished *my* voice could pull him out of his dreams and back into the world. I wished he loved me most, the way I loved him. I wished he were mine.

FINN

Coming up for a fourth breath, Finn's world exploded. Water rushed into his eyes and up his nose; waves slapped him. Three heads broke the surface and his wife's laughter pealed out. They'd bombed him. Toby clutched his mother, gulping, on the brink between laughter and sobs.

'You're on the pizza run, mister.' Bridget swooshed Toby through the water into Jarrah's arms and splashed Finn. 'And later you'll pay for forgetting dinner.'

He dived at her, found her, kissed her. 'Promise?'

'Get going! We're starving.' She leaned in, voice low. 'Take Jarrah.'

Finn lifted his head to look at his oldest son, who was bouncing Toby in his arms. 'Jarr, come for the ride?'

'Sure.'

'Me! Me!' Toby demanded.

'Go on, take all the testosterone. I need some girl time.' Bridget dived, pushing herself away from him, a dark streak under the surface.

Finn stroked to the steps and hauled himself out, glad of the dusk. They were a family comfortable with nudity, but lately he'd realised Jarrah was growing out of that. Going on for sixteen, last thing the boy wanted to see was his parents in the nick. It was a pity; Finn had loved the easygoingness of it in this hot climate. He scooted for a towel.

'Hurry,' Bridget reminded him from the end of the pool. 'I've ordered, and I hear the whimper of chorizo on the chopping block.'

A scramble of pulling on clothes, sprinting to the car, belting Toby into his seat. Finn spun out of the carport, kicking up a bit of gravel for Bridget's benefit. They were boys. It was Friday.

He glanced over at Jarrah as they swung out onto the suburban street. The light striped Jarrah's face and for a moment it wasn't his son there at all. Someone older, stranger, sat in the passenger seat.

'Jarrah?'

They passed a streetlight and Jarrah turned to him in an easy, familiar movement, an eyebrow raised slightly, and the moment was gone. 'Yep?'

Finn swallowed. 'Sorry about dinner, mate. But hey. You avoid my cooking.'

'Yeah.' Jarrah turned away to look out at the garages and driveways and curtained windows flipping past.

'Got any weekend plans?'

Jarrah adjusted the window minutely. 'Dunno. Homework. Might go to a movie with some kids from school.'

A wave of helplessness broke on Finn. Until a year ago, he'd known his son. He was the stay-at-home parent. He'd seen Jarrah more or less every day of his life. But since then, he'd lost him. He still wasn't sure if Jarrah had overheard the furious whispers in the bedroom when Bridget found out, of what Jarrah understood about their sudden decision to move north. Did he wonder why no one ever mentioned the Neumanns any more?

He glanced again at the silhouette of Jarrah's face as they passed another light. They'd had enough change. Finn didn't want any more.

'Dadda,' Toby said from the back seat. 'Where we live?'

Finn took a deep breath. 'Ready, boys?'

'Oh no.' Jarrah rolled his eyes.

'Forty-eight Tumbulgum Road, Mur-will-um-bah ...'

Toby, still unable to get his tongue around the early syllables, hit the car seat with his fists. 'More!'

'New South Wales, Australia, Planet Earth, the Milky Way ...' Finn paused. Were they with him?

'THE CENTRE OF THE UNIVERSE!'

Toby yelled what he could manage, in rough unison. Jarrah at least joined in, if not enthusiastically. Finn felt his shoulders relax. It was all good. They were all good.

BRIDGET

The text comes pinging in on your phone and you pick it up in a reflex action. He's never sent anything you couldn't read out loud to Finn, there's no suggestion of anything going on whatsoever, but you feel guilty anyway. He shouldn't be texting now, out of hours, on a Friday night at the start of a family weekend. He should know better.

No, that's stupid. Why shouldn't a colleague send a text after hours? 'Hours' is such a last-century concept anyway. Work bleeds over into life now. The midnight emails, the Sunday afternoon 'catching up': it's all normal, even for the North Coast sea-change class, supposedly beyond such things.

<Hope she remembered you today ☺>

You pour another glass of wine, aware you've necked the first one in five minutes. Finn won't notice you're on the second by the time he gets back with the pizza. Not that he would say anything.

You usually visit your mother in the nursing home after work on Thursday, but you missed yesterday and squeezed it in today instead. Finn is distracted, and Jarrah's in his own teenage world, so neither of them asked how she was. Part of choosing the North Coast was bringing your mother closer to where she spent her childhood, in the hope it would help her faltering memory. Or at least feel familiar. But today was bad. She didn't recognise you at all.

Only Chen has asked how you feel about it. Nothing wrong with that, is there? Chen has, after all, stepped into the best-friend hole left in your life by Sandra's expulsion. You're both scientists: he the big-picture ecologist to your fine detail biologist. You share a similar sense of humour and a taste for optimism, rare in your profession.

But you know what's wrong with it. He's nine years your junior and you've caught yourself looking at the taut, smooth curve of his arms when he wears a short-sleeved shirt. You swap witty repartee. More recently, your eyes meet and you grin without needing to articulate the joke.

It's a new step, this text. Friday night, and personal, and far too insightful. It's dangerous. You moved here for a fresh start in your eighteen-year marriage. You agreed to put what happened behind you and so far it's on track. Mostly. But you don't stop Chen, and you answer his texts and you glance at his arms and both of you laugh just a bit too long. No one has said anything – not him, not you – and of course it's possible you're imagining it.

But you don't think so.

You'll send back a breezy text. <Nope. She thought I was the nurse.> Except when you go to type it, you realise how unfunny it is.

The second glass of wine has gone the way of the first. You switch to mineral water. They'll be back any second now, and you get yourself together and start clearing the table and throwing down napkins and glasses.

When the landline bleats, you jump and knock your glass over. You snatch up a cloth and multi-task, mopping as you answer.

'Bridge, it's Eddie. Finn's not picking up.'

'Pizza run.' You're not sure you like the way Edmund, with the prospect of making some actual money from your husband at last, seems to have become his new best friend.

'Fuck and bother. He'll really want to hear this.'

You roll your eyes. Edmund loves a drama. 'What?'

'Sculpture by the Quay had a late dropout. I've pulled some strings. If Finn can get that piece finished by Thursday, he's in.'

You've sopped up most of the wine now and you head to the sink, wedging the phone between shoulder and ear to squeeze the cloth. 'Sounds great.'

'Not *great*, Bridget. We're talking major breakthrough. Do you know how many people see this show over New Year? He's picked the steampunk zeitgeist. He'll be keeping you in the accustomed manner.'

You laugh, though not unkindly. Finn's sculpture hasn't ever brought in much more than it costs, but it's made him happy, and meant you could pursue your career while he looked after the boys. It's worked out well all round, as Edmund knows. Sudden artistic breakthrough isn't something you've factored into your plans.

'I'm serious. This is huge. You'll need to step up.'

Edmund can still rile you, after all these years. 'What's that supposed to mean?'

'Put him first. At least for a week, so he meets the deadline. See what happens.'

He doesn't know about Finn's betrayal last year – at least you don't think he knows – and injustice rises in your throat like gorge. 'Listen, I've—'

'Settle. You know what I'm saying. Get him over the line, OK? And now you get to tell him, half your luck.'

You hang up, and moments later you hear slamming doors and feet thudding up the verandah steps. Finn comes in last, behind Toby, who's about to tip into fractiousness from hunger, and Jarrah, whose face is set in studied teenage blankness.

Finn glances at you as he sets the pizzas down. 'What?'

You grin at him, teasing. 'I should make you wait …'

'What, woman?' he demands.

'Eddie called. You're in some minor show in Sydney. Now, what was it again? … Something by the Quay?'

He stares at you, then relaxes. 'Yeah, very funny. They selected months ago.'

'Someone dropped out. Edmund knows the right people. Finish that piece by Thursday and you're in.'

The way his face changes shows you how much this means. He lumbers across the kitchen, banging past the table, and grabs you in a Finn bear-hug that squeezes the breath from your lungs as he lifts you up. You beat him on the back and he loosens his grip and lowers you, grinning like a kid.

And something loosens inside, something hard you didn't know was still knotted so tight. You said you'd forgive him and maybe, finally, you really have. Your kiss lingers with the promise of later.

'Oh, get a room,' Jarrah says, making a face.

You make one right back at him. 'Your dad's only in Sydney's newest outdoor sculpture show, boyo. Worth celebrating. Now get Toby sorted.'

Jarrah wrestles an overwrought Toby into a highchair, where he pounds his fists on the tray of the highchair with an energy that'll turn quickly to tantrum. You quickly slide the pizzas on to platters and Finn cracks a beer, refills your wine, opens a Coke for Jarrah.

You lift your glass high. 'Here's to the steampunk zeitgeist. Cheers!'

Finn clinks his bottle against your glass, and against Jarrah's soft drink. 'Punk-what-what?'

You shrug. 'That's you. So Eddie says.'

Finn fangs down his first slice of pizza in two bites and grins at you with his mouth full. He's a bear of a man, a blacksmith from some medieval village, with his broad shoulders and big belly, everything about him substantial. Smiling back, you make the decision. You'll put this thing with Chen away. You won't reply to his text tonight. You won't think about his arms. You'll throw yourself behind this opportunity for Finn. After all these years of pottering away in the studio, selling a piece here and there, he deserves his chance, and God knows he's talented. He's been carving wood all these years when he should have been metalworking, that's all. He's found his medium now.

It occurs to you things might be about to change drastically. Who'll look after Toby? If this really is Finn's big moment, you need to adjust. You might need a nanny, or a cleaner, or, please God, someone to take over the cooking.

Time enough to talk about that over the weekend, but not tonight. Tonight is about celebrating, about sex, about coming home. You'll switch off the mobile. You'll stop holding back. You'll give yourself to him.

You have no idea, yet, how long it will be before you'll do that again.

17

JARRAH

Mum was always that obvious. 'Subtle as a sledgehammer,' Nanna Brenn used to say back when she was alive. Like I didn't see her whisper to Dad in the pool right before Dad asked me to go with him to pick up the pizzas, as if he'd just thought of it.

I knew what was going on. She was pretending to send us to Great White Pizza, which didn't deliver, because their capriccioso was better and Toby liked the jaws on the front door. The real reason was that Laura Fieldman worked there most Friday nights and I had a crush on her. I guess Mum thought she was doing me a favour.

Laura Fieldman had noticed me all right. Just enough to work out I was into her. Me, Jarrah Brennan, nerd. Her, top of the year ten pack of long-legged, long-haired, long-on-confidence girls who existed in another universe. Just two weeks back I'd walked past them in the quad and a snorting laugh had rung out from one of Laura Fieldman's friends. My face burned. The kind of burn that comes back in the dark and makes you roll over and drag the covers over your head and wish you were dead.

My hunch was confirmed when we pulled into the car park and Dad turned off the engine and tossed his wallet in my lap. 'Can you boys handle it?'

He'd watched me once before trying to stammer out a pizza order to Laura. I guess he didn't want to get in the way. Or it was too embarrassing, watching me make an idiot of myself. I was pretty nervous, so I started mucking around with Toby. I teased him for a moment, standing outside his door pretending I wasn't going to open it. When he started to screw up his face I threw it open. 'Tricked you!'

I'd timed it right. He laughed. I wrestled him out of the seatbelt, picked him up, dumped him on the ground. 'Ready to face the shark?'

Toby looked over at the yawning jaws wrapping the door in a tunnel of teeth, and shivered. He reached up with his arms. 'Jawwa.'

I picked him up and headed in that direction, taking little steps to build the anticipation. He clung on tighter and tighter as we approached, half afraid, half thrilled.

'Feeling brave?' I whispered in his ear.

I took a tighter hold of him and ran, roaring, right into the shark's jaws. Pushed the door open and staggered inside, Toby squealing in my arms, the bell on the door clanking above our heads. Straightened up, laughing.

'Look, here's Little Mummy.'

I hadn't seen them from outside. Five of them, watching us from the window booth. I froze.

'How's your baby going?'

There's always one who leads it. His name was Dave, I was pretty sure. A year above me at school. I'd felt his eyes on me in the playground and known he was trouble. I'd been avoiding him, and now I was cornered.

'Mumma?' Toby asked, confused.

The five of them laughed. Toby laughed too, joining in, and I had to get him away from them. Laura Fieldman was standing behind the counter, her face blank. Hard to know which was the worse option.

'Go on, Little Mummy, go get your pizza.'

Toby squirmed to be put down, arching his back and kicking out. I let him slide to the floor, but grabbed his hand, praying he wouldn't have a tantrum. I tugged him towards the counter, sensing their eyes on my back and the mutter as they tried out some new insults among themselves.

'Can I help you?' Surely Laura had heard them, but she showed no sign.

My voice was an insect squeak. 'Ah, hi. Takeaway? Brennan?'

She checked the docket on top of two boxes. 'Large Hawaiian? Large capriccioso?'

Toby looked up at her. 'Haw-wan?'

Her face lit up in a smile and he grinned back, all toothy charm without even trying. It was an opening, kind of.

'That's us.' I scooped Toby up so she had to look at my actual face as well as his. Toby kept smiling at her as I prised out Dad's credit card with one hand, trying to think of something to say. 'Rotten maths test, eh?'

A snort from the booth near the door. *'Rotten maths test, eh?'* in a high-pitched voice.

Laura Fieldman dragged her gaze from Toby to me. There was a pause long enough for me to absorb the highlights in her dark hair, pulled back into a ponytail, and the precise brown of her eyes, before she said, 'Wasn't too bad.'

She looked back at Toby and I typed in Dad's PIN. A hundred years later the machine ground out a receipt, which she spiked, and a second one that she slapped on top of the pizza boxes. I hesitated, too gutless to face the booth boys.

'Say goodbye, Toby,' I instructed.

'Ba ba!' Toby grinned again and Laura's smile widened.

The door opened, the bell clanged, and another family stamped inside, spilling kids in every direction and giving me cover. I shoved Toby to my hip, snatched up the boxes with my free hand, turned. Did a bit of ducking and weaving to keep the family in between me and the boys. Not that it helped.

'Bye bye, Toby. Bye bye, Little Mummy.'

'Ba ba,' Toby said. Then: 'Dadda.'

A moment away from escape, we were stopped by Dad coming in the door. 'Sorry,' he said. 'I want some garlic bread.'

'Too late. Pizza'll be cold. And Toby's had enough.' I shoved Toby into Dad's arms and pushed past him. I heard Dave call out, 'Bye, boys!' behind me, in the kind of smarmy voice guys like him used when your parents could hear.

I slouched in the front seat while Dad buckled Toby in the back. Across the car park, I could see them laughing at me through the window. Go, go, go.

Dad got in beside me, started the engine, pulled out slowly. 'Friends from school?'

Did he know? 'Not really,' I said.

'What about the girl? Isn't she in your class?'

'One or two subjects.'

'She looks nice.'

'Mm,' I said, in a conversation-closing way. Sure she looked nice, Dad, if you weren't some speck on the hide of year ten. If you hadn't just been called Little Mummy in front of her.

I switched on the radio and cranked up the volume. Nineteen-eighties rock filled the car: Dad's favourite station. I didn't bother asking for mine. Just wound the window all the way down and pushed my face into the wind to watch the streets whizzing past as we headed home. It was getting dark. The pizza burned my legs through the box.

I'd been called a fag plenty of times. Anyone who didn't fit in was a fag. I was used to it. But this was different. They'd seen me with Toby and somehow they knew.

FINN

Finn put the phone down in a daze. Saturday morning continued a run of steamy days trying to set another hottest spring record, and Edmund had rung with a new commission and the chance of a second.

'High four figures,' he said. 'I'll have you up to five soon.'

Finn's belly churned with an unfamiliar mix of excitement and nerves. Maybe the heat was making him delirious. He headed back out to the pool area, where the boys were playing in the water and Bridget was stretched on a deckchair, reading the weekend paper. Told her.

She lifted her sunglasses to stare at him. 'How much did you say?'

'Eddie says hang on and enjoy the ride.' Finn threw himself down into a beanbag, grabbed his hair and pulled so it stood on end and lifted his scalp. 'This happens to other people, Bridge.'

'It's your breakthrough moment, Steampunk.' Bridget sounded like she didn't quite believe it. 'Can you do it?'

Finn suppressed down a squirm of guilt at the time he'd spent carving when he should have been doing metalwork. He calculated. '*Dragon Sentry* took three weeks. Eddie needs the

Sculpture by the Quay piece in five days. Then the commission ASAP after that.'

'Christ.' Bridget blinked. 'But you've already been working on the new piece, haven't you?'

'Yes,' Finn said slowly. 'Ish.'

Bridget lowered her glasses again. 'Better check if I can take some leave. We need child care!'

'What d'you mean? Toby can hang out with me like usual.'

Bridget laughed and shook her head. 'Get real. This is the big league. You can't look after a toddler.'

Finn leaned back in the beanbag and glanced down at the pool where Jarrah was playing with Toby. The kid was giggling and squealing, like he usually did. Jarrah was solemn. He'd been that way a long time. Since he started school, or maybe earlier. Funny how brothers could be so different.

Finn had been the stay-at-home parent for Jarrah while Bridget finished her PhD and worked long hours, tutoring undergrads, marking their endless assignments. He'd loved it, especially when Jarrah was small. Loved carrying him around the hilly streets of Hobart in the backpack, or hiking up Mount Wellington with Jarrah burbling and waving his fists. Loved parking him in a safe spot on the studio floor while he carved. He was good at all of it, except cooking. Bridget had lowered her food expectations and Jarrah knew nothing different.

Finn had wanted more kids. Dreamed of a big Irish Catholic family like the ones his ancestors bred. Bridget was up for it, kind of, though not on the same schedule: she needed more time to establish herself at work. They'd started trying for a second child in a vague way when Jarrah was five. Then her father died and mother started going downhill. Finn never

dreamed it would take another nine years and a miscarriage. They were almost ready to give up when Toby finally came along. Finn hadn't broached trying again. Looked like two might be as good as it got.

A squirt of water hit him on the cheek.

'Dadda!' Toby, armed with a water pistol, Jarrah helping with the aim.

'Right!' Finn got to his feet. He crouched, swung his arms and leaped, tucking up his legs against his belly for maximum impact, knowing his ability to displace a major volume. Hit the water with a whump and heard Bridget's shriek and Toby's squeal as he went under.

He surfaced, grinning. She was sodden. Trying to look cranky, but smiling.

'Gotcha,' he said.

Toby was straining from Jarrah's arms and Finn reached out, grabbed him and swung him onto his shoulders. Then held out his hand. 'Come on, Bridge.'

She shook her head then launched herself at them without warning, straight from sitting. Splashed them all, all over again. Even Jarrah laughed.

'I'll take the boys to the beach this afternoon, and you can get some work done,' Bridget said. 'We'll swing by and see Mum on the way back.'

'But it's Saturday!' Saturday was sacred. Even when she was working hard, even during the PhD.

'Steampunks don't get Saturdays. Or Sundays.'

Finn lifted Toby off his shoulders and handed him back to Jarrah. He waded to the steps and climbed them, his sodden clothes hanging heavy as he rose from the water.

'Hey, this is good news, remember,' she called after him.

It was. It was. But the day felt heavy suddenly. Toby was too young to go into full-time child care. He was only two and a half. Finn had expected another couple of years of gradually handing him over to the world. He wasn't ready to let him go.

'I'll bring you a coffee,' she said, smiling. 'Now scoot!'

At his downcast face, she swam over, pulled herself up and gave him a hug. 'It's your turn, Finn. We're all with you. Go for it.'

Her hair was slicked back, her eyelashes wet. Jesus, she was gorgeous. He squeezed her, lifting her up out of the water. 'I love you, woman.'

'You too, Steampunk. Now make us proud. I'll make some calls about child care before we head to the beach. Maybe we can drum up a nanny or something for the first week.'

The studio, closed up all morning, was stifling. Finn opened the windows and reluctantly pulled on his stiff overalls. Art had never been pressured before, but Edmund was going to stay on his back. He'd been alarmed but pragmatic when he learned of Finn's lack of progress. Suggested that Finn assemble a free-standing clockwork creature that opened and closed a small gate. Audiences could walk through it as part of the outdoor sculpture experience. When the show was done, it could be adapted and reassembled for the first commission. It would deliver just what the customer wanted: an opening device mounted inside their wrought-iron gate, visible from the street but out of reach, triggered remotely once the person inside the house had ascertained they wanted to let the visitors in. Which in itself signified a lifestyle outside Finn's imagining.

Sweat trickled down from his armpits. No welding, he decided. That was for early morning when it was still cool, or nighttime. He'd spread out the components on the floor, see what else he needed and hope to God he could replicate the creation of *Owl* and *Dragon*.

Would he ever get used to the heat? Finn's beloved leather jacket was turning mouldy in the cupboard, barely needed in what passed for winter so far north. It wasn't even summer yet. They'd timed their arrival nicely nine months ago in February for the start of the school year, just catching the last of the heat, and it had nearly wiped him out then. Winter had been superb – cool nights, warm days; he'd have been happy if it stayed just like that.

He heard voices drifting in from the pool: splashing, Toby's high-pitched squeals of delight, Jarrah's voice, barely raised, Bridget's laughter. Whatever happened with the artworks didn't really matter, he reminded himself. Look what he had.

He wouldn't forget it again. He'd taken his family for granted, back in Tasmania. Hadn't thought what he was risking. Hadn't meant to risk it at all. Sandra Neumann was Bridget's best friend and the two families hung out. Finn liked her professor husband Hans well enough, though they didn't have much in common. Jarrah played with their son Oliver. It had been that way for years, and Finn had no idea why, in the course of a long, drunken evening at the Neumanns', something shifted between him and Sandra. He'd followed her into the kitchen to help clear up, and they'd both giggled when their hips bumped at the sink, and the next thing they'd been kissing like crazy.

He'd pulled apart from her – faster than he wanted to, slower than he should have – and shook his head like a dog coming out of water. His groin ached. His wife and her husband were in the next room. All their kids were sleeping upstairs.

Sandra stared at him, guilty and rumpled and suddenly very sexy. 'That can't ever happen again.'

But it did. Twice. Each time hotter and more dangerous. More fumbling, more grinding, more exploration.

The thing was, it took him by surprise. Sure, their sex life had been quiet after Toby was born – but he was sure it would come back once they started sleeping normally again, just like it had with Jarrah. He didn't know why Sandra was suddenly so attractive, until he thought back and realised Bridget hadn't looked at him in that hungry way for a long time.

Finn picked up a cog and ran his hands around its rim. Tasmania was his old life. The long days and long nights of high latitudes, the dusks that lingered for hours, the cold. Woodwork. Leather jackets. Open fires. And family – brother, sisters, father. It was their Irish blood, he reckoned. The Brennans and Tasmania were a natural fit.

Metalwork, it seemed, was his new life. Instead of living in sight of those tall Tasmanian forests, he now resided in a landscape shaped by molten heat and pressure, an extinct volcano, whose crooked core loomed over the town, visible for miles. Now he was a welder, not a carver, and the digital world wanted his machines, wanted cogs and gears, wanted a fitter and turner-turned-artist to remind them how things worked mechanically.

So be it. He'd have been happy in Tasmania forever, and he hated being away from the rest of his family. But after Bridget found out about Sandra and him, she demanded they leave Hobart. Having felt the possibility of losing her, he'd have gone anywhere she wanted.

JARRAH

Didn't really want to go to the beach, but Mum insisted. She wanted to take Toby and me to visit Nan on the way home too. So I got my stuff, chucked some things in a bag for Toby, buckled him into his car seat. Normally I'd recite *The Monster Kings* from the front while he turned the pages on his lap in the back, but today I turned on the radio and pulled down my sunglasses.

'I should have asked if you wanted to bring a friend,' Mum said when we pulled into the car park at Kingscliff.

'Doesn't matter. Billy's busy with homework today.' Billy's few visits to our place meant he was now my 'friend' when one was mentioned or needed.

I carried Toby over the tarmac, the hot wind biting into us, Mum coming up behind with the bags. It wasn't even worth bringing the beach umbrella, not in that wind.

I'd never told her, but I hated the beach. I could swim all right in still water, but that beach was scary. Waves smashed down on the shore as far as you could see. I'd grown up in Tasmania, fair-skinned, swimming only occasionally. Running was what I'd been good at, not water sports. Too late to catch up now.

In front of the surf club the water was full of confident boys – and a scatter of girls – carving up the waves on sharp little surfboards, running up the sand afterwards to shake the water out of their bleached surfie hair and lie down in rows, all flat stomachs and fluorescent swimmers.

Not exactly my scene. And with Mum and Toby, I was horribly visible.

A gust of wind swept down the beach, chucking sand at us as we laid down our towels. Toby screwed up his eyes, ready to howl. Normally I'd have picked him up, wiped his eyes, sorted it. But not any more. I had to be careful. Even with the wind, the beach was full of people. For sure there'd be kids from school here, the ones who were too cool to play weekend sport. Turned away and started plastering disgusting sunscreen on my arms.

'Jawwa!'

Pretended I didn't hear. Stared at the waves, rubbing the muck into my pale skin. Let Toby go from a little howl to a big one, until finally Mum picked him up, patted him, brushed the sand from his eyes. She shot me a look.

'Can you put some of that on your brother when you've finished?'

'I'm hot. Can't I swim first?'

Didn't wait for an answer, just shoved the sunscreen bottle at Toby and left them standing there. Walked down the beach feeling pasty and wrong. Splashed into the waves like I was going out there, and hid in the crowds when the water got to my thighs.

I flopped around for a while, keeping a low profile, ducking my head under the whitewash. Wishing we could just go back home where I didn't feel so exposed. When I reckoned enough time had gone by, I headed back up the beach, past boys and girls with gleaming tans and big sunglasses. Back to Mum and Toby, who was grizzling.

'He's still got sand in his eyes. I'll have a quick dip then we might go for an ice-cream,' Mum said.

I nodded and sat down. Mum strode off in a spray of sand. Toby banged the shovel on the plastic bucket to indicate that I should help with the sandcastle. I knew that game. I'd make one and he'd smash it. For as long as I was willing to keep going.

'Not today.' I put my sunnies on and draped a towel over my shoulders.

Toby hit the bucket harder and I turned my head away from him. A full-scale tantrum was just what I needed.

'Jawwa!'

'Shut up, Toby!' I hissed at him.

His lip trembled and he started to cry. I knew if I took him onto my lap I could comfort him. I forced myself to sit still, ignoring him. It took everything I had.

He was still crying when Mum came up the beach. 'Jesus, Jarr,' she said, picking him up. 'Wanna come for a dip, Toby boy?'

He stopped crying, gave me a disgusted look and clung to her. 'No. Ice-cweam.'

'Yeah, I'm with you on that,' she said. 'Let's get out of here.'

I just about broke into a run to get away from the beach. We crossed over to the ice-cream parlour. Figured it was high-risk, like the pizza place and the beach, so I stood at the other end of the counter from Mum and Toby. Kept my eyes on the ice-cream, didn't look around. Mum didn't want Toby dribbling his all over the seats, so we perched on those stupid white metal

chairs ice-cream parlours always have, and I watched Toby
dribble chocolate down his bare belly, before dropping the last
of it on the ground and launching into a screaming fit.

I let Mum carry him back to the car and wrestle him into the
booster seat. He threw himself around, red in the face, roaring.
I sat in the front saying nothing. She finally got the seatbelt
buckled and slid into the driver's seat. We pulled out, with the
sound of Toby's shrieks blocking all conversation.

The nursing home was on the road out of town. Toby fell
silent about halfway there. It was all right for him. No matter
how forgetful Nan was, she always loved Toby.

Mum parked the car and turned her head. 'Oh, bugger,' she
said softly.

I looked over my shoulder. Toby had fallen asleep, his head
slumped to one side.

'I'll stay here with him if you want to go in,' I said. 'She
never remembers me anyway.'

Mum hesitated. 'Let's just go home,' she said at last. 'I saw her
yesterday. We can come another time, hey?'

'Sure.'

She got the car out on the road and turned inland and I knew
what was coming.

'Is everything OK?' She always asked that kind of thing
when we were driving.

'Yeah, good.'

'Really?'

'Yep.'

'You know you can always talk to your dad and me about
anything.'

'I know.'

Up ahead Mount Warning came into view. It gave me something to look at.

'We'll have to pull together to help Dad,' Mum went on. 'I need you to help me with Toby, especially till we get a new routine organised. Can I count on you?'

'Sure. Can we put the radio on?'

I was happy for Dad; it wasn't that. But I was planning to do less with Toby, not more. I chose my station, the one loud enough so we couldn't talk any more, though she made me turn it down so Toby didn't wake up. I felt sticky and sandy and sunburned, in spite of all that stuff I'd rubbed on my skin.

Little Mummy.

It was late by the time we pulled up. Mum parked outside the gate and looked over her shoulder. 'Look at him,' she said softly.

I turned. Toby's head drooped. His belly was sticky with ice-cream and sand crusted his eyelashes and hair and feet. His lower lip stuck out.

'I'll get all the stuff,' Mum murmured. 'Can you bring him in? You're good at waking him without drama.'

She gathered the damp, sandy piles of stuff out of the boot and headed through the gate and across the lawn. I opened Toby's door quietly and looked down at him.

People love seeing a kid asleep but he made my chest hurt just as much when he was asleep as awake. I couldn't help it. I loved him way too much.

I glanced around, just to make sure I was alone, then put my hand on his head.

'Toby? Wakey-wakey? Home-again-home-again-jiggedy-jig.'

He stirred, blinked, opened his eyes. Looked at me.

For a minute it was like he knew exactly what I'd done. But maybe I'd imagined it, because he blinked again, stretched, then smiled and held out his arms. 'Jawwa.'

There was no one to see me unbuckle him, lift him out, hold him close, ignoring the sticky ice-cream gluing us together. No one saw me kiss the top of his head and the moment of sweetness that came over him when he put his arms around my neck and squeezed me as hard as he could.

'Sorry, Toby.' I whispered. 'Sorry.'

Took my time to carry him across the lawn. I didn't want Mum or Dad wondering why my eyes were red.

BRIDGET

Toby seems to know something's different, come Monday morning. You hear him galloping towards your bedroom even earlier than normal, at the first hint of daylight. He explodes through the door, pulls himself up on the bed and throws himself on you, forcing out your breath with a sudden 'OOF' and poking you in the eye as he tries to peel back the lid. He demands his book and you murmur a recitation, eyes closed, as he lies beside you turning the pages.

'Gain! Gain!'

'Go ask your brother.'

As Toby thunders out of the room Finn rolls over with a sleepy sigh and tries to draw you close. You twist your head to look at the bedside clock. 'Don't go all soft and cuddly. It's time to get up.'

'I'm a steampunk, remember,' he murmurs in your neck. 'Our best time is night. Like vampires.'

He's been a hobby artist too long. You wonder if he knows what he's in for, having to work to a deadline. Like you've had to for years. Has he really got it in him? Tough love is the way to go, you reckon.

'Oh no you don't, mister. Four days, remember? So get up, get the coffee on and get going.'

You shove him. It has no measurable impact on his bulk, but he sighs and rolls the other way.

'Cruel,' he says, stretching. 'Cruel and unusual punishment.'

'Yeah, well this is the price of success, mate. Your wife has to get up an hour earlier and get the household organised and take Toby to some unknown babysitter and go to work late, and she's not used to it. Did you hear me say "coffee"?'

'OK, OK!' He swings his legs over the side and swivels into a sitting position. 'I'll remember this moment in my prize acceptance speech. *I'd like to thank my wife for her utterly stinting support.*'

The sound of Toby's raised voice echoes down the hallway and you judge that Jarrah too has run out of reading patience. You throw back the sheet and get up. In truth, it isn't much earlier than usual for you, but Finn's been making the family breakfast and packing lunches since forever. All you've had to do is eat and walk out the door.

Today it's you who'll do breakfast and lunches and drop Toby off at the one child-care provider in Murwillumbah who can squeeze him in for three days until you find something more permanent. You'll take the fourth day off and stay home to make sure Finn finishes by Thursday, and then you'll make longer term plans. You check the time and decide you can trade off a hot shower for a quick dip to wake you up.

The pool is limpid and cool in the early morning, the air melodic with butcherbird song. You step into the water, gasping, dive under, and swim a couple of laps. Rinse off under the outdoor shower, throw on pants and shirt, and make your way to the kitchen. Finn has coaxed the coffee from his beloved Atomic and he hands you a cup, short and strong and dark, and heads upstairs for a shower. Jarrah, dressed for school, is playing with Toby on the floor. They both look up at you expectantly, and for a weird moment you don't know what to do. You've come to rely almost completely on Finn for household matters. A kind of domestic uselessness, more typical in men than women, has crept up on you.

'Earthlings, for breakfast, eat what do you?'

'It's not rocket science, Mum.' Jarrah stands, lifts Toby into the highchair, heads to the cupboard. He pulls out Weet-Bix, brown sugar, bowls; grabs a banana. 'I'll make his cereal. Then he likes toast soldiers with Vegemite. Can you do that?'

'Manage it, I can. You, what about?'

'Same as Toby. Without the soldiers. Just a straight cut across the middle. No diagonals.'

Is Jarrah teasing? You smile and try to relax a little. 'And lunch?'

'Dad normally makes me a sandwich. Cheese and ham or something.'

'Right. It's not just me who's getting spoiled.' You open the fridge. 'And the bread is where?'

'In the freezer, Mum. Keeps it fresh.'

'Cut me some slack, Jarr.'

He rewards you with a little smile, for which you are grateful. As you construct a sandwich and the boys start eating – Toby spreading most of his food around the corners of the highchair – you realise you're not exactly sure how Jarrah gets to school. You, the early starter, always leave the house first. Does Finn drive him? Does he get a bus? Perhaps he rides his bike. Perhaps it's a mix of all three depending on the day, such as if he has sport on. He used to do athletics in Hobart but for some reason he didn't take it up after the move. He plays soccer at school, you know that, or at least he did earlier in the year. Is the season still going?

Do you qualify as a neglectful mother for not knowing these things?

Finn clomps through the kitchen, kisses you goodbye, and heads outside. 'Work hard, Steampunk,' you call after him.

'Need a lift?' you ask casually as Jarrah puts his bowl in the dishwasher.

'Nup.' He heads towards the door, slinging his pack over his shoulder. 'Bye.'

You turn. 'Kiss?'

He comes back for a quick peck on the cheek. He smells teenage – something sweet like hair gel, and underneath it rank growing boy. Has he even showered?

'Might want some deodorant.' You smile to take the sting out.

'Thanks a million, Mum.'

'Better to hear it from me. Just duck back in and slap it on. Take you a second.'

He trudges back towards the bathroom and you bustle with the plates and Toby's toast, feeling you've passed some kind of test. Proper mothers don't let their sons go to school reeking, do they? You'll get the hang of this. It's not too hard.

You hear the bathroom door slam and he is through the kitchen and clomping down the steps into the garden. You hear the faint click-click-click of the bike as he wheels it out of the shed, then the clang of the garden gate. One mystery down.

'Weed it,' Toby says from the highchair.

You turn to him. 'Not till you've eaten more toast, buster. And let's get that cereal out of your hair, eh?'

You advance on him with a cloth. He squirms as you wipe, and then rewards you with a smile as you release him, and you can't help but smile back with that familiar yet somehow amazing rush of love.

Where did this kid come from? He's bigger than the sum of your parts, far more beautiful than any genetic combination of you and Finn should be. It isn't just a mother speaking: you didn't have this same feeling of disbelief about Jarrah. Maybe it's because you waited so long and nearly gave up, but you swear there's something special about Toby. Strangers stop you in the street, turn to watch him pass, melt when he smiles at them.

'He'll be a heartbreaker,' someone said just last week.

You hope not. You don't think Toby's beauty is the cruel kind. Some essential goodness shines through. If that's not just a mother speaking.

Perhaps it's not a bad thing, Finn's breakthrough. You've missed a lot of Toby's childhood. If Finn really is succeeding, maybe you can cut back on work a little, work from home or something. You've done the career thing for years now. Maybe you need a change.

'Weed it?'

You glance at your watch. There's still the clearing up to do, and you need to eat something yourself and dress for work, then get Toby dressed and pack a bag for day care, and you know from the size of the bulging thing Finn organises to accompany you on every outing that it's no minor thing. The morning minutes have galloped away. You'd planned to make Finn a quick egg and bacon roll, normally a weekend treat, but time's running out.

You clean Toby again and lift him out of the chair. 'Go get your book,' you tell him, and he thunders into the hallway. You stack the dishwasher until a frustrated squeal echoes down the stairs. You run up, locate the worn copy of his book in Jarrah's bedroom and carry Toby back down. You plop him on the ground, spread the book in front of him and turn back to the sink. You can recite the book in your sleep and he's an old hand at turning the pages himself.

Finn's strong coffee has done its work, and by the time the dishwasher is stacked you need your morning trip to the toilet. God, you'd forgotten how the simplest adult act − taking a shower or a shit − is hard with a toddler around.

'Stay there, Toby, and I'll read to you from the bathroom.'

'Weed it gain.'

'Yes, yes, OK,' you say.

You leave him sitting in the sunlight on the floor − which needs a sweep, you mentally note − and raise your voice in recitation as you head down the hall and into the bathroom, leaving the door open.

The sun streams in the bathroom window, promising a hot day. You try to hurry, cursing the timing of your digestive system, calling the words in Toby's direction.

You flush the toilet, drag your pants up, button them, wash your hands. Glance into the mirror. Unmade-up and hair drying like a bird's nest. Is there time to drag a comb through it before teeth cleaning?

You pause the story. 'Teeth time, Toby.'

You grab the electric toothbrush, smear it with paste, rev it up, run it over your teeth. Spit. 'Toby?'

You flick the thing off. Lorikeets squabble raucously over the scarlet stems of flowers on the umbrella tree just outside the kitchen, masking any sound from him. He won't sit for long with his story interrupted. You flick the toothbrush on again, quickly finish your teeth. Grab his toothbrush and load it.

'Toby? Teeth time.'

No answer. You put the toothpaste down and walk towards the kitchen. The birds are still racketing outside, their shrieks loud in your ears as you walk down the hall. Around the corner in the kitchen, his book is lying alone on the floor in the pool of sunlight.

Your belly lurches.

The garden is fully fenced from the road, the pool fully fenced from the garden. That's why you chose this place. He must have wandered outside or upstairs, that's all.

'*Toby!*' The shrill note of your voice should bring him scurrying.

You push the screen door open, step onto the verandah. To your left, the pool gate is firmly shut, Finn's contraption of cogs and gears motionless against the wall. You cross to the top of the short flight of steps leading down into the garden. With a corner of your mind you notice the day is glorious, the colours so vivid it almost hurts to look at them. The lorikeets streak away with a racket, leaving the softer birds to fill the air with melodic chimes and chattering. You take a deep breath to calm the pounding in your chest. Is Toby suddenly old enough to play a game of hiding?

You scan the garden. 'TOBY! COME HERE NOW!' You try to keep the anger out of your voice, anger that he is frightening you, anger that you didn't put him just outside the bathroom door where you could see him.

He isn't in the garden, unless his hiding skills have ratcheted up lately. He must be back inside. Now you're running, back through

41

the living room and up the stairs, calling his name. You reach the doorway to his room, but it's empty and your chest pounds hard. Something's wrong, something's wrong, something's wrong. He's too little to hide like this and you run from room to room, searching frantically, and through your bedroom window something makes you notice the blue sparkle of the pool, a blue that's brighter than the colour of your son's eyes.

JARRAH

For weeks Dave and his friends had been casually circling, checking me out. I'd tried to keep out of their way, especially at lunchtime, sometimes cutting classes or whole afternoons. Didn't catch the school bus unless it was raining, mostly cycled to school. One of Dave's friends caught my bus and all that time sitting still was just asking someone to start on you. I knew that from Tassie.

Someone knocked on the door and took Mr Addison out of the classroom midway through second-period maths. He was gone long enough for a buzz to start. When he came back and looked straight at me, I knew I'd been caught. Worse than caught, by the look on his face. It wasn't a caught-nicking-off-school-once look.

He came to my desk and leaned over. 'Get your things, please Jarrah.'

Getting my things sounded serious, even for skipping school. I couldn't think what else I'd done, but guilt washed over me anyway.

I shut my books, ignored the stares and snickers around me, and headed out the door. Mr Addison followed. I grabbed my pack from my locker and stuffed my books in, hearing the rise of voices behind us from the unattended class. Weirdly, he didn't seem to notice. I hoisted my pack and turned to him.

'The principal needs to see you,' he said and I couldn't read his tone.

He walked by my side down the corridor, up the stairs, past the school office and to the principal's door. The burn in my gut was starting to creep up the back of my throat. Being sent to the principal was bad enough, but being accompanied there was a whole new level of trouble. Calling-your-parents kind of trouble. Detention, suspension, expulsion trouble.

He stopped and knocked. Mr Karlsson opened the door a crack, nodded and stepped out, pulling it quickly shut behind him.

'Jarrah,' he said.

I looked from one of them to the other, trying to work out the degree of my bustedness.

Karlsson took off his glasses. He looked half-blind without them on and I wondered how just a pair of glasses could make someone look so scary.

'Your father is here.' He put the glasses back on like he didn't know what else to do with them. 'He's very upset.'

Karlsson opened his office door and gestured for me to step inside. He was trying to warn me, but nothing could have prepared me for what was in there.

Dad hunched over with his face in his hands, shaking. He lifted his head and I saw my great big father broken into little pieces.

I can't remember how I crossed the room. Next thing I was trying, somehow, to put him back together with my bare hands, gripping his shoulders and saying 'Dad, Dad, Dad.'

He made a noise and reached for me, and I wrapped my skinny arms around him and he said my name, twice, and I couldn't ask. I wanted one more moment of not knowing what made him like this.

He gulped one word. 'Toby.'

My hands tightened on his shoulders to stop him saying it.

'Toby fell in the pool.'

For a wild moment I thought everything was all right. If Toby had fallen in the pool, someone had got him out, hadn't they? It was the very last moment of my childhood. A micro-measurement of time – not even a second – passed and then the instantly adult part of my brain understood they hadn't got him out.

'He's gone, Jarrah.'

He clutched me again as though he was, too, hearing the words for the first time, and the noises he made were terrifying. I don't think I'd ever seen Dad cry, except at Nanna Brenn's funeral, but I could hardly remember that.

It gave me something to focus on because I couldn't understand the notion that Toby was gone. I had to see Mum. That was all I knew.

'Let's go.' I straightened up.

Dad looked up with his ravaged face, like he was the child, and I saw how it was going to be. I walked to the door and opened it. The principal and Mr Addison were still outside.

'We need to go home.'

'The police brought your father here. They're waiting outside to take you both home.' Mr Karlsson put his hand on my shoulder. 'It won't be easy, Jarrah. You'll have to be strong.'

'Yes, sir.' I swallowed Jarrah the schoolkid down to some distant place.

'If there's anything you need, call me,' he said, as if this wasn't a totally weird concept.

'Thank you, sir.'

The bell went with an ear-splitting shriek as I turned back into that room. I helped my father to his feet and he put an arm around my shoulders. His clothes were damp and there were wet footprints where his shoes had been. Pool water. It was the worst thing yet.

I led him, stumbling, to the door and we stepped into the corridor. Karlsson and Addison were standing like bouncers, hands outstretched to halt the rush of students thundering down the corridor towards us. The roar of voices hushed as they skidded to a halt and stared.

I turned away from them, I steered my father the other way, and we shuffled down the corridor and out onto the street, towards the waiting police car, watched by hundreds of eyes as I walked into my new life.

*

We didn't talk on the way home. Dad would start shaking and I'd know he was crying again. I'd reach over from the back seat and hold his hand. The shakes would slow, he'd wipe his eyes and nose on the back of his hand, stare into his lap.

I looked straight ahead at the headrest and the police officer's dark hair sticking up above it. Had I kissed Toby goodbye that morning? I could only remember how Mum had sent me to the bathroom for deodorant. Maybe I gave Toby a high five before that? Maybe I walked out with just a wave? No matter how many times I went over it, I couldn't remember.

46

The car pulled up outside our house, next to another police car. No one moved.

'Dad?' I put my hand on his shoulder and shook him a little.

He blinked like he was waking up. Saw where we were. Saw the other police car. For the first time he moved quickly. Grabbed the door handle, shoved the door open, swung himself around. He managed to get his head outside the car before he vomited.

I got out the other side, rushed around, put my hand on his shoulder. I wanted to run inside and at the same time wanted to run away. None of this was real until I got inside and saw Mum's face.

Dad got up, leaning on the roof of the car like he might fall. Stood for a moment. The vomit stank. The constable who'd been in the passenger seat held out her hand like she was going to lead him.

'Come on, Dad.' I wondered if I'd need to help him, but he took a deep breath and stood straight. Put his shoulders back. Nodded slightly and started to walk.

We got across the lawn and up the steps. The pool area was taped off with blue and white checked tape. More police, crouching by the fence, taking photos, writing things down. I broke into a run down the verandah. Shoved the door open, ran into the kitchen, skidded to a halt.

She was sitting at the table staring straight ahead. Her eyes were red, but she wasn't crying. A woman I didn't know stood next to her.

I meant to say 'Mum?' but what came out of my mouth instead was 'Toby?'

Her head jerked around to me and she drew in a sharp breath. 'He's gone.'

Her head dropped down again. She hunched in on herself, her shoulders curled. 'I'm so sorry,' she whispered.

Dad came in behind me and the strange woman stepped forward. 'Mr Brennan, I'm Detective Inspector Evans. I am sorry for your loss.'

Dad just stared.

'Your wife has given us her statement and we need you to make one too. We can do it now or wait until tomorrow.'

Dad kind of nodded and she gestured for him to go through into the lounge room.

'Want me to come?' I asked him.

The woman shook her head. 'You must be Jarrah? I need to speak to your father alone.'

They stepped out and shut the door, leaving me alone with Mum. More than anything I needed to ask: *How did you let him out of your sight?* More than anything I knew I could never ask that.

The phone shrieked and we both jumped. I looked at Mum, who didn't move.

'It might be the hospital,' I said. 'He might be all right.' I snatched the handset before she could say anything. 'Yes?'

'Hello? Is that you, Finn?'

The tinny voice carried through the silence of the room and Mum put her hands over her ears.

'He can't talk,' I said.

'Jarrah? This is Edmund. I've got some fantastic news for your dad. Will he be long?'

I looked at Mum helplessly. She didn't respond.

I took a breath. 'It's Toby. He's dead.'

As soon as the words left my lips I knew why Dad had vomited. I'd said it out loud. Mum made a noise like she was choking.

Edmund didn't answer at first. 'Oh Christ,' he said at last, his voice trembling. 'Christ, Jarrah. What? Where are your parents?'

'Here. Dad's talking to the police.'

Mum got up. Grabbed the phone from my hand, stabbed the buttons until the call was cut off and dropped the handset on the table. 'What's the time?' she asked me.

The clock was right there. Why didn't she look? 'Nearly twelve,' I said. 'When did it happen?'

She rubbed her face with both hands. 'Um. About nine.'

Toby had drowned three hours ago. The hospital wasn't going to be ringing with the news that they'd resuscitated him. I'd seen her and I knew it was true.

She covered her face and sat very still. Dad cried noisily and messily. The only way I knew Mum was crying was that tears were running down her wrists. With Dad I knew to touch him. With Mum I had no idea.

I hadn't cried. Couldn't. I didn't know what to do next. Didn't know how to even start living in the world without him.

FINN

There was a small scorch mark on the back of his left hand. It must have been from the blowtorch. A little blister was forming under the skin.

Finn studied the hands on his lap like they belonged to someone else. As long as he examined them, he hadn't just broken the news to Jarrah at school. As long as he studied them, he wasn't trying to answer the questions the detective was asking him.

'Could you start by telling me what happened this morning?'

He'd read her name tag but it refused to make an impression on him. Each time he closed his eyes the pictures came again.

'Mr Brennan?'

Finn shook his head slightly, gathered himself. 'I had this new work, this deadline, and Bridget had to get up early and get the boys ready.'

In halting sentences he staggered through the morning. His early trip to the studio, the hiss of the blowtorch, the sound he'd somehow heard over the top of it. The way he ran out of the studio and what he saw when he did. The phone call he made to Triple 0.

When he was done, the woman gave him a glass of water and a tissue. Waited till he'd composed himself.

'Do you know how Toby got into the pool area?'

Finn moaned out loud, a sound out of his control, and shook his head.

'Your wife told us she left Toby in the kitchen while she went to the bathroom, and when she came out he was gone. She checked the pool gate and it was shut. She didn't see him in the pool until she was searching upstairs and looked out the window.'

Everything slowed. Finn heard Bridget pulling a tissue out of a box in the kitchen and catching her breath. He could hear the second police offer pacing the verandah, and the soft metallic clicking of a camera shutter. His own blood washed around his veins, roaring. Bridget had left Toby unsupervised and somehow, in that time, Toby had got into the pool. How? How? How?

In the studio, those few hours earlier, he'd been welding with his back to the pool. If he'd turned his head, even just a little, he'd have seen Toby.

One thing he remembered clearly: he hadn't gone through the pool area that morning. It was bin day. He'd given Bridget her coffee, taken the rubbish from the kitchen, and gone through the garden to drop it in the bin and wheel the bin to the kerb. He'd been closer then to the back door of the studio, the stiff, unwieldy one he hardly ever used. Though he'd have loved a swim, he was conscious of Bridget and the new routine. He'd dragged the studio's rear door open and got to work. Bridget was the only one who'd swum that morning. The only one who'd gone through the gate.

'Mr Brennan?'

Finn reached for the water. 'Just a moment.'

'Of course.'

For the rest of her life Bridget would carry this, and it was too heavy. He couldn't let her. He swallowed and drew a deep, shuddering breath.

'We have a device that opens the gate and closes it automatically.'

'Yes?'

'It malfunctions sometimes. I was meaning to fix it, but I couldn't work out what was wrong. When I went through the pool area this morning, I had a lot on my mind with this new work. I wasn't thinking.'

The detective waited.

'Obviously it didn't close properly after me and I didn't notice. That's the only way Toby could have got in. It must have shut behind him.'

'I see,' she said slowly. She scribbled something in her notebook then looked at him closely. 'Mr Brennan, I have to caution you now that you do not have to answer any questions, and anything you do or say could be used in evidence.'

'What?' Finn shook his head, trying to understand.

'We can continue this interview later with a solicitor if you wish.'

'No,' Finn said. 'I'd rather get it over with. I've got nothing to hide.'

'Could you show me the mechanism?'

Finn stood and the detective followed him through the sliding door onto the verandah. They ducked under the tape. One of the other police officers came out of the pool area to join them and the detective introduced him as a scientific investigator. Finn pulled the lever to demonstrate how *Owl*

Sentry worked. The gate eased its deadly way open, and, after a few seconds, swung shut with a firm clank.

As the investigator took more photographs, the detective shook the gate to check it was latched. 'It's working now.'

'It didn't happen every time, or I'd have fixed it, obviously.'

The thing could well have malfunctioned, Finn thought. How else could Toby have got into the pool area? It was the only thing that made any sense.

'That's all we need for now.' She stepped back and closed her notebook. 'Can you please advise us as soon as you've notified your family?'

They had to start telling people. He'd have to call his father, his brother and sisters, their friends in Tasmania. Thank God his mother wasn't alive. It would have killed her.

He had to stop there. He couldn't imagine the first phone call.

She handed him her card. 'Let us know if there's anything else you remember. A funeral home will be able to help you with arrangements.'

A funeral home. Didn't she know this was his son? Who, three hours ago, had been bouncing around the house demanding someone read to him?

The investigator lifted the tape and gestured for Finn to follow them out. 'Please leave the tape in place and don't go behind it,' he said. 'We'll probably remove it later today, or tomorrow. Constable Feroka will stay to keep the area secure.'

Finn couldn't look at the pool. He had to go inside. Had to join Bridget and Jarrah. He just wanted to hold them hard to his body. His chest hurt as he turned and walked back along the verandah. He wondered, distantly, if his heart might simply halt. He'd be with Toby then, still and blue and cool, and Toby wouldn't be alone wherever it was they had him now, in some metal drawer somewhere.

He reached the glass door of the kitchen and looked inside. He saw Bridget, seated, her shoulders shaking, and Jarrah standing next to her. The boy still wasn't crying, but the look on his face was worse than if he had been.

They were the most precious things left to him, and he'd do anything. Anything. He'd take that weight for Bridget and never put it down.

BRIDGET

You want your mother. You felt the same way giving birth, you remember. A kind of primal need. She was there when you had Jarrah, but by the time Toby muscled his way into the world she was already dipping in and out of the fog of dementia. Now, with advancing Alzheimer's, she is effectively gone from you.

When Finn comes in from talking to the police, the three of you, by some silent assent, move into the lounge room and sit in a row on the couch. Finn in the middle, Jarrah on the right, you on the left. Finn clasps your hand so hard it hurts, and through that small, physical pain you know you still exist.

You notice pieces of Lego rolled under the armchair opposite and you keep your gaze fixed on them. There is still a chance that if you stay sitting there, holding very still, silent, not crying, then you'll wake up and this won't have happened.

Every few – moments? – minutes? – you drift away and then the memory of why you are there washes back through you in another sickening rush. Some part of your brain logs the stress process: adrenaline, cortisol, norepinephrine, flooding your body. Three pieces of Lego under the armchair. One blue, one red, one yellow. Three humans on the couch. Your life is measured now in threes.

Bang. Bang. Bang. Three knocks on the glass door, so sudden and loud that you nearly choke. A woman cups her hands on the glass and peers in, and for a long moment the three of you stare at her, until at last Jarrah stands and lets her in.

'I am so, so sorry,' she says.

Who is she, even? Someone Finn knows? Older, conservatively dressed. You can't place her.

'I'm Meredith Anderson. I'm a volunteer support worker with the hospital and I represent Caring Friends, a foundation that supports families after the death of a child. I wasn't on duty when you came in this morning.'

You cannot make her words mean anything, and eventually, when it's clear no one else will respond, Jarrah says, 'Right.'

'You must be Jarrah?' she says to him. 'And Finn, and Bridget? I understand you haven't been in town long. I'm here to help.'

Her lip quivers and you wish she'd go. Everything is slipping through your fingers; the new world streaming in to replace the old one with shocking speed.

She walks towards you, leans in, puts her hand on your shoulder, letting go when you flinch. 'I know what it's like.'

No one can possibly know what this is like.

She scans the three of you with an appraising glance. 'Jarrah, do you think you could make us all a cup of tea?'

Who is this woman, ordering your son around? You open your mouth to protest, but she squeezes your shoulder again. She's right. You do need help, here in this unfamiliar town two thousand miles from home, with no friends of the real sort.

Meredith isn't afraid of silence. She moves to an armchair and the three of you listen to Jarrah's methodical tea-making. When he carries the tea in on a tray, you know you will gag if anything passes your lips, especially when Meredith, without asking, stirs a sugar into each cup before handing it over. You take the cup and wrap your hands around its warmth. In spite of the day's heat, you're cold.

'I know you're in shock, but there are things you need to do today.' Her voice is gentle.

'OK,' Jarrah says, on your behalf.

'Finn, I understand you've identified your son's body at the hospital and agreed to the autopsy, and you and Bridget have both made police statements. The next thing you need to do is notify your family and friends before they hear some other way.'

One word leaps out. 'An autopsy?'

She nods. 'It is required in a case of accidental death, as the doctor would have explained to Finn.

You try to understand that Toby is now a body.

'Notifying your loved ones is the most important thing,' she continues. 'I can help you make a list, and assist you with those calls, if you wish.'

Your gut contracts. The Brennans. All of them. Not knowing yet.

'The police won't release Toby's name until your family have been notified, but the story will be in the news soon, and these things get out fast on social media. I know this is very hard. Can I help you make that list?'

She takes a notebook and pen from her handbag.

The idea you could tell the Brennans is unthinkable and you're silent. When it's clear Finn can't speak either, Jarrah starts listing names. 'Um, my dad's family, I guess. My grandfather. Uncle Conor. Aunt Mary and Aunt Carmel.'

As the woman writes them down, Jarrah turns his head to you. 'What about Nan?'

You shake your head. You hated how dementia has stolen your mother, but suddenly it seems a blessing. There's no rush to tell her.

The woman won't give up. 'I'll note down the numbers for you. Where can I find them?'

'Mum's mobile,' says Jarrah. 'Where is it, Mum?'

You jerk your head towards the kitchen, and he disappears in that direction. You think Finn must be crying again because you can feel him shuddering next to you. You should squeeze his hand or something.

Jarrah comes back with your phone. 'Some guy from work has texted. Says you're missing a meeting.'

'Let me notify them,' Meredith says. 'Your work may be worried if you haven't turned up.'

You don't really want a stranger calling Chen, but at the pity on her face, you subside.

'How about Jarrah and I go and sort out the kitchen while you and Finn make these first calls? I'll be right here if you need support. You can put me on to people if you want, to help them with arrangements, after you've told them.'

'Thank you,' Finn says. His first words since she arrived.

'After that,' she continues, 'you could take a rest together.'

Finn clutches your arm like he wants to take you down with him, and what will happen when you are alone together? What will happen when you look into each other's eyes? Because each of you has seen Toby dead, and there is no refuge there. And tonight or tomorrow, someone will slice into his skin, examine his organs, take samples.

Meredith hands you the list. 'I'll be just next door, with Jarrah.'

Jarrah follows her out to the kitchen like some capable stranger. What has happened to your family?

JARRAH

It happened to people on television, or those tall black kids at my school – the Sudanese ones – who lost their mother and father and everyone else except an aunt or something. They weren't in my class, so I didn't know them, but I'd heard the stories. How did people actually live through it? The ones who lost their whole family? Was it the same pain multiplied? Could that even be possible?

In the kitchen Toby's book lay open on the floor and his toast crusts scattered across the tray of the highchair.

The woman – what was her name? – patted me. 'Do you think you could stack the dishwasher? I'll just step outside and call your mother's workplace.'

Was she crazy? I slumped on a chair and listened to her making the call just outside on the verandah. There was a Vegemite handprint on the highchair.

She was back in a moment. 'It's better to do something.' She flipped open the dishwasher and sped around the kitchen, passing me things. Over the clank of dishes I strained my ears to listen to Mum and Dad's phone calls. I heard low voices, but not the words. Then I heard Dad start crying.

The woman paused and closed her eyes at the sound. Then

she kind of shook herself and handed me Toby's plastic toast plate. Her eyes were red. 'My heart is breaking for your family. Our foundation provides lots of help and support. You won't have to do it all yourself.'

I shoved Toby's plate in the dishwasher. 'OK.'

When the dishwasher was full I turned it on. Wiped the benches. She even got me cleaning the stove. When it got really quiet next door she went and had a look. Came back a few minutes later.

'I've sent your parents upstairs,' she said. 'They said for you to come up when you're ready. Is there anyone you want to call, Jarrah? A friend who could come around?'

'I'm fine.'

Someone knocked on the glass door and she let him in. It was that guy from Mum's work. I'd met him once. She introduced herself to him. Meredith, and Chen, that's what they were called. He hesitated and nodded at me.

'I just can't believe it,' he said, twice. I think he'd been crying.

'They're resting now,' Meredith said. 'Maybe you can come back later?'

He shook his head. 'I want to do something. I'll make some food.'

She nodded and he starting pulling stuff out of the cupboards and the fridge. It was weird.

'You feel like giving Chen a hand?' she said to me.

'No thanks.'

She put her hand on my shoulder. 'I'm just trying to help, Jarrah. You can come and see me for support. It's free. I know you're in shock now, but it might help in the coming days.'

Did she mean things would feel worse in the coming days? I looked outside. The whole pool area was surrounded with that police tape, flapping in the breeze. There was still one cop under the shade of the palms. He just sat there, staring at the water.

'Are you hungry?' Chen asked.

I shook my head. 'I'm going upstairs.'

'Good,' the woman said. 'Be with your parents. You should stay together.'

I left them in the kitchen and climbed the stairs on tiptoe. At the top I stopped. Down the hall, Mum and Dad's bedroom door was ajar and it was really quiet in there. Did they know I was standing at the top of the stairs?

One of them had made the worst fuck-up that was ever possible. I would never have let it happen, but one of them had. One of them had lost my brother.

My breathing seemed loud in my own ears. I couldn't go in there. My feet wouldn't move. Instead I turned left and crept along the carpet to the open door of Toby's little room at the end of the hall, tucked under the roof with a sloping ceiling.

His familiar smell hit me first. Actual molecules of Toby still circulating in the air. Toby's pyjamas on the floor, Toby's bedclothes rumpled and heaped on his tiny bed – the one he'd only moved into three months earlier – as if he might be hiding under them, tricking us. Toby's plush monster, manky and dribbled on.

When my feet would move, I stepped inside and shut the door. Mum and Dad had each other. I had bits of Toby in the air.

A parent's pain must be the worst, right?

I grabbed the plush monster, lifted up the cotton quilt that had covered Toby in his sleep, and climbed under. Curled into a ball, surrounded by the smell of him. I pulled the covers over my head and hunched in tight. Then I jammed that monster against my open mouth and it ate my howls.

JARRAH

I welcome you here today to pay tribute to Toby Brennan, to mourn the shortness of his life, and to comfort his family for their loss. His mother Bridget, his father Finn and his brother Jarrah have lived among us less than a year. The turnout today is a sign to the Brennan family that though you are new here, you are part of our community, which is full of compassion. Our hearts are with you at this tragic time.

The closest I came to seeing Toby again was when we walked into the chapel at the crematorium at ten o'clock on Friday morning, four days and one hour after he died. There he was, just a couple of metres away from me, in a white coffin that looked too small to hold him.

Earlier in the week the woman from that foundation thing, whose name I kept forgetting, asked if we wanted a viewing. Toby's body would be back from the autopsy on Wednesday and there was time, she said.

Dad just shut his eyes and shook his head.

'You may want to give people the option. You might change your own minds. It can be an important part of your healing.'

Did I want to see Toby? The idea was terrifying. But maybe if I saw him I'd believe he was dead.

'It is a chance to say goodbye,' the woman continued. 'Toby will look very peaceful.'

'After he's been autopsied?' Mum snapped. I think she'd forgotten I was there.

I had a flash of Toby, eyes closed, skin pale. I glanced at Mum and Dad but they were both looking at the floor. If I said I wanted to see Toby, did it mean I was blaming them? Did I need their permission? Was I even brave enough? I was scared that dead Toby would get into my brain and be the only thing I remembered.

The idea of seeing Toby never got mentioned again. Not when people started arriving, not when the house was full of Brennan aunts and uncles and cousins, making food and drinks all through the day and night, crying and blowing noses, hugging me, cooking and eating, cooking and drinking, always food on the table, more and more dropped off every day until we were throwing it out. No one asked about seeing Toby, or not in front of me, though maybe that was what the whispered conversations in the kitchen were about, the ones that stopped suddenly when I walked into the room.

I didn't want to hear what they were saying anyhow. The thing I needed to hear and the thing I couldn't stand to hear was what happened. Who let Toby out of their sight? Which one of them?

No one talked about that.

Then suddenly it was Friday and somehow we were running late for the funeral; suddenly it was all a rush and no one could get organised. We were maybe the last people to get there and we came down the aisle with everyone looking at us, and filed into the front row and sat down. And there was the coffin. When the service was finished, Toby would be cremated. That was the polite word for it. No chance to change my mind.

I'd never seen a dead body. Not of a person. I saw our cat after she was crushed by a car back in Hobart. Gave me nightmares and we never got another cat. I'd had a nightmare about Toby too, the night after that woman asked about the viewing. I knew the body was Toby's, but I couldn't recognise him. Woke up choking. Maybe it was lucky the last time I saw Toby he was alive. Maybe it was lucky I could only imagine what had happened, and what he might look like.

There I was, in full view of every person in the place. Toby out the front in the white box. Mum on the end of our row, me in the middle, Dad next. The two front rows were full of Dad's relatives. Uncle Conor sat next to him, really close. Then Dad's sister Mary and her girlfriend Edie, and his other sister Carmel and Uncle Graeme. Cousins – mostly older than me, who I didn't know well – were in the next row.

Conor was staying with us, sleeping on one of the couches. His wife Helen hadn't come. Edmund was sleeping on the other couch. Everyone else was at hotels, but they spent all their time at our house. Poppa Brenn didn't come.

'He's too old,' Dad said when I asked. 'He can't cope.'

Whatsername asked me all through the week if I had support, if I had friends, did I want counselling. She was trying to be nice. But every time she asked made it worse. No, I didn't have friends. The closest thing to a friend, Billy, was just as outcast as me. He'd texted something during the week that sounded like his mother made him send it, but that was all.

My aunts and uncles and cousins were sorry for me, but it was like they didn't know me. 'You're so much taller,' everyone said. I wasn't. I just looked older suddenly. I could see it in the mirror. Most of them hadn't seen us since we'd left Tassie at the start of the year. Toby wasn't even two then. They didn't know how he'd started talking and suddenly there'd been a person inside that little body. They didn't know how he'd say something and you'd look at him and think: So *that's* been going on in there.

And it was like I didn't know anyone either. Especially Dad and Mum. Dad sat me down the day after and tried to tell me what happened. He could hardly talk. The gate somehow got left unlatched – something to do with that gizmo thing – and Toby somehow got into the pool and somehow no one saw it in time. It was an accident, he said. A terrible accident.

The white coffin. The voice of the celebrant. The sound of people behind me crying.

This doesn't happen to us. This happens to other people.

It was a stupid thing to think. But it wouldn't get out of my head. I'd read about bad stuff in the papers, I'd felt sorry for those people whose lives had been wrecked, and then I'd forgotten them. And now we were them.

When the celebrant paused, I snuck a look over my shoulder. There were about five rows of kids from my class at school. Laura Fieldman was in the middle of the third row, looking right at me.

FINN

I have spoken to family and friends who knew Toby. In his short life he made an impact on everyone he met. Beloved by his immediate and extended family, Toby was an enthusiastic, excited and adventurous little boy. Toby's parents have asked his Uncle Conor to say some words on their behalf.

It never occurred to Finn his father wouldn't come. But since the first phone call, when Finn broke down completely trying to convey the news, he hadn't spoken to his father. He'd called, but John could never come to the phone. Helen, who'd stayed in Hobart to be with him, took the calls and tried to reassure Finn. 'He's in shock,' she said. 'You know he'd be there if he could.'

Edmund and Conor, his agent and his brother, were the ones who stuck hard by him. They let him go only at the end of each evening, when he dragged himself upstairs and joined Bridget and they lay in numb silence. Finn would grope for her hand, or pull her into his arms. They'd cry together. But it was like she wasn't really there.

Even today, as they'd dodged hurriedly into the front row of the chapel, Bridget had let him go in first and then allowed Jarrah to sit between them. There was no arrangement of their

68

reduced family that could be right for this, but Finn wished Bridget were next to him. He couldn't even see her properly.

When the celebrant nodded at Conor to indicate it was time for him to come up and speak, Finn glanced back as Conor stood. As they'd walked in, he'd half noticed the chapel was crowded, but he saw now there wasn't an empty seat anywhere. People were standing at the back. Apart from the people in the first two rows, Finn knew no one.

As Conor fumbled with his notes and tried to steady his voice, Finn found himself blanking out.

Home was Hobart. How had he ever thought he could live elsewhere? They'd had friends, good friends. Family. He hadn't been able to walk around the Farm Gate Market on a Sunday morning without stopping every few metres to catch up with someone. Hobart knew them. He hadn't put in the effort up north. Thought there'd be plenty of time once they settled. He hadn't made a single proper friend, he realised. He was an alien in Murwillumbah. It had been wrong from the start.

He had to collect Toby's ashes and then figure out how to get the family back home. He'd take what remained of his son and they'd climb the mountain and scatter him at the top and know that he looked over them always.

Sandra had called, the day after Toby died. The news must have flashed around Hobart and found her. Finn's sister Mary, tasked with answering the endlessly ringing phone at their house this past week, had come and found him with the handset.

'Oh, Finn,' Sandra said when he took it. Two words, full of compassion, and they were enough to bring him undone.

He took the phone outside, onto the grass, and she waited silently on the end of the line while he sobbed, and even the silence was somehow different, was somehow laden with knowing and understanding and not needing words.

After what felt like forever, Finn recovered enough to blow his nose and breathe.

'I'll come, if you want me,' she said.

Finn had looked up at the house. Bridget stood in the doorway. She wasn't even watching him. She was staring blankly into the far corner of the garden, as if he didn't exist.

'I don't know,' he said.

Sandra paused. 'Hans can't understand why I'm not there. He sends his love to you both. God, I'm sorry it's such a mess. I wish I could just get on a plane. I wish I could help.'

Finn heaved a shuddering sigh.

'Should I call her?'

Finn looked over at Bridget again. 'I don't think she can handle anything else.'

'If it feels right, tell her I'm sending my love.'

'I'd better go,' he'd said. Hung up and felt the most alone he'd ever been.

Except, perhaps, for the funeral. As Conor read, Finn heard the sounds of weeping echoing through the chapel. People who didn't know them, who didn't know him or Toby or their family. Were they the same ones who came in the night and laid down flowers and teddy bears and battery-powered candles in little glasses? The ones who'd left the notes about their little angel, the ones who'd promised to pray for them, who'd turned the front fence into a shrine?

He didn't want it, this kindness from strangers.

BRIDGET

We weren't expecting another baby in the family, and Toby was the one who brought us all together, especially his poppa, who can't be here today. His favourite thing was being read to, and I'd like to share a few words from the book he loved the most.

Here is what you know.

That you cannot tell your mother. Tell her once, and you will have to tell her over and over. You've decided to simply say 'He couldn't come today' if she notices Toby's absence.

That Jarrah is stronger than either you or Finn. He'll get through this.

That the Brennan family blames you. No matter how much Finn explains the malfunctioning gate mechanism, his change of routine, his proximity to the pool – in their minds, you left Toby alone. You can see it in their eyes.

You are grateful to Conor, though. It's unthinkable that you or Finn could actually speak at Toby's funeral, and somehow Finn's older brother manages his short speech about Toby on behalf of the family, reading it doggedly from the page, pausing to breathe deeply and wipe his eyes, amidst the muffled sounds of crying.

It's not you crying. You're frozen. You suppose it could have gone the other way — the funeral might have coincided with your wild weeping, those unpredictable moments that bring a little relief. It feels like you should cry at this terribly public moment.

For half the town, it seems, has blown into the chapel on the winds of this blustery day for Toby's funeral. Behind Tasmanian family and friends at the front stretch rows of strange, sympathetic faces. Chen, close to the front but not in the inner circle of family, not today. Some of your other colleagues. Students from Jarrah's school. Meredith, who seems to have been at your house every day, and one of the paramedics, whose name you will never remember but whose face you'll never forget. The rest — you have no idea. The curious and the sorrowful, the invisible bringers of food and flowers, come to glance respectfully at the tiny white coffin, blink away a few tears, and thank their deity, if they believe, that this hasn't happened to them.

Have you slept yet?

You couldn't on the first night. As if it were the ultimate abandonment of Toby. Some time in the tiny hours Finn fell into a fitful slumber, his snores ripping the air apart, leaving you alone to hate him. By first light you knew what to do. You rose and padded through the house on bare feet, past Edmund, who'd flown in late and was asleep on the couch. You slid open the glass door and headed across the damp grass. In the garage you found what you were looking for, hefty and satisfying in your hands. You carried it back to the house, mounted the steps, and approached Finn's contraption, hanging in its shining obscenity on the wall. You raised the sledgehammer above your head with a strength you'd forgotten you had and let it fall. The first blow smashed through the morning, rocking the timbers of the house from top to bottom and setting shrieking birds a-flight. It was the first thing that had felt right in the twenty-one hours since Toby died, and so you raised the sledgehammer and hit again. The clockwork crumpled and sagged, the sound smashing through the sleepy neighbourhood, the stupid owl's all-seeing eyes shattered.

Because shortly after midnight, fifteen and a half hours after Toby drowned, Finn had told you. Said it was his fault, the thing must have malfunctioned and left the gate open behind him when he went through to the studio, he'd forgotten to tell you it was playing up because he'd meant to fix it; all culpability was his.

'But it was shut,' you said. 'I saw it. That's why I looked for him upstairs first.'

He'd shaken his head. 'It must have closed behind him. It's my fault.'

You lifted the sledgehammer again and let it fall, burying its head deep in the splintered weatherboards, where it jammed. Then Finn's hands were on your shoulders and he was drawing you back, unwrapping your fingers from the handle.

'There are live wires in there,' he said.

You had a wild urge to tear yourself out of his grip, reach in and grasp those wires. It would be a quick death, quick enough that you could find Toby, wherever he was.

Except: you know there is nothing after death. You're a scientist, and there's no evidence that life continues in any form. All that was Toby has been snuffed out.

You wanted to crumple into Finn, but with his own hands he built the contraption that killed your son, and you couldn't

73

bear those hands on you. You pulled away and stalked down the verandah, past tousle-haired Edmund standing with a blanket around his shoulders, past Jarrah emerging from the house with dark-circled eyes. You stalked past them all, into the kitchen, and then, because you could think of not one other thing in the world to do, you put the kettle on.

How would you now spend the hours?

Finn followed you into the kitchen, picked up the stupid Atomic and began his morning coffee ritual, the one that had started your days since forever.

'We need to ring a funeral home,' he said, once the thing was on the stove.

You kept your back turned. The kitchen smelled of food, the linger of cooking and the two casseroles and batch of scones dropped off anonymously just hours after Toby died, now jamming up the fridge, barely picked at.

'Do you want me to take care of it?' He spoke to the back of your head.

'I think you've taken care of enough.' You didn't see if he flinched under the cruelty of your words. 'I'll do it. Are you thinking burial or cremation?'

He made a sound that could only be described as a whimper, a sound that would once have devastated you, and part of you marvelled at how you could do that to him, while the rest of you considered ways to hurt him more.

'The detective gave me a number,' he said. 'A funeral place.'

'Good. I'll call them.'

You wouldn't, you decided some time in that first night, allow Finn to be in charge of anything. You had to set your course to steer through this, a hard and straight course through night and day, in and out of the roaring, terrible weeks and years ahead, and all you can do is hold to that course and see what remains at the end.

Conor comes back to your pew and squeezes in next to Finn, who reaches dumbly across and hugs him sideways. The thing is nearly over. The celebrant says a few more words you don't hear. You take your last look at Toby's coffin. You've made sure it won't roll behind the curtains at the end – such an awful melodramatic touch, you've thought at the few cremations you've attended before. It didn't occur to you that, instead, you will be the one turning and walking away from him.

You stand. Flanked by the Brennan family, you turn and walk down the aisle through the bowed heads. You walk out into the soaking spring rain that's blown in from the sea. The Brennans have lost it completely, and you are losing it too. Thank God for Edmund and Chen, who come to your side like sheepdogs and herd you towards the waiting white cars.

'Are we supposed to wait?' you manage to ask.

'You don't need to do anything.' Edmund puts up his hand in front of you as a flash fires. The local media, in which the story has led the news all week. 'Please respect the privacy of the family,' he calls. To you: 'Get in the car. The people who know you will come home.'

That picture does end up in Saturday's paper. The three of you – Finn, you, Jarrah – clinging to each other, hair rain-slicked, like shipwreck survivors. All looking in different directions.

PART TWO

JARRAH

Time after Toby: seven days. Alarm rang at six forty-five. I'd set it in case I somehow slept after four, which didn't happen. Showered. Dressed in the plainest outfit possible. Picked up my bag from where it'd sat, untouched, for a week in the corner. Headed to the kitchen. Hesitated before walking in. I hadn't been alone with her, or with Dad. There'd always been someone around. And that had been kind of good.

She was at the table, in her work clothes, holding a mug of tea. She held out an arm to hug me. I let her do it for a moment then pulled away.

'You sure you're OK to go back?' she asked.

Nodded. 'You?'

'I've got to do something.'

Knew what she meant. Started getting out my breakfast stuff. 'What about Dad?'

'Edmund's going to help him today, get back to work on his sculptures, I guess.'

Poured the cereal, added milk. Far as I knew, Dad hadn't been back in his studio. The pool area had been locked with a bike chain and padlock since the police took off the tape. I was kinda glad Edmund had stuck around to sleep on the couch.

Made a second bowl of cereal and put it in front of Mum. 'Where is he?'

'He and Ed have gone for a walk. Won't be long. Do you want to wait and say goodbye?'

It was seven twenty-two. I wanted to get to school before the crowd. Walking into the funeral had been bad enough – everyone staring, no escape.

Kissed her on the cheek. 'Tell him I said bye.'

Everything was weirdly normal as I wheeled my bike out of the shed. From outside I was the same kid who'd ridden to school exactly a week earlier. But some other kid had done three and a bit terms there. Some other kid had spent his lunchtimes running away to hide, as though being bullied was the worst thing that could happen to him.

It was a fifteen-minute ride to school. Time to practise wiping Toby from my thoughts. Practise not attracting attention. Practise keeping my face blank. I was good at the last two. But everyone from school had seen me bawling my eyes out at Toby's funeral. *Little Mummy*. There'd be no hiding now.

School was nearly empty. I locked my bike, strolled through deserted corridors, opened my locker with a clang that echoed along the hall. Dumped my pack on the ground and started unloading.

'Jarrah?'

Spun around to face Laura Fieldman and two of her long-legged friends. They must have been casing my locker, waiting. This had to be bad.

'We're so sorry about your brother, Jarrah.' Laura came closer and put her hand on my arm. The two girls behind her, whose names I hazily thought were Jade and Eve or Evelyn or something, were nodding with the same sympathetic looks on their faces that everyone in the world now used on me.

'It must be so awful for you. I can hardly imagine. But Jarrah, we're here for you, OK?'

'Um. Right.'

'D'you want to come and sit with us till the bell?'

'OK.'

It felt like a set-up. Gathered up my books and shoved my bag in the locker. Laura linked her arm in mine and led me down the hall and the other girls followed us out to one of the desirable alcoves that lined the playground. Laura pulled me down next to her.

'We copied some notes so you can catch up,' she said. 'I mean, like I'm sure they'll make allowances for the exams, but it might help.'

'Yeah,' I said.

I don't remember what else we talked about until the bell rang. The only clear thing was Laura looking at me with her deep brown eyes, saying, 'You're so brave.'

Maybe I was wrong. Maybe it wasn't a set-up. I'd expected Laura to lead me to the pack, to be torn to bits. But she and her friends stuck to me the whole day. Lots of the girls in the class, and even a few of the boys, came up throughout the day to add to the sympathy. People I'd never spoken to – whose names I didn't know – hugged me, or patted my back or my shoulder. Dave and his creepy mates ignored me. Billy, previously the closest thing I'd had to a friend, came up at lunchtime.

'Hi, Jarrah,' he mumbled, red-faced.

I hadn't heard anything after the one text, though I'd seen him at the funeral. I'd presumed he had no idea what to say to me. I'd have been the same, in his position.

'Hi, Billy.'

He looked helplessly at the girls flanking me. 'Um, how's it going?'

'OK.'

There was an awkward silence as we both realised he couldn't hitch a lift with me on this rise in importance. Laura and co had taken me and left him behind, and that was it.

'I'll see you round,' he said at last.

'Yeah, good,' I said. We looked at each other a bit desperately, but I couldn't help him. Later, when things went back to normal, I'd find him again.

Geography. Fifth period meant it was now more than a week since Toby died. If I clenched my jaw as hard as I could and stared at my textbook, I wouldn't cry. It was like walking a tightrope. I didn't have any brain left over to think about igneous rocks. Just enough to think this about Laura and her friends: they were enjoying my tragedy. Not in a cruel way – they really were sad for me – but they liked the attention. Briefly, I was the most important kid in the school.

When the last bell went, Laura came with me to my locker and watched while I stuffed things into my bag. 'You live near me, don't you? How do you get home?'

'Bike,' I said.

'Why don't you come on the bus tomorrow? I get the seven forty-five. I can save you a seat.'

I nodded in a vague kind of way that didn't promise anything.

'I'll see you tomorrow, Jarrah.' She stepped close and, before I realised what she was doing, leaned in and kissed me on the cheek. 'Bye,' she murmured.

I still felt like a million invisible eyes were watching, so I didn't touch my cheek or stare after her in shock. I moved things around in my locker for a few minutes and then closed it, hitched my pack over my shoulder, and headed towards the bike racks, keeping my head down so I didn't have to look at anyone. I couldn't stand any more sympathy.

On the way home it felt good to stand up on the pedals and use my whole weight to shove the bike in the direction I was riding. In a week or two, I reckoned, everyone at school would be back to normal. I'd be back eating lunch with Billy in some place no one could see us. It was like a swap-card craze, or when someone broke an arm. For a few days or weeks no one could talk or think about anything else, and then suddenly it was all over. That would be me. Laura and her friends would forget me, and I'd sink back to my normal level.

In the meantime, I guess it kind of took my mind off things. Kind of.

BRIDGET

Today you will return to this thing called your day job. You finish breakfast, put your plate and cup in the dishwasher, say goodbye to your husband (you even peck his cheek) and Edmund (is the man ever planning to go?), check your handbag, check your mobile, find your car keys, get into the car, and drive yourself to work. Koala extinction is an almost appealing prospect, with the relief from feeling that it promises.

But in the car park you cannot get out of your car. You forgot that work meant people. You forgot the open-plan office and your colleagues. You cannot unlock your fingers from the steering wheel. That grip and the diagonal pressure of the belt across your chest are the two things holding you together.

Meredith was right: you hadn't thought this through.

She's been dropping in most days and found you alone in the garden on Sunday morning. For the want of something to do, you were weeding, and she got down next to you and helped, and told you about the foundation she represented, where as far you understood, parents with dead children tried to help each other feel better. You'd sensed she wanted to tell you her own story, but you threw your hand up instinctively to stop her saying more.

'Just know there's support available,' she'd said. 'Emotional, legal, even some financial.'

'Legal?' you'd asked.

'I could come with you to the coronial inquest when the time comes. Be with you for any further police interviews.'

'They told us they were done.'

'Well then, that's good.' She looked at you with sorrow on her face. 'Why don't you tell me about your work?'

You didn't feel like talking, but you sighed and went ahead. For a decade you'd lectured in wildlife ecology at the University of Tasmania, and researched infectious diseases in native mammals. The catastrophe of Tasmania's devils, ravaged by facial tumour disease, kept you awake at night for years, supplemented by general scientific concern about the demise of the world's pollinators, the way the high latitudes were heating far faster than predicted, and the resulting tipping points of the global ecosystem. The same big pictures keeping most scientists awake at night. You used to wonder why the whole human race wasn't lying awake worrying; why they couldn't see beyond their individual lives. Now you know.

You told Meredith about the new job, the one that drew you up from Tasmania. A chance to get out of the tightening vice of twenty-first-century corporate academia, to do something small but real: assessing the scope and extent of the North Coast's geographically and genetically distinct population of koalas, and writing a plan of action to increase their chances of survival.

'A government job,' she'd said thoughtfully. 'That's good.'

You didn't know what she meant, but she explained: compassionate leave entitlements, flexibility, time in lieu.

'You can probably have as much time off as you want,' she said.

You'd stared at her in shock. 'I'm going back tomorrow. What else am I going to do?'

She'd shook her head and hugged you, one of those long, warm hugs. A female hug, the kind you would have had from a mother, or an aunt, or a best friend, if you'd had any of those things. Finn, the extroverted, has his family ringing constantly. Your much smaller number of old friends have been scarcely brave enough to call you once in the face of this tragedy, and so returning to work is all you know to do.

Chen appears next to your car. He must have been watching for you. He opens the door and crouches so your faces are level.

'Are you sure it's not too soon?'

Eyes straight ahead, hands locked. 'I can't stay home.'

He exhales heavily. 'I know. Walk in with you?'

Your knuckles relax and your hands slide from the wheel. You manage a nod and he holds the door while you unbuckle, gather your things, swivel, get out. You close the door and press the button to lock.

He takes hold of your arm. 'Hug?'

Before what happened, you'd never hugged. Over the past week he's hugged you without reservation, but one hug might bring you down this morning, and you decline.

Walking up the steps, your knees shake. Chen opens the door, lets you pass, follows you in. It's too early for Christine to be in reception and you pass into the open-plan office ungreeted. Your desk is in a cubicle at the far end. You're early, like always. Only four people are in. You can do this.

The pattern is the same as you pass each of them. Eyes meeting yours, confusion spreading across their faces, the visible battle as they decide what to do. One looks down again quickly, blushing. Two adjust their features and give you sympathetic nods, murmuring. The fourth goes to rise, but a gesture of some sort from Chen indicates no, not yet, and she reverses the move.

You make it to your desk relatively unscathed and Chen leaves you to make tea. You open your stubbornly retained paper diary and stare at the expanse of a week. There are things written there, matched against times. Meetings that might have been significant from the perspective of a week ago.

You place both hands flat on the desk to hold yourself steady. If you breathe, this will be possible. You will plan your day, and your week, find some structure to buttress you through the infinite hours, some sense of motion or meaning. Something.

When Chen returns with two steaming mugs you're still clutching the desk and he winces at the sight of you.

'Here, let me help.' He wheels in a chair and squeezes it next to yours, starts up the computer and looks down at your diary. He puts a finger on the first meeting, checks the names, turns to the emails avalanching to your inbox, types a search query, finds four relevant messages, sends their attachments to print, collects a slender sheaf of papers.

'Step by step,' he says. 'Read them. Agenda first. Use a highlighter pen, mark them up.'

'Why will I be attending, again?'

He gestures at the spread of the week in your diary. 'Because you need things to do. No one expects anything from you. If there's anything you want to say, make a few notes.'

He continues, scrolling through emails, marking things in the diary, printing, putting messages that need responses to one side. You won't be able to do any of it. Every appointment, every list, every pile of paper is another step away from the life that had Toby in it. Already you have turned into someone he wouldn't know, someone you don't recognise.

'I'm just across the way,' Chen says. 'Text me and I'll be here in fifteen seconds. And Bridget – no media, hey? Or social media. No Google.'

He's been a friend this past week. Keeping you afloat when everything in you wanted to sink. Edmund must be doing the same for Finn. Who is helping Jarrah?

Your heart crumples under the weight of this, though you've tried, in the terrible week past, to reach for him. He's been distant, unreachable, remote. He acts as though he's fine, he doesn't collapse into the sudden weeping that overtakes you and Finn. You can only cling to the thought that Jarrah's a boy, not a parent, and normal life will at some time begin again for him. He'll grow up and heal – he'll be all right.

A chime alerts you to the meeting about to start. You collect your papers, a pen, a pink highlighter, and your mobile phone. Knowing now what life can serve up, you've become one of those people you used to despise, who need to carry it everywhere.

The office is now full of people, though unnaturally quiet, and quieter yet as you rise and walk towards the meeting room. Along the way, and as you enter, stilted expressions of sympathy. The hesitation of your co-workers as they murmur their sorrow. You appreciate that they want to acknowledge it while not going any further. You wouldn't know what to say either. A few of them add 'If there's anything I can do …' and you nod.

The meeting begins and you sit straight and stare at the agenda, and occasionally you refer to the notes, and mark something with the highlighter, but essentially you are far from the room. They are careful to ask you nothing, demand nothing, not look at you for too long. You are grateful.

On return, your desk is piled high with offerings for morning tea. The workplace equivalents of beef casseroles and chicken soups: muffins, cookies, chocolates. At least there are no flowers. But what will you do with the rest of the day?

'File,' Chen says. 'Your desk has been a mess for months.'

You stare helplessly at the mound of paper on the desk, already defeated, but he reaches past you and plucks the first sheet from the stack. He reads the first few lines aloud. There is a date mentioned.

'Last week,' he says. 'Too late.' He lets it slip into the recycling bin. 'Done. Next.'

The tsunami of paper is something that defeats you even in a normal week, and you'd have said, if anyone had asked, that you'd be utterly unable to cope with it today, this day, this Monday. But Chen prods you into a kind of momentum, and after he leaves, you work slowly down the pile, somehow falling into a state of mind in which pieces of paper and the order in which they should be stored are accessible to you, something like doing a jigsaw puzzle.

The problem is a stack of papers, each filled with a demand. The solution, as Chen showed you, is simple: take one more step. Any that are too demanding are put in the too-hard pile – he's given you permission to create one – any that are intractable or unimportant are binned, the rest are filed.

You work through lunchtime. Especially through lunchtime, when people might feel they have to talk. At two pm, just as you're slowing down to avoid the end of the filing, your phone rings. Your boss wants to see you.

In his office he stands to greet you and nods solemnly, waves you into a chair and goes through the usual expressions of sympathy. He's awkward; this is not his forte. He's visibly relieved when he can move on to business.

'You want to get out of the office, Bridget?'

You feel a moment of panic. 'What?'

'Chen and I have discussed shifting the koala fieldwork forward. He can start it this week. You'd work with him in the field for a month or so, doing the grid analysis.'

Your mind turns slowly. This is menial, assigned to the most junior workers, the new graduates. 'Um. I didn't think I was doing the fieldwork.'

He leans forwards. 'Chen thinks you need a straightforward task, and some fresh air. I agree – if that's what you want.'

They'll be glad to get you out of here, because no one knows how to speak to the devastatingly bereaved. After a month of office sympathy you'll be heart-attack material, if today's allocation of muffins and biscuits is anything to go by. That's the kind of joke you once would have made. No one has mentioned death, or children, or unfortunate accidents. Many water-cooler topics to avoid. Yes, on the whole better to get you out. Bless the government and its flexible jobs and discretionary budgets. Chen has come up with a way to protect you.

You agree and shake Rob's hand. A month's reprieve. By the time it's over, the shocking intrusion of your bereavement will have passed for the rest of them, and some kind of return to normal might be possible. For now, you are in quarantine.

FINN

After Bridget drove off in a crunch of gravel, silence settled over Finn and Edmund. For the first time in a week the house was otherwise empty. Parrots shrieked in the blossoms outside and the smell of coffee hung heavily over the kitchen. It had begun tasting evil – dark and metallic – but Finn couldn't yet accept the loss of the morning elixir that had sustained his adult life and so he forced it down.

Edmund rinsed their mugs and stacked them. 'I'll head back this arvo. What say we get a bit organised?'

He meant well, Finn knew. And Eddie was right. Bridget had gone back to work, Jarrah to school. Without something to get on with, Finn would crumble.

'I guess we missed Sculpture by the Quay,' he said, realising it for the first time.

'We'll shoot for next year, don't worry,' Eddie said briskly. 'Let's get your studio sorted first and go from there.'

The studio, beyond the pool. The zone where no one went. He'd locked the pool gate with a chain and padlock after the police removed their tape, and it had remained that way since The Day.

He would have walked around to the back entryway, but Edmund took his arm and nodded at the gate.

'You've got to go in sometime.'

The padlock yielded with a clunk. Finn lifted the chain, feeling the greasy weight of it in his hands, slung it over the fence, and pushed the gate open. The pool lay beyond, clear and rippling gently in the morning sun. The monster in their backyard. There should have been some evidence, surely, of what happened there? But apart from a scattering of dead leaves across the bottom, the water beckoned as invitingly as it ever had.

Soon, Finn knew, he'd have to carry out maintenance. Scoop a vial of water and drop in the indicator chemicals, wait until the colour showed the level of acidity, then splash the required chemicals into the pool to maintain its balance. But no chemical test would show what had happened.

'Want me to go first?' Eddie said.

Finn nodded and followed, eyes fixed on Eddie's neck. The man had outstayed everyone else. Even Conor had left yesterday to go back to work. Eddie had stepped up from agent to friend. Finn assumed he owed this at least partly to the man's past with Bridget, or, more likely, to his potential earnings from Finn's art, but he was grateful.

They skirted the edge of the pool, Finn avoiding its brilliant, sparkling blue. Edmund reached *Dragon Sentry* and pulled the lever to open the sliding doors. They stepped through, neither turning to watch the doors close, though the sound of the latch locking behind his back made Finn flinch.

On the floor, pieces of clockwork, strewn. The welding torch flung aside. A stagnant coffee on the bench.

Until a week ago, the studio had been his sanctuary. His first proper workspace: the shelves he'd constructed, the welder with its lanky argon tank, the hoist, taken from a previous life lifting engine blocks from unresponsive cars, its hook now dangling in the service of Finn's art. The double-doored outlook straight into the pool area. The one direction he hadn't glanced that morning.

'Can I make a suggestion?' Edmund asked softly.

'What?'

'Do some carving. Take the pressure off. The commissions can wait.'

Finn blinked back to the moment. 'I don't think I can do anything.'

'You need something, Finn.'

Finn picked up the torch, hefted it experimentally, hung it back on its hook and disconnected the welder.

'What about another place to work?' Edmund asked. 'You could hire a studio.'

'We're not staying here.' It wasn't until the words were out that Finn knew he'd actually made the decision. 'I'm going to sell the house. We're going home.'

*

The mountain had been the decider, when they first saw the place.

The four of them had flown up together for Bridget's second interview with the Primary Industries Research Institute. It had been raining, and from the plane Finn had glimpsed sodden cane fields among the clouds. Being Tasmanian they were used to rain, but when Finn stepped out of the plane, the humidity hit him like a slap, slick with aircraft fuel. He sweated across the tarmac, damp where a grizzling Toby sagged, heavy and uncooperative, on his hip. He had screamed for much of the flight, from ear pain, Finn thought.

'Is it always this hot?' Jarrah had asked.

'No,' Bridget said over her shoulder. 'On the days the volcano's erupting, it's hotter.'

Finn gave his oldest son a warning glance. No complaints, at least not before her interview. She'd gone on about the extinct shield volcano straddling the state border, the biodiversity hotspot, the volcanic-core-turned-mountain, and other facts that had failed to move the male members of the family. Jarrah trailed behind them into the terminal, pink-faced and irritable.

They collected the hire car, manoeuvred their way out of the car park, headed south. Turned into Tweed Heads for lunch. Found a place that served fish and chips and seafood on the river, where they could sit under cover, out of the rain.

The seafood was, compared to Tasmania's, worse than average. The rain pissed holes into the river's surface. Dangerous-looking pelicans cruised by, eyeing their scraps. Finn was still sweating uncomfortably, his shirt sticking to his skin. Bridget went off to change and came back looking odd and tightly buttoned in her new suit, which didn't suit the climate.

'Let's go,' she said. 'I need thirty minutes of air-con before I go in, or I'll be a puddle.'

They wound through Tweed Heads towards the Pacific Highway. He already hated the town Bridget had picked for them on the basis of this job, its proliferation of nursing homes, and its proximity to where her mother grew up on the Gold Coast. One big retirement village, trying too hard. Jammed up against its twin town on the other side of the border, big brash Coolangatta, trying even harder. Two different time zones to add to the culture clash. Flat and hot and humid and wet. How could he live here? How could Bridget think this would work?

It was his own fault. He and Sandra hadn't had actual sex – it was just kissing that got out of hand. Neither of them wanted to lose their marriage. It was one of those stupid things. Or, in fact, three of those stupid things. The second and third times they weren't drunk. Finn was no good at lying and Bridget fast saw something different between her husband and her best friend. Then she got it out of him and snapped. So she was calling the shots for this move, and he had no choice but to go along with it.

As the highway briefly curved southwest, the rain tailed off and the cloud lifted. Beyond the flat sugar-cane plains the knobbled crag of rock rose – shocking, massive – against a backdrop of ranges.

Finn stared. 'What the hell is that?'

Bridget smiled. 'Wollumbin. Cloudcatcher. Better known as Mount Warning. I told you, remember? That's the solid core of the volcano, what remained after the rest wore away. Those mountains all round? The caldera. Forty clicks across. Imagine that erupting.'

They dodged the screaming B-doubles, turned off the highway and followed the sinuous curves and switchbacks of the Tweed River straight towards the mountain. As the rain passed, the whole place gleamed. Steam rose from the roadsides and cane fields, and the brilliant shades of green hurt Finn's eyes. Even Jarrah and Toby gazed around with interest.

He wished Bridget luck as she got out of the car. Pumped the air-con higher and took the boys on a drive, winding out of town and following the signs to Mount Warning. They passed from cane fields to pasture, to trees, and pulled up in the car park at the mountain's base, surrounded by thick, dank rainforest. A hidden creek trickled past, and signs warned against attempting the climb late in the day, or climbing at all for those who respected Bundjalung tradition. They stared wistfully up into the canopy, trying to spot the summit.

This was supposed to be a sea change, with a beach house. Bridget had chosen Tweed Heads, or one of the coastal villages south of it, for their new life, and had found a nursing home for her mother. She'd picked out a couple of houses on the coast and suggested they do a drive by while she was at the interview. But as they headed back into Murwillumbah, Jarrah was searching on his phone.

'What about this one, Dad? It's just round the corner.'

He tilted the screen and Finn saw purple weatherboards and red trim in miniature, a lush garden, a pool.

'Don't you want to live near the beach, Jarr?' he asked, just in case.

'Nup,' Jarrah said. 'Do you?'

'Nup. Let's check it out.'

He'd known, even before they pulled up out front and peered through the bushes into the garden. Even before he found out about the extra room – separate from the house and overlooking the pool, perfect for his first real art studio – he'd known the purple house would be theirs. Bridget had got her way with moving to the North Coast, but Finn and the boys chose living inside the volcano.

*

From the kitchen Finn could hear the real-estate agent's feet upstairs, her efficient clip-clip-clip as she followed Edmund around, the pauses as she stood in open doorways, counted bedrooms, assessed the presence and absence of built-in wardrobes, checked the aspect of windows and proximity of bathrooms. She came down the stairs behind Edmund, stepped through lounge, bathroom, living area, kitchen. Stopped and glanced in the direction of the pool.

'Shall I?'

Finn nodded. Of course she knew. Everyone knew. Even if she didn't read the local papers, a fool could tell something dreadful had happened in their home. Flowers jammed every surface, the most delicate wilting, the robust long-lasting varieties blooming obscenely, the air stinking of vase water and pollen. The mess of sympathy cards, stacked in piles. The shattered boards, the twisted remains of *Owl Sentry*, the chained-up pool gate, the shrine spilling on to the road out the front.

Edmund took her to the pool. They were back in less than five minutes.

'Mr Brennan, it's a beautiful house,' she said. 'Charming paint job, good aspect, full of character.' She sat down. 'But let me be honest. It'll be a difficult sale. Tragic events affect a property. The kinds of people who'll be interested will drive a hard bargain. It may take a while, and you may need to take quite a loss.'

Loss was all relative, Finn thought. 'It doesn't matter. I want to get us out of here. We can leave it empty, can't we?'

She shook her head. 'Empty sends the wrong message. You want it to look normal.'

'What about tenants?' Edmund suggested.

'You will have some of the same issues,' she said. 'There'll be … resistance … to living where there's been a tragedy, though if the rent is low enough you'll get someone. That doesn't send a good message either. You might do better with a house-sitter who could keep it nice for inspections. Depending on the issue of cost.'

'There's a bit to think over,' Edmund said. He was getting good at stepping into the conversational gaps caused by Finn's silences, buying Finn time to gather his thoughts. 'Anything else?'

'I see you need some repairs,' she said carefully. 'If you'd like help to get the house inspection-ready, my son Tom's a handyman. He's good. I can ask him to call by this afternoon and give you a quote.'

Finn nodded, though he wasn't really following. 'Inspection-ready?' he repeated at last.

'Here's the thing,' she said. 'We don't want you to look desperate. It's a great home and we don't want to draw attention to what's happened. So the house needs to be clean and tidy, the garden in good nick, the pool looking clean and maintained. And you should to do some … clearing up … in your son's bedroom.'

Finn got to his feet and went to the window. It was impossible to sit still, and he didn't want her to see his trembling chin.

'I know how hard it is,' she said to his back. 'My husband died of an aneurism and his life insurance had lapsed. I had to put our home on the market within a month. Tom and I have some idea what you're going through.'

Finn turned. He'd thought there was something behind her professional face.

Angela slid her card on to the table and stood. 'We'd try selling off-market first. No signs, no advertising. I'd just bring around qualified buyers who would be interested.'

Finn nodded. 'I'd like to go ahead. I just need to talk to my wife.'

'There's one more thing. You'd be best to clear away the flowers from out the front.'

She shook his hand and Edmund walked her out, leaving Finn alone. From the window over the sink he could see the pool.

Bridget's income had always sustained them. His artworks had only ever been cream on top. Nowhere near enough to pay a mortgage, let alone rent them another home in the meantime. But now Edmund had people who wanted to pay thousands for his work. Surely those sales could get them out of here and back to Hobart?

He paced up and down until Edmund came back in. 'Let's talk about those commissions.'

'If you can fulfil the first commission, the other client will come on board.'

'I thought they were definite?'

Edmund shrugged. 'They were based on getting into Sculpture by the Quay. But the first one has signed, and I think I can get the other one over the line.'

'I need enough to get us home and cover us while Bridget looks for a job.'

Edmund thought for a moment. 'Tell you what. Dismantle *Dragon Sentry* and adapt it for the first commission. It'd be easier than starting from scratch.'

Finn nodded. That he could do. It wasn't art. It was a ticket out.

Edmund was visibly relieved at the prospect of action. 'Let's get that handyman started. Your time's better spent working. He can get rid of *Owl Sentry*, patch up the boards, get the gate latches replaced. I'll feel better leaving once that's organised.'

He came and stood next to Finn, so close they were almost touching. 'If you like, I can clear away the shrine?'

Finn nodded. He knew what it was: the town's expression of sympathy. But he couldn't bear it any more. Each time they stepped out of the gate, it was an accusation.

JARRAH

Soon as I turned into the street I saw the stuff was gone. The teddy bears, the flowers, the cards tucked into the wire, the candles smoking in their glass jars. Disappeared.

No one knew, but I'd been adding to it. A flower or two I picked on the way home, and I tried to make sure there was always a candle burning – not one of those battery ones, but a real one. Someone had left a little glass lamp and I put new candles in and lit them, morning and night, when no one was watching.

Now all that was left was a patch of brown grass where the flowers had been lying for a week, a few crushed petals, a dead match or two.

Never knew what would be gone when I got home these days.

Kicked the gate open and wheeled the bike in. Added four pm to the list of times I hated. Getting home used to be my time with Toby, while Mum was at work and Dad in his studio.

I wondered what Dad had done all day. I was close to the house when a bang on the verandah made me jump. Hadn't noticed a guy crouching below the gizmo, holding some kind of tool.

'Who are you?' I blurted.

He jumped and turned around, spanner in the air. 'Man, you startled me. I'm Tom.'

Like that was meant to mean something. He was younger than I'd first thought – not much older than me. I kept staring.

'I'm doing some repairs,' he added. 'Your – dad, is it? – wants some things fixed up before the sale. Hey, give me a hand to lift this thing off the wall?'

'Isn't Dad here?'

He shook his head. 'He and the other guy have gone out.'

Dropped the bike on the grass, clomped up the three steps to the verandah and went over next to him in front of the smashed metalwork hanging from the splintered weatherboards. Tom had tidied it up, unscrewed it and spread a paint-covered sheet below to catch it.

'Take it there and there.' He gestured. When my hands were gripping the thing, he took hold and nodded at me to lift. It came away from the wall, trailing wires and screws, and we crouched and laid it on the sheet.

'Thanks,' he said, bending over it with the spanner. 'I'll be right now.'

Stood up, backed away. Walked past his bent back and into the kitchen. Wondered where Dad and Edmund had gone. Ate a huge bowl of cereal overflowing with milk as if it would give me the answers. It didn't.

I vibed him to go and it worked. He knocked on the door ten minutes later.

'Tell your dad I'll be back first thing in the morning with the timber. I reckon I can knock it over tomorrow.'

'Right,' I said. 'Before the sale.'

'I dunno. That's my mum's side of things. I'm just the grunt.' He brushed his hands on his overalls and looked at me through the screen. 'Sorry about your brother, mate.'

That took me by surprise. I'd never met the guy. Did every person in town know what had happened? This handyman – Tom – said it without looking weird or embarrassed or anything.

'Yeah.' I did a stupid kind of nod. 'Um. Thanks.'

'See ya.' He turned on his heel and was stomping down the steps before I could answer. He headed across the grass, head up, like he didn't care about a thing. Not much older than me, but out of school, doing his own thing.

I went outside. The thing was gone. I couldn't see what he'd done with it. There was just a smashed, splintery hole in the wall. There was no chain on the pool gate and no one else home.

First time I'd been in the house by myself.

I went to the gate and swung it open. The pool cleaner was plugged in, chugging around the bottom of the pool, sucking up all the dead leaves blown in over the past week. I stared into the water like it might have answers. It wouldn't have happened while I was at home. I'd never have forgotten Toby long enough for him to get into the pool area, fall into the pool and drown.

Dad's car pulled up out on the street and I bolted. I was sitting at the kitchen table like nothing was wrong by the time he came up the steps.

'Hey,' he said. 'I just took Eddie to the airport. How'd you go today?'

'Didn't know we were selling the house.'

He stopped dead for a moment then sighed. Went over to the kettle and lifted it. That thing wasn't for boiling water any more. It was for bad moments.

'Some guy called Tom said he can finish up the repairs in the morning in time for the sale.'

The water gushed out of the tap. He filled the kettle right to the top, a bad habit that Mum used to hassle him about. Boiling two litres of water every time he wanted a cup of tea.

He turned the kettle on. 'Nothing's been decided, Jarrah.'

I didn't say anything while the kettle hissed and finally boiled in the silence. He sloshed the water into a mug, jiggled the bag, added milk. Then looked at me. 'You can't honestly tell me you want to stay in this house.'

I shrugged. 'Where would we go?'

'Where we belong, of course,' he said. 'We need family and friends, Jarr, at a time like this.'

It sounded like a line he'd rehearsed. But I got it. I got why he'd want to be with his brother and sisters. I was an only child again. I had cousins in Tasmania and they were OK, but they weren't brothers. Toby was the person I'd been closest to in the world. If I had a brother, I'd want to be with him.

'I don't want to put more pressure on your mother,' Dad said. 'I'm just looking at all the options, working out what we can do, how we can get home as easily as possible. It'll be all right.'

It wouldn't. Moving was never going to make it all right. And the last place I wanted to go was back to Tasmania.

'I'll talk to your mother when she gets home. Can you keep it quiet until then?'

'Whatever.' That wasn't something I was allowed to say to my parents, before. I got up. 'I've got homework.'

'Give me a hug.'

I didn't want to. It wasn't like our family didn't hug – we did – and Dad was famous for being a bonecrusher. That was the problem. I didn't think I could handle one of his hugs. But his chin was trembling and I couldn't stand that either. I clenched my teeth and stepped into his hug. I stepped back as soon as I could, scooped up my schoolbag and headed upstairs. Shut the door and flopped down on my bed.

Dad had family in Tassie, and I had Oliver Neumann.

The worst thing was, our parents were friends. It'd been bad enough to face him at school, where he was a couple of years ahead of me, but then we'd go to the Neumanns' for Sunday barbecues. Toby was still little then, and after lunch he'd fall asleep in his car capsule and we'd be waved off to 'play' in Oliver Neumann's bedroom as the olds opened another bottle of wine.

'Don't fucking come near me, you pervert,' he'd say, and get on the computer. I'd sit in the chair across the room at an impossible angle from the screen while he surfed, stopping when he found something to hassle me about.

'Ever touch me and I'll fucking kill you,' he said often enough.

What was it about me? I didn't want to touch him. I'd never have thought of it if he hadn't gone on and on. I'd spend hours perched on the edge of his chair by the desk, praying he'd find something to watch and forget about me.

'Check this out, perv,' he said one time. 'Stupid parents have no idea how to block stuff.'

The image that came up was three naked men. It took me a moment to understand what was happening and where their penises were and I felt sick.

'Like that, don't you, faggot?'

'It's gross.' I turned away from the screen, but not before I saw the bulge in his shorts.

'Don't look at me like that,' he snapped. 'Like you want it in your fucking mouth.'

That time I did something. I walked across the room, opened the door and let myself out.

'Don't think you can run away from it, Jarrah,' he yelled after me. 'Doesn't matter how fast you are.'

I was down the hall before he could follow, and downstairs. The olds were still laughing in the living area. I found a big built-in cupboard down there, in the laundry, and wedged myself into it. It smelled of clean sheets, and I shut my eyes and tried to get rid of the picture of those men. I stayed there for two hours, until it was time to go home and I could sneak out.

It didn't work. I still remembered it. I still remembered the look on Oliver Neumann's face as he laughed at me. The main thing I'd achieved since we came to Murwillumbah was avoiding seeing that look on anyone's face.

Tasmania. Home, Dad called it.

BRIDGET

You are weary to the cartilage of your joints, the marrow of your bones, the vessels of your blood. Too weary from deciding what to do each minute of your working day and the prospect of deciding what to do each waking minute of your evenings to face anything else at all. Too weary to summon outrage when Finn tells you he's had an agent appraise your home.

'I'm looking at our options. Trying to take the pressure off you,' he said.

It's impossible to think of working again in the department, or at the university, living back in Hobart with its familiar hills and valleys, Mount Wellington looming overhead, the harbour lapping at its feet, the little houses crowded on its hills, backyards largely free of swimming pools in that chilly climate. Safe, familiar.

'If I can get enough commissions, say two or three, we could go straight away,' Finn says. 'It doesn't matter if you don't have a job.'

Without a job what machinery would grind the moving hours past? Without some slender thread holding you to the world, who knows where and how far you might fall?

'I need to work, Finn.'

He nods. 'Sure. But we've got to get home.'

You turn and put your hands on the bench. Outside the sky is all kinds of vermillion and orange, streaked with light, speckled with flying foxes streaming from their roosts into the evening. You remember that Hobart smelled of lavender and brine and empty oceans and Antarctica. Here smells like Asia: shiitake mushrooms, frangipani, mildew and bat shit. You've been foreigners all along, out of your element. If you'd stayed at home, this would never have happened.

When you fall into bed not long after dinner, Finn reaches for you and for the first time there is humming intent in his hold. You've wept, separately and together, each night for the past seven, but there's been no desire. Now, suddenly, you feel it flaring in him.

It might be comfort, perhaps, and release. Connection, skin, breath, life. But you've stitched together someone to be and those threads are so thin and stretched that anything might snap them. You've created a person who might be able to get you through, a person who can forget, for some moments here and there, dragging her drowned son from the water.

You can't think of that. You can think of Finn and the gate and the stupid *Owl Sentry*. You can think of your older son, your ordinary son. It wasn't Jarrah who blew your world. Jarrah was, and continues to be, exactly what you'd expected from a child. The most normal kid you could imagine.

Toby, on the other hand, did nothing but surprise you. He hurtled into the world, uncontainable. A force of nature, Finn used to call him. Like he was going to reach out and devour the world. So dangerous, you now know, to live like that. To treat the world without fear. It *should* be feared.

Finn reaches for you and as his body presses against yours he could be a stranger, coming at you so tentatively, trembling.

'Please,' he whispers, and he draws you against him slowly, not daring to demand. You almost wish he'd stop asking, stop making you the decider and just take you. Fuck you so hard you could get lost in it. Fuck you past this agony.

Your traitorous body feels him and some primal biology kicks in so you are suddenly ravenous. You roll on top, straddle him, feel his surprise and matching desire. You can't kiss him, not that, but after just a few moments of grinding together you position yourself and thrust down so he impales you. You groan, deep and guttural, just as he does, you rise up and come down furiously, hands on his chest. From indifference to hot and hard and slick in seconds, agonising and irresistible at once. You're rutting like animals that have tasted death and want nothing of it.

You're going to come; you can't believe it. When you do, it blazes through like rage and you look down at his face. In that second you hate him with your whole being. His eyes roll back a little and he arches and cries out and in your mind you've killed him and it's gore, not sex, that slicks over your body. It's the only punishment that matches the crime, your rage's obliteration of him.

You slide off and he pulls you down and sobs, hulking sobs in the space between your breasts. Then he falls silent, and a moment later twitches, and you know he's dropped into post-orgasmic sleep. You lie next to him, shuddering deep inside. It's dangerous to be open to the world and dangerous to be open to him. Coming, you felt the start of a primal shriek you couldn't afford to utter. And so you roll away from him, clamp your legs

109

together, clench your jaw and fight down that shriek, wrestle it down to its dark hiding place and shut the lid on it.

He sleeps, damn him, like a child, sweaty and restless and deep, whimpering and crying out but never waking. Toby used to sleep like that, bringing you to wakefulness often with his thrashing and murmurs. He'd wake in the morning revitalised, while you were shredded. Orgasm has stoked your rage and focused it more freely on Finn, who dares to sleep, dares to breathe, dares to sweat and weep and pant and ejaculate.

You'd thought that after a week you might have been able to comfort each other, but your fury is deepening and widening, becoming inexorable, soldered onto the foundations of your being. It's becoming the buttress to your grief, its equal and opposing force.

The clock flips its way around the hours, glowing red in the dark, and the night noises outside swell and subside, and the darkest, quietest hour arrives and somehow, eternally, passes. You can't be close to Finn, but you can't be too far away from him either, or what holds you upright will collapse.

He wakes at the first hint of light in the sky, some time a little after five. You hear him swim up to consciousness, his crusted eyelids cracking open, his tongue moistening his lips, the scratch of his nails on his belly. It's repulsive.

You're up on your elbow, facing away from him, watching the window. He rolls into your back, reaches out a hand and cups the curve of your hip bone.

'I want you to sleep somewhere else.'

In the silent, shocked moment that follows he removes his hand from your skin. The only other room is Toby's. Still untouched. You can feel his incredulity in the air between you.

'The studio,' you say. 'There's room for a bed.'

'What will Jarrah think?'

You almost want to laugh at this. 'He'll think the world's gone to shit, Finn.'

You get up and begin to dress, keeping your back to him.

JARRAH

'How's it, Jazz? Weekend OK?'

I hated people asking me that. But it was Laura, and she took my arm and looked at me, all soft and concerned, and I didn't mind so much.

'OK.' My standard reply. Meant I could probably get through the day without falling apart. Not that I did fall apart. Not in front of anyone. Hadn't cried since Toby's funeral, not in public. Maybe that's why they'd all forgotten.

They were all such kids. It was ten days since the funeral and it was like half of them had forgotten my brother was dead. Their lives just went on like usual. They got upset about stupid stuff, excited about stupid stuff.

Except Laura. She hadn't forgotten.

'Meet me after school?' she whispered into my ear.

'What for?'

'You'll see.' She winked and went off to class.

Life after Toby, nothing was the same. Not that life was good before he died, but I kind of knew what to expect. Knew Laura was out of my reach. Knew the dangerous kids, and kept out of their way. Knew Billy was as lonely and weird as me, and we sometimes made a bigger target together than either of us alone – was careful not to hang out with him too much.

Now the dangerous kids ignored me, Billy wasn't cool enough to hang with me, and Laura was my best friend. On the morning bus she saved me a seat. She'd look down the aisle to catch my eye and smile. When I sat down, that question: *How's it, Jazz?* In the afternoon I watched her drama club rehearsals, or did my homework in the booth at the pizza place while she worked, and got dropped off home afterwards by her mother.

No one my age had ever looked at me like she did. I'd figured out how to control my face so she couldn't see the effect it had on me. I sat next to her on the bus, our legs touching slightly. Sometimes she rested a hand on my shoulder, or touched my arm. She did it easily, like I would have touched Toby, like being rejected had never entered her mind.

I guess it hadn't. When she walked down the hallway at school, people turned and their smiles were real. When Laura knew the answer to something in class, she just put up her hand and said it. She didn't hide being clever. She did her homework but she wasn't a perfectionist. She wasn't a suck, but she was well behaved. She was normal, she was pretty, she was clever, she was popular. She even got on with her mother, who, by the way, was really nice to me.

Wish I could have enjoyed it more. Sometimes, for a second, I nearly forgot about Toby. It was worse then, because it hit me again in the guts.

I met her in the afternoon at the gate, thinking we'd walk to the bus stop. She gave a funny kind of smile without really looking at me.

'Let's go,' she said, and headed in the opposite direction so fast I had to hurry to keep up.

There was a scrappy bush block at the back of the school. The edges were full of rubbish and weeds, and the place smelled of bats, because about a thousand of them slept in the trees all day and kept most people out. But there was a spot in the middle no one seemed to know about, away from the bats, where a little creek ran through a patch of tall trees. Kind of like a forest. I'd spent a few lunchtimes there.

Laura stopped at the edge, glanced back to make sure I was following, picked her way through the rubbish and found the twisting track. The ground was covered in dead leaves, and it was loud in there, with the bats squealing and flapping their wings as we walked under them. I followed her through the trees till we reached the creek. She stopped, dropped her pack on the ground and stepped down the bank till she was standing a little below me. The water was rushing and brown, swollen from rain the night before. She had that same smile as she turned. Stretched out, took my hand, pulled me towards her until we were nearly touching.

'I know you haven't …' she said softly.

I could hardly breathe. She wanted me to kiss her. I had no idea how. My stomach churned. Wanted to bolt like an animal, crash through the trees, break out into the sunshine and sprint home.

She laughed a little. 'You're shaking. It's not that scary!'

She was so close I could feel her breath on my neck. She dropped my hand, lifted her arms, put them round my neck. I wanted to kiss her but couldn't move. Scared of doing it wrong.

She pulled me in until our lips met. She closed her eyes but I kept mine open, feeling like I might fall over. When she slipped her tongue into my mouth I had to stop myself jerking away with the strangeness of it.

I was nearly sixteen years old. I must have seen millions of screen kisses and a few real-life ones, but they didn't help. I was a late starter. I should have been prepared but it felt weird.

I took hold of her waist and kissed her back, trying hard.

She broke away. 'Easy, Jazz. Nice and slow.'

OK, so less tongue. I tried again and she kind of softened in my arms. I was getting the hang of it. It wasn't bad, actually. She moved closer and I felt the brush of her breasts against my chest like an electric shock.

After a few minutes she stepped back and opened her eyes. I tried to read her face. Was I hopeless?

'Um,' I said. Stopped.

'We'd better go,' she said. 'Mum's picking me up at four, after extra maths.'

'Extra maths?'

She shrugged. 'Skipped it. Wanna lift?'

'Yeah.'

I had no idea if I'd done it right. Wanted to kiss her again but wasn't brave enough. Worried I hadn't cleaned my teeth since after breakfast – no one cleaned their teeth at school, did they? – and that my breath was gross.

She grabbed my hand: that was something. We walked side by side on the narrow path, with me scraping past the trees. As we got near the edge, realised I didn't want to go out there again. Strange though the kiss had been, for the first time I wasn't thinking about Toby for a few minutes.

I stopped, pulled her round. 'Hey.'

She stepped in, put her palms on either side of my face. I knew what to expect this time and I leaned in to meet her. Shut my eyes and focused on the feeling of her lips on mine. Let my mouth open more naturally.

It was shorter, but when she drew back she was smiling.

'Fast learner, Jazz-boy. Now come on! Mum'll be there.'

She tugged my hand and we broke into a run. I didn't mind the branches slapping me in the face. I was smiling too. Our second kiss wasn't so weird. I'd felt more like a teenage boy kissing the girl he worshipped. It was good.

FINN

Finn rested his shaking hands on the bench, breathing through his mouth to minimise the stink of ozone and molten steel. That had been the smell filling his nostrils when he'd first heard the sound. He'd released the trigger, raised his goggles, and heard it again. The sound no one should ever hear. The sound of Bridget finding Toby.

He clenched his jaw. He wanted to tear the torch from its moorings and fling it over the fence. Or turn it on *Dragon Sentry*, lying dismembered on the bench before him, and melt the contraption down to nothing. Once, Finn had been able to sculpt so that the world receded and the only reality was wood and steel and the stink of ozone and molten copper. He'd never get back there. It was too dangerous to let world and time disappear. Nothing would erase the fact that he'd welded with his back turned to the pool while his son had drowned.

Had he really promised Edmund he'd create more of these things? So pretty, so gleaming. So deadly. In the absence of another explanation, it seemed *Owl Sentry* had indeed failed. How else could Toby have got into the pool? Even the police seemed to have no idea. DI Evans had interviewed them both

117

again, and the tone of the questions was more sinister, but it was clear she didn't know either.

It was no good. He stripped off the goggles and threw them on the bench. Straightened, stretched the kinks from his back, strode to the door and crossed over to the house. He had to think. When she was at work during the day, he could pretend he still lived in the house instead of across the chasm that now separated him from Bridget. The pool literally lay between them.

Finn readied the Atomic and put it on the gas. He felt sick as the machine heated up and the smell of hot metal permeated the kitchen. Acid burned in the back of his throat. He turned off the gas, carried the machine to the door and hurled it into the garden.

As the thing bounced across the grass he saw Meredith closing the gate behind her. Finn groaned softly and closed his eyes. Was it too much to ask, that he could lose it for a moment and be unobserved?

When he opened his eyes she was advancing on him.

'Finn,' she said in her low voice. At least she didn't try for a breezy greeting.

'Rough day,' he said, not looking at her.

'I was passing. Thought I'd see how you're getting on. It can't be easy, working out there.'

Finn started to cry. It spilled over without conscious decision, weeping of the hopeless kind, a stream of tears soaking his face.

'Let's go in,' Meredith said, putting a hand gently on his arm.

He allowed her to turn him and usher him up the steps. Without really knowing how, he found himself sitting at the table while she bustled around with kettle and milk and mugs.

118

'You'll find tea goes down better with this.' She pulled a small bottle of brandy from her handbag. The smell of alcohol at ten in the morning made Finn dizzy. He took a gulp of brandy-laced tea that burned all the way down.

'You always carry that?'

She smiled, a small, sad smile. 'Unfortunately, yes.'

Finn took another gulp. 'I had an agent around last week to look at selling the house. We haven't signed or anything. But she's just called to say she's got someone keen, who's only in town today.'

'So you're leaving?'

Finn nodded. 'I guess so. But she wants me to clean out Toby's room.' He groped for a tissue, honked his nose, and took another gulp of tea.

'When does she want to bring them?'

'In an hour.' Finn felt his chest heave. With the flowers and candles and teddies out the front gone, Toby's room was their own private shrine. Changing it from the day Toby died seemed an irrevocable step, and one that Bridget should have a say in. But the idea of texting or calling her to ask felt monumental.

'Do you want me to help?' When he didn't answer, Meredith passed him another tissue. 'I promise you, I'll do it with love.'

Love was a word that hadn't been said between Finn and Bridget since Toby died. He'd been too afraid to say it, too afraid of her response. Afraid the hate in her eyes would be articulated. He'd moved across the pool to the studio without complaint and endured the unendurable nights over there the same way. He was far enough away that she wouldn't have to drive him further. A safe distance from which to wait and see what happened.

119

He looked over at Meredith, she of the brandy bottle in the handbag, and the foundation for dead children, and the understanding face.

'I can't go in there. Could you do it?'

'Yes.'

'I think there are some boxes in the garage somewhere.' He gestured vaguely.

She stood. 'I'll take care of it. Why don't you clean up the living area and run a vacuum around the place? The two of us can get it looking fine in an hour.'

Finn watched her cross the lawn, open the garage, locate some boxes and carry them back. She'd appeared at the exact moment he needed help. She had brandy in her handbag. She was willing. So why didn't he like her?

BRIDGET

Your second working week and the days have fallen into a pattern. You back the car out of the garage and drive to the office. You meet Chen in the car park, transfer into a state-owned four-wheel drive and head out to areas identified as likely or known koala habitat. Your body moves; you eat. You appear to be alive.

Chen makes you do all the driving and presents you with a list of tasks every day. At first you feel a vague prickle of resentment that he seems to be treating the time like a holiday. After a few days you realise it is deliberate: Chen is accepting boredom so you can stay busy.

He seems OK with looking across and finding you weeping. He doesn't try to stop you; he doesn't say anything about time healing. He doesn't even offer you tea. So far he is the only person who can stand to simply be with you. You've never known, before, what a rare quality this is.

Today you bash along a rough bush track, and as you emerge on the steep side of the enormous caldera and look down at the tilted cone rising from its centre, you're struck by the deep unfamiliarity of the place. The country of Toby's death is obscenely fecund; you turn your back for a season in this place and a little shoot of a plant will be towering over your head. You once liked its warmth and fertility. But as fast as this land gives, it takes away again, snatches life back, tramples it, breaks it down, claims it. Anything dead is humus before you can blink.

At lunch you feel dangerous. Perhaps because you're dangling your legs over the lip of an old volcano, perhaps because your fury at Finn is starting to bubble hot and deep. Chen has brought lunch, as always: rice paper rolls wrapped around chicken and noodles and mint; falafel and hummus in flat bread, expertly made, stowed in a small cooler with an ice brick so they emerge fresh and tasty. You can barely bring yourself to eat anything cooked by Finn, but thanks to Chen's lunches you're getting nutrition.

'How come you're not married?' you ask, picking up a pebble and casting it overarm into the valley.

He shrugs. 'Job plus PhD doesn't equal much time for anything else. You know that.'

You make a rueful face. 'Guess I was already married when I started mine, but six years of study was still a big ask for Finn.'

'I got into the habit of being on my own.' Chen glances sideways at you. 'And then – well, the people I like always seem to be committed.'

Flirting with danger feels suddenly stupid and you back off. 'Well, you're a great cook.'

He picks up another rice paper roll and asks, more gently than you deserve: 'Have you told your mother yet?'

*

The nursing-home matron comes out to reception to meet you, her face a picture of compassion, her arm outstretched to pat or

122

grasp or hug. On the phone she's promised to keep your secret about Toby. Agreed the news would be traumatic – and might have to be repeated to your mother many times.

'We're so sorry,' she begins, and you back away, nodding yes, yes, to head her off.

'No one's slipped up, have they? She hasn't found out?'

'She doesn't know a thing. The staff have all been briefed.'

'Good,' you say, turning away and setting off down the hallway. You can do this.

'Bridget,' she calls after you. 'She's drifting today.'

She's seated by the window in her comfortable armchair, looking out into the garden. You stand for a moment at the door to her room, steeling yourself. You never know how she'll be from one visit to the next. Never mind that you're not the same person who came in a couple of weeks ago, simply tired from work and thinking that made for a bad day.

'Oh hello,' she says. You focus and find her looking up at you and smiling.

You force yourself to smile back, blinking back tears you weren't aware of. 'Hello, Mum.'

'I'm not your mother, dear,' she says, with a sympathetic nod. 'Don't you know where she is?'

'No,' you say slowly. 'No, I don't know.'

'Never mind. Come and sit down and wait for her. I think she was just here.'

'Thank you.'

You sit next to her and share the view. It's pretty. This isn't a bad place, not at all. You were lucky to get her in here.

Unstoppable tears slide down your face.

Someone wants to buy your house. Finn blurts it out as you climb the steps to the verandah, talking to fill the silence as you try to absorb his words. Have you even agreed to selling?

'I know we haven't talked about the price or anything, but she had someone interested and wanted to bring them around, and it just went from there.'

He tells you their offer. It's insultingly low: far less than you paid. What kind of person wants to profit from your misery like this?

'We should take it,' Finn says. 'Cut our losses. We could be back home in a month.'

You shake your head, more in disbelief than refusal, and walk past him into the living room, noting its sudden neatness and the absence of flowers. You throw your bag down, kick off your shoes, push into the kitchen and pour a frosty glass of sauvignon blanc.

The house feels hot and airless. Once upon a time you'd have swum after arriving home on such an evening. Now it's become normal to act like you don't have a pool at all, as if across the safety fence is no-man's-land, mined and impassable. For the want of somewhere to go you head back out to the verandah, passing Finn and walking to the end furthest away, warning him with an upheld hand to keep away. You lower yourself into the creaking wicker armchair and allow a long mouthful of wine to slide down your throat.

Finn gets up and goes inside. You take another, larger, mouthful of wine. You've been waiting for it all day, thinking about it in the comfort and risk of working beside Chen for hours, counting koala scats, searching for scratch marks, peering up into trees. You want Chen nearby, and then you're relieved when the day is over. Relieved until you step into your house and must confront Finn and your barely contained rage, and Jarrah, who seems to stay just out of your reach.

You need to make a decision. You need to think.

If you sell the house, Finn can lead the way back down south. He could find you somewhere to live, get things ready while Jarrah finishes the school year and you keep working until something turns up in Hobart. You and Jarrah could move out of Murwillumbah, take a holiday house at the beach for a month or three, drive into work and school.

But.

What if, once separated from Finn, you don't want to rejoin him? The distance between you is taut and stretched, quivering. It holds you together, for now. Without that tension, you might collapse. Or escape. Doesn't he sense the danger of leaving you?

The door bangs and Finn steps out with another beer. He looks at you, eyebrows raised, asking permission. You nod and he lumbers towards you and lowers himself into the adjoining chair like an old man.

You launch right in. 'We can't afford it. We'd hardly buy back into Hobart with the money we'd lose.'

He doesn't answer but tilts his head back and takes a long swig. You know all this without looking at him directly, with your visceral awareness of how his body moves itself near you.

'What about Jarrah's school? We can't take him out now. It's only the start of term four. He's got to finish the year at least.'

A parrot lands in the umbrella tree near the verandah. These things are weeds, you've learned this week – harmless in cooler climates but rampant attackers in the subtropics, invading the bushland, growing without reason or limit. The birds don't mind; the noisy miners and lorikeets make the most of the free food bounty. Shyer birds, Chen tells you, are getting rarer as the brilliant extroverts take over.

'Edmund would be the first to say you can't bank on making money from your art. My job pays the mortgage, remember?'

His silence is unnerving. You expect him to mount a case, to challenge each of your reasons for not selling, but he says nothing, leaving your arguments to fall flat. Two can play that game. You go back to your wine and your contemplation of the garden. You'll sit it out.

You've both finished your drinks by the time Finn turns to you.

'I just can't live here, Bridge.'

Your heart contracts. There's so much pain in his voice and for a second that's all you hear – the agony of this man you've loved, the father of your children.

'It might be the only offer we get. I want to take it. I want us to go home.'

How can you argue against what is, clearly, Finn's bottom line? You want another glass of wine so badly that your throat aches, but you can't get up. The two of you sit in silence with your empty glasses. More lorikeets land in the umbrella tree and shriek their joy as they slash into the spikes of tall crimson flowers, shredding the petals and letting them fall to the lawn.

'It must have taken you all day to clean up the house,' you say.

JARRAH

Time after Toby: fourteen days. He was gone to the land of the monster kings. Did he miss me? Did he want to come home?

They thought I didn't know, but Dad was sleeping in the studio. He'd sneak over there after I went to bed and sneak back early in the morning so he was in the kitchen drinking coffee when I got up.

Hearing him go at night was my signal. I'd watch from the window, and once he'd shut the studio door behind him, I'd get out of bed. I'd stand by the door and listen to make sure there was no noise from Mum, and then I'd tiptoe down the hallway and open Toby's door. It used to squeak but I'd found some oil and put it on the hinges and now it was silent.

I'd get into his bed and pull the covers up. I'd take his book out from under the pillow and open it, and I'd read to Toby in the dark, in a whisper. As if, by reading it often enough, I'd remind him to get back in that sailing ship and come home to us.

Until tonight.

Got home from school late. Watched Laura's drama rehearsal and then her mother collected us and dropped me off out the front. It was dark as I opened the gate. Smelled mown grass. The path was clean, and as I climbed the steps, clomped over the verandah and stopped by the door, everything seemed tidy. Had Dad done it? Thought he was supposed to be working on that stuff for Edmund.

I could hear them from outside. Mum's voice, raised: 'How dare you?'

Dad's voice, lower. 'They were coming. It had to be ready.'

'I wasn't ready!'

'Look.' His voice was so low it was hard to hear. 'The sooner we sell, the sooner we can get out of here. I didn't want to bother you.'

'So you let her come in here and—'

I pushed the door hard, making plenty of noise as I stamped inside. They stopped talking.

'Jarrah,' Dad said.

'Hi.' I dropped my bag on the floor. 'Sorry I'm late.'

They hadn't realised I was late, I saw from the stricken look Dad gave me. He'd become hopeless at hiding his feelings.

Mum tried to cover it up, reaching out her arms. 'You could have texted.'

I gave her a quick hug. 'Dinner?'

'Um, yeah,' Dad said. 'What d'you feel like?'

I felt like anything except a thawed-out casserole, and I was pretty sure that was all we had in the fridge. Obviously dinner wasn't a priority.

'I'll just have a snack,' I said. 'Had something while I was out.'

They sat still and silent while I poured a bowl of cereal and sloshed milk on it, wondering how long I could live on that stuff before I got deficient in something. It wasn't exactly relaxed in the kitchen. My back prickled between my shoulder blades, like it did when someone was watching me. I didn't want to know what they were fighting about. I didn't want to know what Dad's move to the studio meant. I'd googled the divorce rates for people whose children died and found the usual crap you get when you ask a question like that: somewhere between twenty-five and eighty per cent, which was no help. Anywhere in that range sounded bad.

Finished the cereal, shoved my bowl in the dishwater, slung my schoolbag over my shoulder. 'See you.'

'Um, Jarrah,' Dad said. 'You know how we talked about selling the house? Someone came at short notice to see it. I had to put a few things away in your room. Sorry. Hope you don't mind.'

'Right,' I said, not looking anywhere in particular.

There was more they wanted to say, I knew, but I didn't want to hear it. Headed out of the kitchen, up the stairs, into my room and shut the door firmly so no one got any idea of following me.

Dad had done a teenage tidy-up: shoved everything into the cupboard and shut the door. I let it all spill out again and sat down on the bed.

My phone chimed. About as common as a supernova. I dug it out of the bag. Laura. She'd asked for my number a few days earlier, but it was the first time she'd texted.

<howz it jazz?>

It wasn't exactly a question I could answer by text, but it seemed like I shouldn't just ignore my first text from a girl. I didn't know any of those abbreviations, but I made sure to turn off the caps and not use commas.

<⊗ bus tomorrow?>

<yup>

<cul8r>

It took me a moment, but I worked it out, and actually smiled a little. Maybe my use-by date wasn't coming as fast as I thought.

I put some clothes away and took the chance to rip down my movie posters and shove them in the bin. They belonged to some kid I once knew; that's how it felt. What I really wanted was something of Toby's I could hang on to at night when it got bad. That plush monster he loved, the one that was sitting on his bed. I cracked the door open and listened. The TV was on downstairs; they couldn't hear me. I tiptoed down the hall and silently twisted Toby's doorknob. I didn't need to flick on the light. Could tell from the streetlight coming in the window. His little car-shaped bed, the one he'd only had for three months, was made up with some plain cover I'd never seen before. The books and toys that had scattered the shelves and the floor were gone. There was no plush monster anywhere.

I stepped inside, shut the door behind me. Crept to a drawer and opened it. Empty. They were all empty. Everything that had belonged to Toby was gone. Like a kid's room would look if no kid lived in there. Like something in IKEA.

I wedged myself into the space between the bed and the chest of drawers. Drew my knees up to my chest and made myself small in the dark.

He was gone. He was gone and he was never coming back, not sailing over the sea from the magic island, not on the shoulders of one of those monsters, not even in my dreams, where he never appeared.

Shivered, though it wasn't cold. Thought I'd already lost everything, but that wasn't true. There was always something else to lose. Toby was gone and my memory of him was being taken away bit by bit. Soon the house would be gone. By the looks of it, Mum and Dad wouldn't last long either. I put my head down on my knees and pressed my eyeballs into my kneecaps until they hurt and I saw horrible spirals and blurs of light and dark on the back of my eyelids. Would I live with Mum, or with Dad? Would they both go back to Tasmania or would they end up in different places? It didn't seem real. But I knew how things that didn't seem real could suddenly get that way.

Toby must have held us together. Without him, we were like the particles after the Big Bang, flying apart, spreading at the speed of light to different points in the universe.

FINN

Finn knew he should be grateful. After a discussion that dragged on all evening Bridget had eventually agreed, but demanded he ask Angela to try for a higher offer. He'd hated risking the loss of the sale, but he made the call.

Angela got back to him the next morning. 'They've come up fifteen grand,' she said. 'But they want the front of the house patched and repainted so you can't see where the mechanism used to be.'

The words wouldn't quite come clear in his mind and Finn felt stupid. 'What?'

Angela paused. 'Look, it stinks. I'm sorry. It's the best I can do. Tom can start straight away on the repair and painting if you want to proceed.'

'We want to proceed. Christ, we don't want to lose it. How soon will they exchange?'

'Within the week, or maybe two. But I can't push too hard, or I'll scare them off. It wouldn't take much. Trust me, OK? I'll send Tom around shortly.'

Finn hung up and went outside to stand on the verandah of the crazy purple house with its red trim, the house that had promised so much and seemed like their friend. Maybe, away from this place that had betrayed them, and back in Hobart, he'd be able to work again.

It wasn't hard to hide his lack of progress from Bridget. She never came into the pool area or the studio, and she never asked about the sculptures. Edmund was so careful not to make demands on him that fobbing him off hadn't been too hard either. But the truth was, he couldn't work. He had no idea what Bridget's working days were like, but his were agony.

He wanted to rage back at her; of course he did, he was human. But if he allowed himself, then he might accuse her, and he knew they could never have that conversation. He had to put it out of his mind. And so he walked the house during the empty days. He raked the lawn and pulled weeds, he went to the shops. Sometimes he went out for coffee, dark glasses on, hat brim low, newspaper held high so he wouldn't be recognised. He cleaned the studio and fitted his tools into their places. He used the computer to scroll through real-estate sites, looking for houses in Hobart. It seemed much more expensive than he remembered, and those sessions would send him back to the studio to fiddle with pieces of metal, rearranging them uselessly. He avoided Toby's neat bedroom, and he didn't ask Bridget where she was keeping Toby's ashes.

Tom arrived within an hour of Angela's call. He methodically laid a drop sheet the length of the verandah and taped the edges. Set out paint tin, brushes, tray, roller, clean rags, stirrer. He had the correct tool for levering the lid off the tin of paint and he placed the lid, wet side up, where it wouldn't get in the way.

'Did Mum tell you they want it painted a different colour?' he asked.

Finn looked down at the tin of pale paint, then up at the vivid purple wall. 'No.'

'They'll repaint the whole house once they buy it, so they've asked for the front to be done in Clotted Cream. I'll have to undercoat it first.'

'You're in charge.'

Finn sat on the step, pretending to drink his coffee while watching Tom's preparations obliquely. The boy took up a clean brush, dipped it in the paint, stood and slid the brush along the join of two weatherboards. Paint spread out in a pale trail behind the brush, smelling clean, chemical, optimistic.

He was paying the boy to paint so he had time to finish the sculpture. But Finn wanted nothing more than to apply that thick coating to the wall, blot out any evidence of what had happened, focus on the simple job of moving the paintbrush in a straight line, covering up one colour with another.

'Can I give you a hand?' He felt foolish the moment he said it.

Tom showed no surprise. 'Sure. I'm doing the joins first and then I'll roller the rest. There's another brush.'

Finn picked up the brush. It was used – old paint stains speckled the handle – but the bristles had been meticulously cleaned. He dipped it into the paint, lifted it, placed it against the timber. As he drew out the first line of paint, he inhaled the scent and felt inexplicably relieved.

The two of them worked easily together. Found their way around each other without hassle, timed their refills so they didn't collide, took up where the other had left off. As the cutting-in work moved towards completion, Tom poured a slab of paint into the tray, worked the roller back and forth until it was saturated, screwed it to the end of the long pole. He moved down the other end and began rolling the boards, the paint matching up the gaps with a pleasing symmetry.

Finn let himself fall into the rhythm of the brush, senses alert, mind stilled. He was aware of the movement of his arm and the way his body supported it. The sounds of the birds, the humming of small insects, the occasional croak of an errant frog, the rustle of undergrowth as one of the water dragons moved through in search of that frog. A tapestry of sound in which he was central and the brush and the paint were central too. The task being done.

'Do you miss your father?' he asked, as Tom passed close with the roller.

Tom's rhythm didn't falter. 'Every day.'

'How long's it been?'

'Two years, three months.'

'And no better?'

Tom stopped at the end of the row and lowered the roller. 'Of course it's better. You think it'll never get better at first, but it does. Only thing is you hate yourself when you feel better. Like it's disloyal.'

Finn nodded; that he could understand. 'I can't talk to my son, Tom. I don't know what to say to him. I don't know if he's OK and getting on with his life or what.'

Tom went back to the paint tray, topped up the paint, pressed the roller into it and soaked it again. 'Can't you do stuff with him?'

'Stuff?'

Tom gestured to the wall. 'Like this. Practical stuff.'

Finn lowered his brush. 'He used to like running, but I'm too fat to run. Anyhow, he's busy.'

'What's he doing?'

'I don't know. He's hardly at home any more. I think he has new friends.'

Tom started on the next row. 'New friends, you reckon?'

Something in his voice caught Finn's attention. He hadn't thought much about Jarrah's new friends, in truth. He'd seen him getting out of a car once or twice – there'd been a girl in the front seat and a woman, presumably her mother, who'd waved him off. But no one ever came into the house. He knew nothing much about any friends, new or otherwise. Just the girl from before, the one Bridget told him worked at the pizza place. Maybe she was the girl in the car?

'Could *you* talk to him, Tom? You're close to his age. You know what he's going through.'

'No one knows what you're going through,' Tom said, his voice wary. 'Nothing anyone says makes much difference.'

'You're right about that,' Finn said wearily. He put the brush down, suddenly exhausted. 'I should go and get some work done,' he said, wiping his hands on a rag. 'Thanks for letting me help out.'

Tom flashed him a small smile. Finn headed along the verandah, steeling himself to cross the pool area and do some actual work.

'Don't leave him alone too much,' Tom said from behind him. 'Even if you think that's what he wants.'

BRIDGET

No matter what they give you to bring sleep, it never lasts. You dread this time. You refuse to open your eyes, refuse to let your body stretch or move or, in any way, act awake. After the first few times you don't need to look at the red burn of the numbers on the bedside clock to know. Three-thirty, give or take. The deathly hour, the hour of regret and sorrow and revenge, the hour of buried rage resurfacing. The hour when you relive finding Toby, over and over, and wonder if those images will ever burn themselves out.

You haven't even made it to the pre-dawn hours this time. It's a little after two and you've been awake for God knows.

Someone is buying this house. Already some guy is painting the front wall, covering up any trace of what happened. Soon you'll walk out for the last time, hand over the keys, take the money and go. Home, Finn keeps saying, like this has been a poorly conceived holiday to a dangerous destination where war suddenly broke out, and now you're being airlifted to safety by the embassy.

You slide out of bed, stand, pull on a dressing gown, cross to the window. The moon is setting against the faint chatter of fruit bats as they feed on the lemon-scented gum blossoms out on the street. The rest of the human world sleeps, while the absence of Toby slowly dismembers you.

You have dreamed all this. You'll wake and he'll thunder down the hallway and scramble into bed beside you, his hand will pat your cheek and he'll babble in your ear. It's impossible he doesn't exist.

You have been a scientist all your adult life, but one thing you now know: there is no consolation in science. It offers nothing to help you understand or live with this. Your body does not know science. Your body believes that if you search long enough you'll find Toby out there somewhere.

As if pulled by some force, you stride to the door, open it, pad down the hallway past Jarrah's door, enter Toby's room. His absence – now total – is a vortex that wants to suck you in. You stuff your fist in your mouth and it's only the thought of Jarrah two rooms away that forces you to control the harsh sound that wants to come. Until yesterday you could come in here and still smell Toby. It was unendurable, and you came rarely, but now you want it back.

You have to keep moving. The lounge room is cold and dark, the kitchen the same. Your body is animal in its need for comfort, a caged creature pacing its pain into the ground. You want Finn, suddenly and physically. You need his body against yours, his arms around you, his bristled chin on your cheek, the way he has never said anything to blame you. The urge is so strong, so beyond your control, that you follow it, through the lounge, out the door, along the verandah.

And then understand, viscerally: you have to pass the pool to reach him.

You lift the new, efficient latch, push the gate open, step into the pool area, feeling the rough sandstone under your bare feet. You let the gate close behind you. You plan to skirt the pool as widely as you can on your way to Finn, you plan to avert your gaze, but you can't help yourself. As you tiptoe by, you glance down into the water and it all comes back.

You'd thought perhaps you were starting to make progress these past few days, but the memory smites you. You stagger and chlorine burns up through your nostrils and into your brain.

Before you can flee, something flickers down there in the water. The moon's reflection glistens and the water moves slightly, as if some small thing has disturbed its calm surface, setting tiny ripples in motion.

You are suddenly very still.

There is nothing alive about a swimming pool. It's a closed loop of finely balanced chemistry calculated to obliterate organic life. When operating normally, the pool's system ensures anything organic is burned into oblivion before it can multiply.

Yet, looking down into the dark water, you'd swear you could almost hear its voice, an impossible siren song hidden in the ripples, drawing you in. You lower yourself to hands and knees, put your face close to the water's dark surface and stare into its merciless depths.

Toby went into those depths. He followed the siren call to the water, down with the mermaids and the white whales and the giant squid and the seals and the selkies and all the nameless things of the sea. And it seems to you that water is always trying to lure its children back, whispering through human dreams, as if your lungs recall breathing water, your old gills strain under the surface of your skin, the webs between your fingers and toes twitch and try to grow, your limbs dream of weightlessness. You are made of water and you can never leave it.

If he's anywhere, surely he's here?

You know it's not true; it can't be. Your brain is mining memories of childhood fairy tales, pushing you to madness. Yet you lower yourself until your belly is pressed against the sandstone edging and your face is just centimetres above the water, and you stare as if you could pierce the surface with your gaze, as if you could look into it and see Toby's face in those shadows of light and dark.

Because you are hanging over the surface your tears fall straight into the water and it happens again, the ripples, the movement of light and dark, and it seems you can see into the depths and almost hear his voice.

Toby?

You lower your hand, feeling the moment it breaks the surface tension of the water and the cold moves up your fingers.

You're touching him. For a second you're sure of it, and you reach in until the water laps around your wrist and you can feel him in there, as if he's looking up at you.

'Bridget?'

Finn's low voice, real and shocking, snaps you out of the moment, wrenching you back into the world where your son has gone and the pool is a body of lifeless, disinfected water.

'Are you all right?'

You scramble to your feet, shaking, and back off. 'Get away from me.'

You turn and run away, fumbling with the gate and letting it clang behind you. You take the steps at a run, crash inside the house and flee to your bed, forgetting that Jarrah's sleeping, forgetting everything except that for one moment you reached out your hand and touched Toby.

JARRAH

I felt like I should know if Laura was my girlfriend but I didn't. At school she was just the same as before we'd kissed. She didn't mention it.

Two more afternoons went by. On the first I sat in the booth at the back of the pizza shop and did my homework during her shift. Dave and his mates were in the front booth, but they ignored me. Or at least they didn't say anything, and I kept my head down. On the second afternoon I watched her rehearsal again in the school hall. Laura was playing Coral in *Away*, the play we were studying in English. She'd never be a great actress – even I could see that – but she wasn't bad, and I didn't mind watching.

There wasn't a minute alone with her. In her mother's car, dropping me home after drama, she sat in the front seat, so there was no chance to hold hands, or even exchange a look.

'I'll see you tomorrow?' she said when her mother pulled up outside my place. 'I've got rehearsal, if you wanna come?'

I got out, shut my door, leaned down to her window. 'Yep.'

'Bye, Jazz,' she said.

'Bye, Laura. Bye, Mrs Fieldman. Thanks for the lift.'

The car swooshed off in a way that didn't answer any

questions. It was still light, and the evenings were warm. In the old days I would have had a swim.

How would I even know if Laura was my girlfriend?

I pushed open the gate and headed in. The handyman guy, Tom, was crouching on the verandah, which was suddenly cream, and the place stank of paint.

I trudged up the steps. 'Hi.'

He looked up from wiping the brushes and smiled. 'Hi.'

'Looks good,' I lied.

He looked at me with an eyebrow raised and then back at the wall. 'Yeah.' He stood up and dried his hands on the legs of his shorts. 'I hear you like running?'

I blinked. Back in Hobart I'd won a few athletics prizes. I'd thought being a fast runner would help. But you know what they say about vicious animals: running just makes them attack you. I hadn't run since we moved north.

'Uh, I guess. Used to.'

'There's a loop track that starts in the next street. Up to the big park and back. About six Ks. Wanna come?'

It was a weird offer. I took a step backwards. 'Oh, no thanks. I've got homework, you know?'

'Easy!' Tom put his hands up. 'No big deal. Your dad thought you might wanna.'

I was right to be suspicious. I wondered if it was part of Tom's job for Dad. Paint the verandah, mow the lawn and cheer up my son.

'What would Dad know?' I moved past him and put my hand to the screen door.

'Running stopped me going nuts when my father died.'

I stood still.

'How old are you?' Tom asked.

'Nearly sixteen.'

'I was nearly seventeen when Dad died.'

The house was empty. I didn't have homework. I'd done so much homework to pass the time, I was reading chapters we hadn't reached in class. There was nothing for me to do and no one to do it with. Since Laura and I had started catching the bus, I hadn't even ridden my bike.

I pushed the door open. 'I'll get changed.'

*

I started out fast, but after two kilometres I had a stitch. My face burned and I was panting.

Next to me, Tom breathed easily. He wasn't even sweating. The track had gone round the grassy streets of the neighbourhood, past the barking dogs, and come to the big park. We ran under a tall pine tree where the noise from the parrots in its branches was nearly deafening.

Tom slowed and glanced over at me. 'Break?'

I was glad to stop, though I tried not to show it. Put my hands on my hips and bent over, breathing hard. It hurt, but physical pain was bearable. I just hoped Tom wouldn't take this as a sign to ask how I was coping or whatever other dumb ideas Dad might have put in his head.

I snuck a look at him. He'd put his foot up against the tree and was stretching out his hamstring, looking up at the parrots. Not smiling, exactly, but happy. It was Wednesday afternoon, he'd finished work, he was fit. He'd probably be going to the pub with some mates later, or maybe he had a girlfriend he was taking out to dinner.

'Let's get going,' I said, straightening up. 'No pain no gain.'

He laughed. 'You believe that bullshit?'

He swung around and took off and I had to sprint to catch up. He was faster than me and I couldn't get into a rhythm going side by side. Kept falling behind and speeding to catch up. Six kilometres was going to wear me out.

It was better when the track wound down into the bush and I dropped back and ran behind him instead of trying to match his stride. I found a rhythm and my legs settled. The stitch disappeared. I panted and my muscles burned, but I remembered how you could get to that feeling like you were floating. It didn't take long. A week or two of running and I could be back there.

We pounded through the little valley and up the other side. I couldn't remember when I'd last sweated like that from exercise. It was dripping down my sides and my forehead and it felt good. Whatever Tom thought, the physical pain was good. I lifted my knees higher, forced my legs to work harder. We were back in the streets and I sped up. Tom heard me coming up behind and grinned as I caught up.

'Bout time.'

I didn't answer. Was going to pay for this tomorrow, I reckoned, but it didn't matter. I remembered how I used to dig down for that last bit of strength, and it was still there, right where I remembered. My legs pumped. I drew ahead of Tom and rounded the corner of my street. A quick glance over my shoulder showed him twenty metres behind, red faced but not giving up. There wasn't far to go and if I slowed down he could still catch me. I was looking at my feet, I realised, and remembered what I'd learned back in Hobart. Look at the finish line. Look at where you want to end up.

The light was fading as I raised my head. I saw the hedge that hid our house, the little wooden gate, the big gum tree with the white branches, the driveway.

Parked in it, a police car.

FINN

The faint noise of footsteps on the verandah broke through Finn's concentration. He laid the gears on the bench and wiped the grease from his hands with a rag. For the first time he was making progress with disassembling and adapting *Dragon Sentry*, though his gut churned the whole time. Finding Bridget by the pool in the night had shocked him into action. He had to get them out of here.

The noise resolved into knocking. Never again, Finn thought, would he be oblivious to distant sounds. The slightest clank or thud sent him onto high alert, senses quivering.

He pushed open the door and stepped out, blinking in the afternoon sunlight reflected off the pool's surface. Through the glare he could make out two figures on the verandah.

'Hello?' he called.

'Finn Brennan?'

The voice was familiar, and as Finn started to walk around the pool one of the figures stepped towards the gate. A uniform. There was barely time for him to register the colour – blue – before a wave of fear engulfed his body. Was it Bridget, or Jarrah?

He broke into a run towards them, reached the gate and wrenched it open, yelled into her face: 'For Christ's sake, what is it?'

The woman held up both hands to stop him. 'Nobody's hurt.'

Finn's heart was thundering and an awful weakness swept over him. For a moment he thought he might pass out. He pressed his hand to his chest to try and squash the pain there.

'Do you need to sit down?'

He knew their faces. The female constable had driven him to the hospital and then to the school. The man had spent the afternoon of Toby's death sitting in the shade in the pool area until the police tape was finally taken down.

'Yes, I ...'

He staggered inside and slumped on the couch. One of them got him a drink of water, and they sat silently for a few minutes until the hammering in his ears and chest subsided a little and he nodded.

The woman put her hand on his arm and Finn thought she was trying to comfort him with her firm grip, until she spoke.

'Mr Brennan, you're under arrest.'

A short, snorting laugh escaped Finn. 'You're joking.'

'You are charged with manslaughter by criminal negligence. You do not have to say or do anything, but if you do, it may be used in evidence against you. It may harm your defence if you fail or refuse to mention something that you later seek to rely on in court. Do you understand?'

The urge to laugh vanished and his heart started up again.

'We need to take you down to the station. Are you ready?'

She gestured towards the door and Finn stood, unresisting, unable to gather his thoughts.

Footsteps thudded up the wooden stairs outside. Jarrah burst into the room, slammed to a halt, looked frantically from Finn to the constable. 'What's going on?'

'It's all right, Jarrah.' Finn tried to reach for him, but the constable stopped him from moving.

'I'm sorry, but your father's under arrest,' the constable said.

'For what?' Jarrah demanded. When no one answered, he said it again. 'Tell me!'

'Manslaughter by criminal negligence.'

Jarrah blanched and his hand flew to his mouth. 'Is it Mum?'

He was thinking the worst, just as Finn had. Worse than the worst, by the look of him. Finn wanted to reach out and grab him. 'Jarrah, nothing's happened. Don't worry.'

'Is Mum all right?' His face worked.

The constable stepped forward. 'This is a legal matter related to your brother's death. Is there an adult who can stay here with you while we take your father to the station?'

Tom had come in behind Jarrah. 'I'll stay.'

'We need to go, Mr Brennan.' The male constable pulled gently but inexorably on his arm. Finn strained against his hold, twisting to look at Jarrah, who was sickly pale under the flush of exercise. He forced himself to be calm. 'Call your mother,' he said over his shoulder as they led him towards the door. 'She'll know what to do.'

In his own ears, his voice almost sounded normal. The cops flanked him down the stairs and out onto the grass.

149

BRIDGET

A text from Jarrah: <You have to come home>

Chen has just pulled up by your vehicle in the car park when it pops through. You call Jarrah immediately but he doesn't pick up, and so you snatch your things from the back of the four-wheel drive, leap into your car, skid out of the car park and floor the accelerator.

Your mind races through scenarios as you drive. It could be as small as a lost key, as major as death. You swing into the driveway, opening the door before the car has stopped, and leaving it gaping as you run. You take the verandah stairs in a leap, wrench the sliding door on its tracks, roar into the kitchen.

Jarrah is at the bench, talking on the phone, his face white and stunned. This is no lost key.

'What?' you demand.

'Mum's here,' he says into the phone. 'Can you talk to her?'

He shoves the phone in your direction. The painting guy is leaning against the kitchen wall, you notice, as you grab the phone and Jarrah slumps onto a stool.

You press it to your ear. 'Someone tell me what's going on!'

'Bridge, it's Eddie. Jarrah says Finn's been arrested.'

You breathe properly for the first time since receiving Jarrah's text and steady yourself against the bench.

'Jarrah says he's been charged with negligence.'

'Negligence?' It doesn't sound too bad, you think. Like carelessness. 'Is that serious?'

'It's manslaughter by criminal negligence, Mrs Brennan,' the painter interjects, loud enough that Edmund can hear.

Edmund's silent for a moment. 'Christ. That's serious. You need a solicitor. Have you got one?'

'Um …' You try to think. 'Someone's doing the house contract, I think.'

'That's no good. I'll find someone who can get over to the station. You should go too. You'll need to get whoever I find up to speed.'

'OK. Gotta go.' You hang up.

'What do they mean, manslaughter?' Jarrah blurts. 'Like they think he killed Toby?'

'No!' You say automatically. Try to give him a hug but he's wooden in your arms. 'It means they think that what he did to the gate, with that opening device, was wrong.'

'Dad said it was an accident.'

He's staring at you, his face even whiter, and you wonder what he thinks happened. Finn took the job of explaining it to Jarrah and you never asked what he told him.

'Of course it was,' you say. 'Look, I've got to get to the station.'

You glance over at the painting boy, but your mind refuses to supply his name. 'Can you guys stay here? Watch a video or something?'

'Can't I come?' Jarrah asks.

You shake your head. 'It could be hours, Jarr.'

Hours in which you and Jarrah will sit in some hideous waiting area, and you'll be powerless to avoid his questions. You look again at the painter. The boys are both wearing running kit; they've obviously been hanging out.

'Do you mind staying here with Jarrah?'

He gives a brief smile. 'No problem, Mrs Brennan.'

'Thank you.' You pick up the keys from where you've thrown them on the bench. You don't try to hug Jarrah again. 'It'll be OK.'

Jarrah gives you a disbelieving look, and as you step out again into the warm late afternoon, you know it's a stupid thing to say. Nothing is OK. Haven't you all learned that? Better to think that whatever is happening can always get worse, suddenly and drastically.

The mobile rings as you turn out of the street and you pull over to answer it. A fine for using the phone while driving is the last thing you need.

'Bridge, I've found you a local solicitor. He's headed to the station now. He'll do for tonight. Are you on the way?'

'I'm in the car.'

'It's a serious offence. He's going to need you.'

You feel a stab of resentment at the suggestion you're neglecting Finn. 'I understand.'

'Do you really?'

You hang up. At some point Eddie changed sides, aligned himself with Finn, against you. Damn him. He must know Finn's been banished to the studio.

You pull out, narrowly missing a car you didn't see coming. A blare of horn, a finger stuck in the air, a shouted insult. It's

152

almost a relief. No one has dared to do such a normal thing to you in your grief. You thrust your middle finger up in reply too and settle into the lane.

Manslaughter.

It isn't a word you've dreamed of applying to what happened. 'Accident' was what everyone said, to keep some of the horror at bay. Someone, you remember, gave condolences for the fact that Toby had 'passed'. You hated that word.

Drowning was worse, suggestive of gasping, struggling, the flood of liquid into the lungs. Drowning, you thought, was the worst word. But now, according to the law, Toby was slaughtered.

Edmund's words are slowly sinking in. You should be grateful to him. Who else could – from a distance – track down a solicitor and get him to the police station in a matter of fifteen minutes? But you hate him. It's unjustifiable and irrational, you know, but you can't help it. You hate the world, and everyone, and Finn. Now it's not only you who blames him. The state is on your side. The state believes he's guilty.

The station looms up ahead on the left. You turn in, park. Switch off the engine and sit, hand on the keys, staring sightlessly ahead. What can you do for Finn? You don't want to comfort him. You can't reassure him you'll be by his side through this.

You reach for the door handle but your fingers won't work. They won't pull out the lever to open the door, allow you to swing your legs out, stand, walk to the entrance of the station and step inside. The phone rings again. Edmund. You let it peal three times. Just before it goes to voicemail you swipe.

'I can't do this,' you say before he can speak. You push the red stripe on the screen, wishing for the days when you could hang up a phone with force.

Chen's number is top of your frequently called list, and you type a message.

<I really, really need a drink. Can I come over?>

The reply, instant: <Of course>

It's not right. If you're not staying here for Finn, you should at least go home for Jarrah. But you need someone whose world hasn't been destroyed. Someone who can withstand your fury.

JARRAH

Pizza, she said. And left me with him. Christ, I'd only met the guy twice. We'd been on a jog together. I hardly knew him.

'Look, don't worry about it,' I said, as I heard her reverse-crunch on the gravel, then slam into drive and speed off. 'I'll be fine. I'm sure you've got plans.'

'Not really,' he said.

'I've got homework.'

He drummed his fingers on the bench. 'Don't reckon you'll get much homework done.'

I poured myself a glass of water, offered him one too, gulped it down while I tried to figure out what to do. The sweat was cooling on my T-shirt. A swim would have been nice. My hands shook as I lowered the glass to the sink. Because I'd just run six kilometres for the first time since forever? Or because of the moment when the woman said 'manslaughter' and I thought she meant Dad had killed Mum? Or because Toby's death somehow wasn't an accident?

'Let's get a pizza,' Tom said. 'We can bring it back and watch telly.'

'All right,' I said, giving in. But in fact I was glad. I didn't want to sit in the house by myself for hours waiting for them to get home. Way too much time to think.

Tom drove an old ute, the floor covered in soft-drink bottles and empty chip packets. He swept a bit of junk off the seat and I shuffled my feet around and buckled the belt.

'Any favourite place?' he asked, starting up and shoving the column shift into reverse.

'Domino's,' I said. Laura might be on shift at Great White Pizza and I couldn't face her.

We drove there in silence and Tom parked. He looked over at me. 'You look like shit. Want me to order? You're not vegetarian or anything are you?'

I rolled my eyes. He hopped out of the car, slammed it behind him, disappeared inside.

It was a hot evening, like summer already. I was still in running clothes. My T-shirt had dried and the air felt good against my skin. It was the only good thing.

I didn't think things had got so bad. Sure, they were sleeping apart. I'd been imagining them splitting up in a vague, horrible kind of way. But for a second I totally believed Dad had killed Mum. And it seemed like the police thought Dad had somehow killed Toby. I didn't know any more what they could do, my parents. I didn't know them.

Finally Tom strode across the car park, a huge pizza box in one hand, a two-litre bottle of Coke in the other, and slid them onto the seat between us. He saw my red eyes.

'Let's get out of here,' was all he said.

Thank God he didn't ask how I was feeling, like Laura probably would've.

It was starting to get dark when we got home. The house felt weird and empty and blank. I hesitated on the steps. Didn't want to go in.

Tom barged up beside me, slid the door back, stepped in, looked back. 'Don't let all the mozzies in,' he said with a jerk of his head.

I shut the door behind me and followed him to the lounge room. He put the box on the coffee table, flipped it open, fumbled for the remote. The news came on as he headed to the kitchen for glasses. I didn't want to see any news. I flicked it over to some game show.

I hadn't eaten pizza since Toby died. Tom had ordered Hawaiian. I poked at it and picked up a slice. Tom came back in, cracked the Coke and glugged it into the glasses. He scooped up a slice and took a huge bite.

I bit into mine. One bite was enough to take me back to the last Friday night Toby was alive. We were sitting around the kitchen and I was stretching the cheese on my third piece of pizza, stringing it out between my mouth and my hand until Toby was laughing so hard he was nearly choking.

I tried to chew but my chest started heaving and I nearly choked too. I forced that bit of pizza down and swallowed. Then my shoulders started shaking. I'd never felt like that. I didn't know crying could be like someone grabbing you by the shoulders, lifting you off the ground, and shaking you so hard that your teeth knocked together.

After a while I realised I was sort of lying down, and I turned my face so it was buried in the cushions and curled up. I couldn't stop crying.

I felt something. Tom must have moved. He didn't do anything weird, just moved to the end of the lounge, against my foot. Didn't say anything. Just a few centimetres of contact. Nearly nothing. But he stayed there.

FINN

A line of sweat trickled down Finn's back in spite of the air-conditioning. His new solicitor, Malcolm, sat next to him, and made notes on a lined yellow pad. It all seemed to be happening at a great distance. DI Evans, who'd seemed quite sympathetic on the day Toby drowned, was now set on grilling him.

'How many times did the gate malfunction?'

'Um. Two. Or, no, more than that. Four. Might have been five.'

'What did the malfunction involve?'

'Opened and then didn't swing shut properly.'

'And that was because of the device you installed.'

'I think so. Yes.'

'So you knew the gate didn't shut properly but you didn't do anything about it?'

'I was planning to. And we normally checked it was shut, you know. Manually.'

'Are you familiar with the New South Wales *Swimming Pools Regulation 2008*?'

'I'm not sure. What is it?'

'It requires every swimming pool to have a certificate of compliance. Does your pool have one?'

'You would have had one with the purchase of the house,' the solicitor interjected. 'It's required by law now.'

'Then, I suppose so,' Finn said.

'Has your pool been inspected since you installed the modifications to the safety fencing?'

'No.'

It went on and on. Once or twice the solicitor stopped him from answering. At last DI Evans sat back in her chair.

'That's all the questions we have at the moment.'

Malcolm laid his pen down. 'It's a pity someone has decided to make an example of my client at this tragic time.'

'Yes, it is tragic, but the law has changed.'

'And do you grant my client unconditional bail?'

DI Evans nodded. It took another hour to photograph, fingerprint and paperwork Finn, then he was free to leave. They emerged into the subtropical dark, the warm air washing over them after the station's chill. Finn took a deep breath.

'I'm sorry, this must be a dreadful time for you, Mr Brennan,' Malcolm said. 'They're idiots. I don't believe this can go far. Someone up high wants to try it out, but I don't think they have the evidence. Come on, I'll give you a lift.'

Finn blinked and shivered. He'd hoped for Bridget, but there was no sign of her. He got into Malcolm's car obediently.

As they pulled out, he sent her a text: <on the way home>

He'd chosen to take the blame from Bridget. As if he hadn't been to blame at all. But that decision felt so remote now. What had he told the police on the day of Toby's death? He strained to remember. What was real and what had he made up? He'd absorbed the story of the gate-opener failure until it felt true. Perhaps the failure of *Owl Sentry* was real. What else explained it?

The solicitor followed Finn's terse directions and pulled up outside the house. 'We'll talk in a day or two. Try not to worry too much.'

Finn nodded, remembered to thank him, got out and turned towards the house. The car eased away and he stood at the gate, his hand on the row of pickets, looking into the garden. The garage yawned empty; a ute was parked out the front. No sign of Bridget's car. Over at the house, lights were on and Finn heard the faint tinkle of television. Jarrah must be there.

How could he go inside?

It was one thing to try to shoulder the burden, but another to be accused by the law. It no longer seemed like a noble act, what he'd done in trying to take the blame. He *was* to blame. The gate hadn't worked. And he'd turned his back.

Finn trudged across the grass and climbed the stairs. Through the door he saw the boys sprawled on the two couches, watching television, pizza box spread on the table. Like any pair of teenage mates. He opened the door and they both swivelled. It wasn't a normal night, Finn remembered, looking at Jarrah's pale, strained face and red-rimmed eyes.

'What happened?' the boy asked.

'They just asked some questions,' Finn said. 'The solicitor says it will blow over.' He hoped to change the look on Jarrah's face, but his words weren't doing it. 'Where's your mother?'

'Isn't she with you? She went to meet you ages ago.'

Finn felt cold. 'No.'

Tom got to his feet. 'I'd better go. See ya, Jarrah. Bye, Mr Brennan.'

'Bye,' Jarrah said.

'Bye,' Finn added automatically. And caught himself as Tom reached the door. 'Thanks.'

'No worries,' Tom said. And was gone.

Jarrah turned to face the TV again and Finn stood still. Nothing in his experience told him what he should do.

After what felt like an eternity, Jarrah glanced up again. 'Want some pizza?'

'Yeah.' Finn wasn't hungry, but he sat on the couch Tom had vacated, flipped open the box, conveyed a cold slice to his mouth. Instructed his jaws to bite and chew. Faced the television, upon which some show played that made no sense at all.

He was on the second bit of cold pizza when the landline rang and he felt a rush of relief. It must be Bridget. He jumped up to answer it.

'Mr Finn Brennan?' An unfamiliar voice.

'Yes?'

'David McNally, *Northern Gazette*. What's your response to the charge that your son's death is the result of criminal negligence?'

Finn pressed his finger to the red button and cut off the call.

'Was that Mum?' Jarrah kept his eyes on the TV.

'Someone trying to sell something.' The phone rang again but Finn turned his back until it stopped. 'If it rings again, leave it.'

He went into the kitchen, closed the door behind him, and sat heavily at the table. There was no curtain at the window and his skin prickled as if he were being watched from out in the darkness. He stood up again and turned out the light. It was a relief. He could relax his face, let his body slump. Allow despair.

He couldn't face ringing Bridget. He pulled out his mobile and texted her again.

162

The message went with a little whooshing sound. When no reply came, Finn stared at the phone in the dark. It was late. Would his father be awake? Every time Finn had called, Helen or Conor had answered; his father was never well enough to come to the phone. That's what they said.

He pressed the number.

'Hello?' Conor's voice, anxious.

'It's me. What are you doing there?'

'Finn. Shit, you scared me. I've been keeping an eye on Dad.'

'Is he OK? Can I talk to him?'

Conor paused. 'He's devastated, Finn. I don't think he could handle talking.'

'Jesus.' Finn rubbed his face. 'Should I come down?'

'You've got enough to cope with. Why don't you leave it till Dad's stronger?'

'I just want to see him.' Finn's lip was trembling like a kid's.

'I know. I just worry it'll be worse. For both of you.'

'OK.' Finn took a deep breath. 'I'd better go.'

'Are you all right?'

'I'll be fine.'

He hung up. What the hell was going on down there?

No reply from Bridget. Finn laid the phone down on the bench where he could see it and waited. At ten-thirty Jarrah put his head in the door. He didn't ask why Finn was sitting in the dark.

'I'm going to bed. Night.'

'Are you all right?'

Jarrah shrugged. 'I guess.' He turned away without another word. He hadn't even asked where his mother was, Finn realised.

163

He gave Bridget another hour, but she didn't reply. Shortly before midnight he gave up. He stepped out into the cooling night, made the journey through the pool area, past the silent water, into the studio. Smelled the trace of molten metal as he undressed. Lay down and stared into the dark.

At four-fifteen, he looked at the clock. She still wasn't home.

BRIDGET

It's past the darkest hour and moving towards dawn when you pull up on the street and get out of the car. A cold front came through in the early hours and the clouds hang heavily overhead, misting the night. The first few drops of rain spit on your face as you stand there, still, looking up into the sky.

After being with Chen, you can breathe.

You know what Finn will think. You've been out virtually all night with a man. There can only be one explanation. You hope to make it inside before Jarrah wakes up and possibly comes to the same conclusion. Before Jarrah has new questions to add to the litany of unasked, unanswered ones crowding your lives.

Nothing happened, you remind yourself. If Finn accuses you of anything – if he dares – you have that to hurl back at him. Nothing happened with Chen. Nothing.

Well, that's not quite true.

You'd paused in ranting about Finn, about his arrest, about the disaster your lives have become, when Chen changed the subject.

'I never met Toby,' he said. 'Can you tell me about him? Was he like Jarrah?'

The question floored you. No one asked that. Once Toby was gone, no one dared ask you to remember.

'No, nothing like Jarrah. Toby was like … curious. Had to know how things worked. It was like he had a grown-up brain in a kid's body, with a kid's vocabulary, and all he wanted to do was grab the world. You couldn't stay angry with him though, even when he was bad. People just loved him.'

Chen smiled. 'More like you or his dad? You're both interested in how things work.'

You'd never thought of Finn and you in that way before. 'I don't know. Neither of us ever had that much energy.'

'Who did he look like?'

'He had eyes like mine. Hair from Finn's side. But didn't look much like either of us. Or his brother.'

'Would you be OK to show me a photo?'

You dug out your phone and handed it over. 'Scroll back and you'll see him.'

He was quiet, stopping to look, scrolling again. You moved next to him and looked over his shoulder, but one photo that closely framed Toby's grin was too much. You walked away.

'Sorry.' Chen put the phone down.

'Don't be. I like that you want to see him.'

He looked up at you, his face soft. 'Can you tell me what happened?'

You'd told it several times. To the police, to Meredith, to people who knew, to the family. You'd learned it the way you'd learn a story or a speech, so that you could say it without reliving those moments, so it wouldn't destroy you.

You steadied yourself and opened your mouth. But what came out was a child's whimper.

'I don't know.'

And you started to sob. 'One minute he was reading on the floor and the next minute he was gone and I don't know how he got out there, there was no way for him to get into the pool, the gate was shut when I looked and so I went back inside and looked in there.'

Chen took hold of you and wrapped you close and let you cry. When your weeping came to an end you stayed in his arms a little longer. In truth, you wanted him to lead you into the bedroom. You yearned for the comfort of skin contact with another human. He wanted it too, you were pretty sure. But instead he got you tissues, refilled your wine, sat down so you were a little way apart.

'Where do you think Toby is now?'

You rolled your eyes. 'Nowhere. You know that.'

'Is that what you feel?'

'It doesn't matter what I feel.'

He leaned back. 'I was really close to my grandfather. When he died, I wasn't so sure any more. I felt his presence sometimes. Especially in his room.'

'There's no evidence …'

He shrugged. 'There are some interesting studies under way showing continued awareness after brain death.'

You stared at the ground for a long time before you could say it. 'I've been in the pool. I felt him there.'

Chen didn't seem to find the notion of your haunted pool ridiculous, but speaking it aloud was unsettling. You realised how late it was. You'd barely make it home by dawn.

Now, standing outside the house, you're relieved things went no further. Staying out the entire night after Finn's arrest is inflammatory enough, never mind actual infidelity.

The light is just beginning to shift from black to blue, the first cackle of early kookaburras drifts down the street. You slip your shoes off, sling your handbag over your shoulder, pad softly across the lawn, picking up dew on the soles of your feet. Climb the three steps. Cross to the pool gate.

The timer is all out of whack and the pool light gleams. Way back, Finn installed a soft green underwater light to look more natural than the previous cold blue illumination, and he set the timer so it came on in the evenings. It was subtle and beautiful, and all winter you were looking forward to night swims in summer. Now the water flickers moodily and you want nothing more than to push open the gate, step inside, drop to your knees and reach in for him.

You hold still. Soon the day will start. Soon you'll have to face Finn and find out what this all means.

Before that, you want one more thing for yourself.

You ease the catch up, inch the gate open, step through, close it with an imperceptible click. You move, one barefoot step at a time, towards the pool, to a spot where you think Finn won't be able to see you if he wakes and looks outside.

You kneel, bring your face close to the water and gently push your fingertips past the surface resistance, feeling the coolness reach the webbing where your fingers join your palm.

You mouth: 'Toby.'

In response, a soft but unmistakable volley of metallic clicks. Not in the pool, but out there somewhere, in the garden or the street. You jerk your hand out of the water and come back onto your heels. Push your hair from your eyes and look through the fence, trying to find the source of that sound. It comes again. It takes your brain another few seconds to understand what you're hearing. A camera shutter.

You push yourself to your feet, run to the gate, ease it open and hurry softly along the verandah into the house. You risk one more glance before you open the door and this time think you see the glint of a lens out on the street. You duck inside and slide the door shut behind you. Stand still, heart hammering, as if hunted.

'You're home.'

You physically jump at the sound of his voice from the lounge. 'Fuck, Finn. Why don't you have a light on?'

'Why didn't *you* turn one on?'

You take a shuddering breath. 'There's someone out there taking photos.'

'Did they see you?'

'They took a fucking picture of me!'

'I think it's the press. A journalist phoned last night.'

'What did you tell them?'

'Nothing.'

Silence falls between you. Is he going to ask where you've been? You get in first. 'So what happened at the station?'

He spreads his hands in a helpless gesture. 'They want to test some new laws about pool fencing, Malcolm says. He doesn't think it will go anywhere. He says not to worry.'

You snort. 'And Malcolm is?'

'The solicitor Edmund organised.'

'What now?'

'I'm on bail. There'll be some kind of hearing, I think.'

You need to know more, but you're exhausted. Birdsong rings out in the garden, piercing the quiet, letting the day in. It's nearly light; you can see him slumped on the lounge, smell the pizza boxes still sitting there.

You heft your bag and head to the kitchen. The night falls away behind you, into the same place as the circumstances of Toby's death, the place that can't be approached. Let Finn think what he likes. He has more to lose by asking than you do.

JARRAH

Woke with an early-morning stiffy and lay there till it went away by itself. I hadn't done – that – since he died. Hadn't wanted to. But after 17 days I was feeling it. Plus, I had Laura to think about.

Weirdly, I thought differently about her. Before we were friends I'd pictured her taking off her top, or something like that, when I did it. It had been kind of fuzzy, like a dream. But now that we'd kissed, it was real. Didn't know how I felt about it. Scared as well as excited.

Thing is, I didn't know what to do. Knew nothing. Only way I could think to find out was to look for porn online. The family computer was set up with parental controls, supposedly for Toby's benefit, though maybe it was really for mine. I suppose I could have looked on my phone, but I kept remembering that time in Hobart with Oliver Neumann. It was disgusting and I couldn't get those pictures out of my head afterwards. I didn't want that again.

Anyway. Worrying about Laura and my morning stiffy was easier than thinking about the night before and Dad.

It had kind of been working, not asking and not knowing whose fault it was. I didn't have to hate one of my parents more than the other. But the police arrested Dad, so it must be his fault.

It was like a worm had got into my heart in the night. Like the ones dogs get, the worms that breed until there are millions of wriggling white things in there, so the dog's heart hasn't got room to beat and it dies. The first worm had got into mine while I was asleep and I could feel it starting to spread. The worm of blaming Dad.

Crept out of bed and dressed in silence. Didn't want to see Mum in case we were now both on the same side against Dad. Grabbed my pack and eased open my bedroom door. It was all quiet out there and Mum's door was shut. I'd glanced at the clock when I heard her park the car, and it was nearly morning. If she was asleep, she'd probably stay that way for a while.

I tiptoed down the hall, down the steps, through the lounge and outside. No one stopped me. Pushed open the gate, rolled my bike past Mum's car and took off.

No one much was around at school. I sat in Laura's alcove, pulled out a book, tried to bury myself. Don't know how much later Laura tapped me on the shoulder. I raised my face from the words and tried to squash down my morning thoughts of her.

'You're early,' she said.

Felt my lip start to quiver and quickly got a grip. 'Thought you had rehearsal?'

'This arvo, you know that.' She threw down her bag and dropped on to the bench beside me. 'Walk after school?'

My throat got tight. Fear or looking forward to it – they both felt the same. 'Sure.'

She tilted her head and smiled a secret smile behind her hair. A smile that hurt inside my chest and for some reason made me think of Toby. I tried to find something to say that wouldn't pull me down.

'Done that English homework?'

'Yeah,' she said. 'Need some help?'

That, thank God, took us through to her friends arriving and the blast of the bell, and I was OK and the day was going to be all right.

I thought.

Made it through to lunchtime. Got a roll from the canteen and sat with Laura and the girls again, eating while they chattered around me. A nod every now and then was enough when they were all together.

But I started to feel weird looks from around the playground. Three kids hunched over an iPad stared at me, then looked down as soon as I caught their eye. My back prickled. What was going on? By final period it felt like everyone in class was looking away as soon as I lifted my head. When the bell went I grabbed my things and headed to the door.

Laura was waiting outside. 'It's in the paper. About your dad being arrested.'

Trapped, I looked around for escape. Passing kids stared at us.

'Are you OK?' She reached for me.

My arm burned where she was holding it. I pulled free. 'Gotta go.'

'Do you want a lift home?'

'I'll meet you after rehearsal.' I spun around, pushing against the tide of kids pouring down the hall. Fought my way through them, found the door, stumbled outside. It was raining, so no one was out there. I put my head down and ran along the path, keeping close to the edge of the building to avoid the line of windows looking down on me. Scuttled around the playground over to the fence and found the hole leading to the little forest. Scrambled through it, scratching my arm on the rough edges, getting muddy. Ran along the track into the trees. Found my old hiding place under a tree, out of sight, surrounded by bushes. Tucked myself there.

The rain kept falling. I was soaked and muddy anyway. It didn't matter.

Had this crazy idea if I sat there long enough, Toby would come toddling down the path, his fists in the air. *Weed it, Jawwah! Weed it!*

He'd like it there in the forest – it was like the island where the monster kings were, overgrown and out of bounds, no grown-ups to be seen. He'd come around the corner and see me and his eyes would light up and he'd run and I'd sweep him up and throw him until he laughed and laughed and put his arms around my neck. Then I'd throw him on my back and run with him.

Fuck.

I never knew when it would hit me like that. Could be OK for a day, two days. Then it came: a Toby moment. Hurt so much it made me dizzy.

After a while my phone pinged. Probably Laura, and I didn't know what to say to her. But I wiped my eyes on my arm, opened my bag, pulled it out. A number I didn't know.

<Hi Jarrah you ok? Run? Tom>

How the hell did Tom get my number?

Laura would want to talk if she found me. I couldn't stand it.

<got no shoes>

<At your place will get shoes pick you up where?>

174

Didn't want anyone knowing my hiding spot. Texted him a street corner. Pushed my way out through the weeds, scoring a few more scratches along the way. Because of the rain there was no one out. I waited at the corner, my hair slicked down and dripping, my clothes sodden. Tom pulled up and I opened the door and squelched in.

He had a copy of the newspaper on the dash, folded. 'Seen it?'

I shook my head. 'Everyone at school has, but.'

He put the car into gear. 'Take a look if you want.'

Don't know what I expected, something about Dad I guess. I unfolded the paper and half the front cover was a photo. Mum, in the dark, looking down into the pool. The pool light was on, shining up on her face. The headline: WHO'S TO BLAME?

I snapped it shut. I'd been doing OK at school, but I knew what it'd be like now. The whole school talking about my parents. How did Dad do it? Would he go to jail? All that attention back on me because they thought my dad killed my baby brother. Didn't matter what the truth was, I knew that much.

It was still raining when Tom pulled up under a tree a long way from school. He'd found my shoes and handed me my shorts and singlet too.

'Stalker,' I said.

'I got 'em off the line. Didn't go in your room, don't worry. And your dad gave me your number the other day.'

I stood in the shelter of the car door to change after Tom got out. The clothes would only be dry for a few minutes. I didn't care. I wanted the rain. I wanted a storm.

Tom was stretching his leg on the bonnet of the car. 'Ready?'

I looked at my watch. 'Gotta meet Laura back at school in an hour.'

'Laura?' He raised an eyebrow.

'Girlfriend.' I said.

Tom grinned. 'Let's go then.'

We did. We ran and we ran and we ran.

FINN

The plane banked in a sweeping curve, tilting so Finn saw the sun glint off the harbour, silhouetting the spindly span of the bridge against its brilliance. He shut his eyes and leaned his forehead against the window. A headache pinched the base of his neck and his eyelids felt scraped.

Edmund had called at seven-thirty, after Jarrah left for school and before Bridget woke. He had a Sydney barrister friend – owed him a favour – who could fit in an emergency appointment that day and would work with the local solicitor. Edmund even booked the flight. All Finn had to do was throw a change of clothes into a bag, leave a note on the fridge and call a taxi to the airport. It was a relief to escape before Bridget woke. Before he had to ask where she'd been all night. And with whom.

And then he'd go on, Finn decided, down to Hobart to see his father. Needed to hear his voice. Needed to hold him. Needed to counter the fear that Conor's words had sent shooting through his body, no matter that his brother said to stay away.

The bump on the tarmac jolted Finn back to the present and he opened his eyes as the plane's brakes went on and his body, animal–like, braced. Was it a copout to run without waking

Bridget? Was he a coward for not wanting to know how she'd spent her night?

Three options Finn could figure: she'd been alone, with Meredith, or with Chen. She didn't know anyone else up there well enough. He didn't want to think about the third option. Had no right to be suspicious. He was probably way off track. If Bridget thought he'd been worrying about her fidelity she'd be even more furious. He couldn't ask her. Shouldn't even be thinking it. What was wrong with him?

It was a relief to see Edmund waiting at the gate. When he gave Finn a hug and thumped his back, Finn fought back the urge to hang on for too long, and stepped back, swallowing hard.

'Fucking hell, Finn,' Edmund said. 'Not fair. Not on top of everything.'

Finn spread his hands helplessly. 'That solicitor you got reckons it won't go far.'

Edmund nodded. 'Hope he's right. Let's go. My mate said to come straight to his office.'

Sydney. Loud, hot, concrete, metallic. Traffic streamed. Horns blared. Doors slammed. An assault, and yet welcome. Something, in the place of the awful silence at their house, broken by the hideous on and off schedule of the pool pump. The radio shouted at him. Finn had time to register his name before Edmund flicked it off.

'What was that?'

'Talkback. Everyone's got an opinion. You don't need to hear it. Skip the papers too, and be glad you're not into social media.'

Finn shook his head, dazed. He was being discussed on public radio. His private, secret choice to protect Bridget was spinning out of control.

It was forty excruciating minutes before Jack Ferguson QC could see them, and there was nothing reassuring in his manner. He grilled Finn on everything that had happened, then sat back in his chair thoughtfully, scanning his notes.

'The solicitor said it wouldn't go anywhere.' Finn had repeated this to himself during the night until it felt like solid truth.

'Perhaps.' Jack flipped through some papers and extracted a document. 'Testing a new law will get attention. This coronial joint inquest into toddler drownings recommended the charge be introduced, and they've been waiting to try it in court.'

'But Jack, I've looked at that report,' Edmund interjected. 'The coroner said none of the parents in the eight deaths he examined would have been subject to such a charge.'

'True.' Jack found the page he was looking for and read aloud. *'The existence of such a criminal charge would however emphasise the importance to the community in general of taking matters, such as the maintenance of pool fencing and gates, seriously, and the public condemnation of the failure to do so when a life is lost as a result.'*

He lowered the paper. 'The aim is to reduce deaths by making pool owners aware of how serious their obligation is, and to remind them this can happen to anyone. There's been one charge of manslaughter in relation to this, which didn't proceed, so they're still waiting for a test case. While the judge will be cognisant of your loss, Mr Brennan, it doesn't mean he or she won't make an example of you for the greater good.'

'And what would that mean?' Edmund asked. 'Are we talking jail?'

Finn flinched. However hard he tried, he just couldn't catch up. He still barely understood he'd been arrested. Hadn't even thought ahead to a court case, let alone jail. *Don't worry*, the solicitor had told him. *Don't worry.*

'It's a very serious charge,' Jack said. 'A criminal conviction and a custodial sentence are certainly potential outcomes. We'll put up a strong case for the committal hearing in the Local Court. That's where the magistrate decides if it will go on to a full trial. Obviously we'll be trying to get the charges dropped. That's what's happened in other comparable cases.'

'Right,' Finn said.

'Your local solicitor will do a lot of the legwork and I'll consult with him from this point onwards,' Jack said. 'There'll be a mention in the Local Court this week or next to set down the date for the committal hearing.'

'How long's this going to take?' Finn asked.

Jack shrugged slightly. 'A committal hearing – up to six months. If it does go to trial – well, we'd be looking at a year or two. Maybe more.'

'Um, right.' Finn still couldn't take it in. 'A year, did you say? How much will it cost?'

'Don't worry about that now,' Edmund interrupted. 'We've taken enough of Jack's time this morning.'

Moments later Finn found himself outside on the street, cars roaring past, pedestrians pushing and shuffling around them.

Edmund took his elbow. 'Lunch.'

They set off, winding through the crowds. It was too busy to walk side by side, and Finn fell behind, watching the back of Edmund's head to keep oriented. He had a bald spot developing there. Had Bridget ever grasped his hair the way she used to grasp Finn's, during sex? He hadn't thought about the two of them together for years. Ancient history. A short fling two decades earlier, way before Finn was on the scene. Bridget had introduced them and Edmund had become his agent – as a favour to her, Finn presumed. Edmund had always been starry-eyed about Bridget. All Finn could see now was Bridget with Edmund, in horrible clear images. Maybe that was easier than imagining where she might have been all night?

Edmund led him into a pub and through to a beer garden. Left Finn alone for a few minutes and came back with beer and salt and vinegar chips.

'It's in between breakfast and lunch. Start with this.'

Finn took a long swallow. The cool slip of beer and the chips' sharp salt on his tongue were things to focus on. 'I need to know about the cost,' he said.

'Cost doesn't matter. You've got to fight this. With any luck you'll win at the committal and it won't go to trial. And here's the thing: Jack wants a sculpture, so you can pay this first part of his fees in kind.'

'What kind of sculpture?'

'Something in your steampunk style. That will take care of the committal hearing.'

Finn put down his beer. 'If there's a trial and this goes on for two years, what kind of money am I looking at?'

'Being straight: a lot. But let's go one step at a time.'

A myna landed on the back of the chair next to Finn, looking at the half-finished chips spilling from their packet on the table. Head tilted to one side, bright black eye weighing up risk and opportunity. The sounds around Finn rolled heavily, like a slowed-down soundtrack.

'We've sold the house,' he said at last. 'Terrible price, but I guess there'll be some money from that we can use.'

'Already?' Edmund raised his drink. 'First, the committal. Finish the first commission and do the sculpture for Jack. Let's reassess after that. I can help you out. It'll be OK.'

Finn took a deep breath, and a second one. His heart was thudding so hard it hurt and his stomach was turning over and over. The beer shifted in his gut, a swallow away from hurtling back up.

'How's Bridget doing?' Edmund asked.

'They've sent her out on fieldwork, get her away from the office. That woman from the foundation has been around a bit, I think that helps her.'

'Is she with you on this? Do you need me to talk to her?'

'She's with me.' Finn picked up his glass again, glancing casually at Edmund and then away. His phone vibrated in his pocket. He'd become scared of the thing. Scared of its silence. Scared of the fact that he didn't know how to call Bridget and tell her he might end up in jail.

He fumbled it out. 'Hello?'

'Finn, it's Angela. I saw the papers. Are you OK?'

Finn nodded numbly. 'I'm in Sydney. Just saw a barrister.'

'I'm really sorry, Finn, I know this is a terrible time, but the sale's fallen over. They saw the news. They were teetering and that pushed them over the edge. It's off.'

Nothing had changed around him. The myna was still considering a pounce on the chips. The three women at the next table laughed uproariously. Over in the corner, an old guy drank by himself. The world went on. Finn had enough presence of mind to swipe and end the call. He laid the phone carefully on the table.

'The buyer pulled out,' he whispered.

They sat in silence. The myna darted forwards, snatched a crinkled chip, fluttered out of reach.

'Come and stay,' Edmund said suddenly. 'All of you. You've got to get out of there. You can leave the house on the market or rent it out, whatever. We can find somewhere for Jarrah to go to school, and Bridge can start looking for a job.'

Maybe Edmund was right, Finn thought. Nothing good could come of that place. Maybe once they got the hell out things would change. Maybe he'd find some path to Bridget again, draw her back before the gulf between them went too wide and too deep.

'I can stay with a friend and give you the place to yourselves,' Edmund urged. 'Call Bridget now. Tell her and Jarrah to pack and fly down. You don't even need to go back.'

Finn raised a wry eyebrow. 'I'm not game for that, not without talking to her. Anyway, I want to fly on to Hobart. I need to see Dad.'

'Some advice,' Edmund said. 'Stay here tonight. Tomorrow, go back north. Talk to Bridget, get organised, get out of there. You could be back here by the weekend. Visit Hobart once you've sorted this.'

Finn sat back. Would Bridget come around? What would Jarrah feel about it? It was gut-wrenching to realise he had no idea.

BRIDGET

Rain drums on the window as you wake slowly, trying to hold the first moment between rising out of sleep and actual awareness. The most precious moment of the day.

The second moment is the one that takes you out. When you remember, and the movie begins reeling behind your eyes, the unravelling of that day, the reliving. And then, the testing. Today, what level of pain? What resources have you marshalled – if any – through the night to help you? Will the day knock you to your knees or will you be able to stagger through it?

All this before you open your eyes.

It feels late. It was daylight by the time you fell into bed, and amazingly you dozed off. You lift yourself a little, force your eyes open and peer at the bedside clock. It's ten-seventeen. Against the odds, you've managed a few hours' sleep.

It's a work day. Chen will also have had just a few hours' sleep, if that. He said to text him if you wanted to work and he'd pick you up. It's too early to know if you can. It's a one-step-at-a-time day. Think no further than the next action. First, open your eyes. Second, move your body from the bed. Third, shower.

The house is echoingly empty. Jarrah will have gone to

school, of course. But you sense Finn's absence from the studio even before you find the sticky note on the fridge.

Gone to Sydney. Edmund's organised a barrister. Then seeing Dad in Hobart. Back on the weekend.

You stare at it stupidly. Finn was arrested yesterday, you remember. Once upon a time it would have been the biggest problem you'd faced.

Next step: breakfast. You can do this. Toasted muesli and milk, the simplest possible meal to prepare. You pour muesli into a bowl and open the fridge. It's stuffed with leftovers and dropoffs and handouts, people's kindnesses, most now seeping in their plastic, furred with mould. Still you can't manage the simple act of scraping the offerings into the bin. You find the milk, shut the door on the whole mess of it, and tilt the carton. A glob falls onto your muesli. How milk could possibly go off in your fridge at the rate Jarrah drinks it you don't know, but that's breakfast ruined. You fight the urge to heave the whole lot at the wall, smash the bowl, let it all run down to the floor.

You can't go to work today, that much is clear. You abandon breakfast, settle for a cup of black tea, carry it outside and sit on the verandah. The rain hasn't slowed. Steady, soaking, grey. The smell of mould rises from the cushion beneath you, straight up into your sinuses, turbo-charging your headache.

What made you come here?

The job, you'd say straight off. Of course it was the job. An opportunity to get out of academia and use your skills in the real world again. If it hadn't popped up just at the height of your fury with Finn and Sandra, just days after you discovered they'd been fooling around, you might never have considered it. But there it was, blinking in your inbox. The perfect way to get your family out of there, leave your ex-best friend in the backwash, escape the claustrophobia of Finn's family and the university and Hobart's relentless cold. And, if you were being honest, a perfect punishment for Finn.

You couldn't stay in Hobart once you worked out what was going on. No matter how Finn protested that they hadn't gone the whole way, no matter how Sandra wept and begged for forgiveness, the betrayal had gone too deep for that. Best friend and husband. Double betrayal, no matter how you read it. You were a modern woman, but not that fucking modern.

You weren't leaving only to punish them. Deep in your bones you yearned for heat, light and fecundity. And there was one more thing. A feeling you couldn't define when you looked at your oldest son and saw a pinched look on his face. You had some instinct to get him out of there.

You made sure you burned the bridges, selling the house and cutting Sandra out of your life. But instinct was wrong. It told you to bring them here, then turned on you and wrecked your lives.

You check your mobile, wondering if Finn has called. A slew of texts shrieks for attention. You pick Chen's.

<It's all over the news are you ok?>

You've become adept at avoiding the news – especially the local news outlets, where you starred horribly for a week after Toby died. You check the computer. Your own face, there on the front page of one of the national papers. Your private moment, looking into the pool, displayed. The photographer's trophy.

You get to your feet. You can't go to work, but neither can you sit.

*

At the nursing home's front desk the receptionist looks at you and blushes. Looks away, looks up again. She slides a newspaper out of sight.

'Your mother's good today,' she says. 'She'll be pleased to see you.'

A slip in the deception would be easy enough with that kind of thing lying around. You gesture with your chin. 'I hope she hasn't seen it.'

'Of course not,' the woman says with a wan smile.

Your mother is up, dressed and in her armchair. She turns and smiles when you enter and her gaze is frighteningly lucid.

'Darling,' she says. 'I've missed you. Where have you been?'

You kiss her on the cheek. 'It's been crazy at work. But you remember I was here last week, don't you?'

She nods. 'You haven't brought the boys for so long.'

You stiffen. What boys does she mean? Jarrah and Finn? Jarrah and Toby? The cousins from her Irish childhood, who are weirdly clear in her mind now?

'I'll bring them later in the week.'

You settle into the visitor's chair. Conversation with a person who has dementia is a new art. You can't ask your mother what she's been doing lately. There are no future plans to refer to. And your secret throbs and gives off heat.

'They grow up so fast,' she says musingly. Turns her gaze to you. 'You're looking dreadfully old.'

'Thanks, Mum,' you say. 'Would you like a walk?'

'I'd like a cup of tea,' she says firmly.

'I'll find one,' you say.

You flag down the nurse pushing the tea trolley and he makes you two cups, extra sugar in your mother's. You set them down, make sure she can reach hers, pick yours up.

'I'm going swimming with Toby later on,' you say, as you take a sip. She's the only one you can say it to.

'He's such a good little swimmer, isn't he!' she says. 'Like a fish.'

*

The rest of the day alone at home is interminable. How has it come to this, that you have no friends? There's no word from Finn in Sydney. You're not sure where Jarrah is. He's rarely home in the afternoons any more. Will he be home for dinner? Where is he spending this time?

When the gate finally clicks in the late afternoon you snap to alert, feeling a rush of anger at Jarrah for disappearing. As footsteps clatter on the verandah and the screen door scrapes, you rise up out of your chair.

'Where have you been?'

Two people follow Jarrah inside, halting you.

'Mum, this is Laura and her mother, Mrs Fieldman,' Jarrah says, and you can tell your stridency has embarrassed him.

Laura. You remember now, the girl Jarrah had the hopeless crush on. Standing here in your kitchen larger than life, prettier than you vaguely remember from seeing her behind the pizza counter. A girl out of his league, but here nevertheless, smiling a little nervously at you. You pull yourself together, hold out your hand.

'Laura,' you say and try something approximating a smile. 'Good to meet you.' You glance at the mother, standing a few steps behind.

'Adele,' she says smoothly, and reaches a kind hand to shake yours. 'I'm sorry about barging in on you like this, but we've been taking up so much of Jarrah's time, it's only fair we introduce ourselves, in case he's been forgetting to tell you where he is.'

Kind woman. In a sentence she's let you off the hook for snapping at Jarrah, and for not knowing his whereabouts. Plus she doesn't allude to the fact that your picture is plastered over the newspaper.

She makes a few minutes of polite chat and then she and Laura excuse themselves and leave, heading back to their car and their presumably nice, normal, stable home, and some kind of family dinner. It's nearly eight pm and you've drunk two glasses of wine and eaten half a packet of rice crackers and cheese.

'Hungry?' you ask Jarrah.

He shrugs in that teenage way you can't stand. 'I'll have some cereal.'

He stands with his back to you, shaking cereal out of the box until a mound of it almost overflows the bowl. Sloshes milk onto it from the carton you remembered to pick up, spilling some on the bench, starts to eat noisily, standing up. You bite down the urge to point out to him that now he's seeing a girl like Laura, he should stop eating like a starved ten-year-old.

'She seems nice,' you say instead.

He nods, mouth full.

'Kind of her mother to bring you home and come in. I didn't know you'd been spending so much time with her.'

'Mm.'

You're sure he's shoving in mouthfuls as a pretext for not answering. How to ask what you want to know without being

189

a stupid parent? You reject the first few questions that occur to you as being idiotic and finally come up with: 'I guess she likes you too, then?'

He blushes with such a theatrical cheek-reddening you could almost laugh.

'That's fantastic, Jarr,' you say, and you mean it. That a girl like Laura could even notice him is miracle enough; that she would feel sorry for him is likely; that she might even be attracted to him *is* fantastic. It makes you weak with relief.

'Are the two of you an item, then?'

'I dunno.' He shovels in another mouthful of cereal. 'Maybe.'

You actually smile, your muscles creaking from disuse. 'That's great.'

He doesn't smile back. He finishes the food, sticks the bowl in the dishwasher and looks back to you. 'Where's Dad?'

'He went to Sydney to see a barrister. He'll be back on the weekend.'

'Is he going to jail?'

You hear the fear in his voice. 'No,' you say, too quickly. 'It's a technical case, that's all. It probably won't even get as far as court.'

You have no idea if this is true, and clearly Jarrah doesn't believe you. He looks at you for a moment, then turns his body away. 'Night, Mum.'

You glance at the clock. 'Bit early for bed isn't it?

'Homework.'

'Don't I get a kiss?'

He comes back to you, leans in, brushes your cheek with his lips. He seems taller since Toby died. You remember suddenly the sweet way Toby smelled. There's a trace of it, almost indiscernible, somewhere in Jarrah's teenage scent.

The kitchen seems large and echoing once he's thudded up the stairs and closed his door. You pour another glass of wine and drink half of it to build your courage before calling Finn.

His number rings out to voicemail. He hasn't changed the message; those calm, measured tones are a shocking reminder of happier days. You hang up silently, turn off the light and drink the rest of the wine in the dark.

At nine pm the pool light switches on automatically. After the photographer you meant to change it, but you forgot to struggle over to the pool shed, tucked away in a weedy corner beside the studio, potential home to snakes and rats and oversized tropical things that crawl.

You'll do it now, you decide, after three glasses of wine. You find the torch app on the phone, slip on a pair of thongs and head out across the grass. The pool pump and filter live in a rickety metal garden shed. You lever the door open, holding back so that anything alive can get out without attacking you. Flash the light inside. Locate the damned switch. Turn it off. Shove the door closed and turn off the torch.

The night closes darkly around you in a damp embrace. You stand still, allowing your eyes to adjust, feeling the warm air lick the bare skin of your arms. You could never do this in Tasmania. Nights where you could go out bare-armed were few. That biting cold, seeping up from the south, was always only a breath away.

It isn't just warm; it's hot. Sweat trickles down your back. No breeze, just the heavy moist air and the stars, hot and bright above. You take a deep breath and your feet move. You decide to let them walk where they want, and they seem to know something you don't. Without hesitation they take you back across the grass, up the verandah steps, across to the pool gate. You raise the latch, swing the gate open, step inside.

Without the light on, the pool seems menacing, and you feel somehow invisible, safe from watching eyes. Your feet take you to the edge and then, before you can react, step into the water and land on the first step.

You step back out again in a flash, heart pounding and horrified. You can't go in there, not in that water.

Your feet tingle and the rest of your body, like an unthinking animal, lets you know that it desires immersion. It's dark. Finn is hundreds of kilometres away. Jarrah's room faces away from the pool. No one will know. You slide off your T-shirt, unclip your bra, hook your thumbs into your shorts and underpants and shuck them off.

The night welcomes your bare hide.

You step into the water again. It reaches the midpoint of your shin and all the hairs on your body stand straight up at the contact. You won't think. You take another step down, and the water rises to mid-thigh. Another, and it shockingly comes right up your body to your waist, making you gasp. You hesitate for a moment, smelling the faint trace of chlorine, and then you let it take you.

How could Toby have sunk? This water takes you gladly, holds you, buoys you. It laps around your neck with the lightest touch, and you take a deep breath and go down.

Toby's world, with its strange, amplified sounds. You open your eyes and in the dark you can see only glimmers and whorls, blurred. You reach out both arms and the water holds your entire body, like a lover. Like a womb. Like you once held Toby.

He's there.

JARRAH

Decided to skip school on Friday, the day after the newspapers. Wasn't hard. Cycled around the block, waited until Mum drove off and headed back. Hadn't worked out what to do with myself, though. The house was empty and echoing and sad. Made a hot chocolate and sat at the table. From there, if I looked out the window, I could only see a bit of the pool fence and a stripe of water through a whole bunch of leaves. If I turned my head, I was looking through the sliding doors that opened onto the verandah, through to the other side of the garden and the path to the gate and the road. The pool was off to the side, on the small end of the house. You could nearly forget it was there.

What happened that day?

From where I was sitting, I couldn't see into the pool and I couldn't see the gate. If Mum had been in the kitchen, she wouldn't have seen anything in the water. But Dad's studio looked right into the pool. Why didn't he see Toby?

Got up, went out and stood at the gate. There was no sign now of the thing that had once opened it. Just a latch on top of the post, the type you had to pull up. I opened it, stepped in and let go. It clanged shut behind me, hard enough to make the fence shake.

Headed through the pool area, taking a wide path to stay as far away from the water as I could, and opened the studio door. It was a mess. Stuff everywhere. Empty coffee cups. Half-made bits of whatever you called those things he was meant to be making. Even I could tell it wasn't the mess of someone making art. I'd forgotten he had that big breakthrough. Some outdoor sculpture thing that was going to change our lives. Well, it did that.

I sat down on the unmade bed and looked out the double glass doors. You could see more than half the pool, even from there. Mum or Dad – or both – had looked away from Toby and somehow he'd got into the pool area. Who found him and what did they do? Dad had been wet when he came to get me at school. He must have been in the water.

Dad kind of told me it was his fault because of the gate, but I thought the whole thing was an accident until he was arrested. What did it mean? Something more than an accident, I guess. I didn't know, but it made more sense of why Mum wouldn't sleep with him any more. Could she ever forgive him? Could I? I didn't even know what for. Didn't know if I wanted to know. Talk about fucked up.

Looked like Mum and Dad were going to split. Couldn't imagine where we'd go and how we'd live. Or what would happen while we were still waiting, stuck there together, Mum and Dad hating each other.

That studio felt like Dad's hell. Had to get out of there, or I'd start thinking about slitting my wrists or something. Got up, ran past the pool, got to the kitchen. Made another hot chocolate in the microwave. Felt kind of scared. Being alone in that empty house felt like it could make me do anything.

My phone pinged.

<not at school? OK?>

Laura. Chucking me a lifeline.

<cant do it today ☹>

A few minutes passed. Imagined her hiding the phone under the desk, waiting until a teacher looked away.

<will I come over?>

I stared at the screen. If Laura snuck out of school and came over, no one would know. Mum was at work; Dad was in Sydney until tonight. It'd just be the two of us.

<yeah> I sent, before I had time to think any more.

<CU>

Shit. It was too late to change my mind. I just wanted to hang around the house and not feel bad about crying. Or not crying. But that felt kind of dangerous too. Like if I went too far down, I wouldn't get back up again. Laura would take my mind off it. But what would we do?

Headed upstairs to my room. Didn't know if we'd hang out there, but I wanted to check if it was too gross.

It was pretty bad. Clothes everywhere. Crusted muesli bowls. Nearly as sad as Dad's studio. Started picking up clothes. Easiest was to throw everything into the wash. I clattered the old cups and bowls together and put them out by the stairs, stacked up other stuff lying around. Looked at my bed. Unmade since who knows. Hair on the pillow. Gross. But way too scary to think about changing the sheets or anything. Pulled up the covers to hide it all. She probably wouldn't even come upstairs, I told myself. We'd probably watch TV or something.

What would we do? I'd never had a girl over, let alone when the house was empty.

Clumped downstairs clutching the bowls and cups. It was a stupid idea. Laura wasn't the kind who wagged school anyhow. I couldn't believe she'd suggested it. I was crazy to say yes. Grabbed the phone so I could text her not to come. Remind her she'd get in trouble if she got caught sneaking out of school. She probably didn't even know how to sneak out without being seen.

'Hello?'

Too late. She was right there, outside the screen door.

'That was fast,' I said, going over.

'I pinched Jade's bike.' She smiled, but looked kind of nervous.

'Wow. Bike thief and truant. Double criminal.' Straight away wished I'd kept my mouth shut. God, the dumb things that came out before I thought about them. Slid the door open and she stepped past me into the kitchen.

'Are you by yourself?' she whispered.

'Yeah,' I said, like it was nothing. 'Mum's at work. Dad's in Sydney. I'm in charge.'

Stood awkwardly while she looked around. 'Got any coffee?'

That was something I could do. Didn't drink coffee, but Dad had drilled me so I could bring them espresso in bed on Sunday mornings. Hadn't done it for a while, but I remembered.

'Flat white? Latte? Long black?'

'Latte,' she said. Watched me flick on the stove and start preparing the Atomic. 'What's that? An antique?'

'Pretty much. Only way to make real coffee, Dad says.'

I ground the beans. Laura watched over my shoulder, sniffing. I liked the coffee smell too, even though I didn't drink it. Stuck the head in the machine, put it on the stove.

'Just takes a minute,' I said, watching it like it wouldn't work otherwise.

'I'm missing maths,' she said, behind my back. 'Needed an excuse to skip it. I couldn't finish the homework. Guess I'll be in trouble for that too.'

I hesitated. Didn't want to sound too dorky. 'I could have a look at it with you?'

The Atomic started to hiss. I was about to turn my head to see why she didn't answer when she came up behind me. Slid her arms around my waist, put her face against my back, and leaned on me.

Couldn't put my arms around her, or do much except kind of lean back into her. I slid one hand down and put it on her hands, which were clasped on my stomach. My other hand gripped the edge of the stove to keep me up. Also, I knew the Atomic was going to start dripping out coffee any moment.

'Where do you think they go, Jarrah?' she murmured.

They?

On cue, the coffee started gurgling.

'Don't know.' All I could feel was Toby had gone. The church stuff didn't mean anything. I didn't know if heaven existed, or hell. It all sounded like something humans had made up to suit themselves. If there was something afterwards I hoped it'd be more than just rewards and punishments.

I squeezed her hands. 'Um, the coffee—'

'Don't want it any more.'

She let go and stepped away and I felt cool all along the parts of my body where she'd been pressed. Flicked the stove off and turned. She was standing at the window and I couldn't see her face.

197

'What did you do with your brother's ashes?' she asked.

I swallowed. Toby's ashes were one of the things I forced myself not to think about. 'Nothing, yet. I guess they haven't decided.'

'Have you looked at them?'

'Nope.'

I'd thought of it. When the box first came home I was desperate to look inside. But it never felt like the right moment to ask.

She turned. 'Don't you want to know what they look like?'

'Guess so. But I don't know where they are.'

She came over, grabbed my hand. 'Let's find them.'

We started in the lounge room. Looked inside the cupboards and at the back of the shelves. Nothing. Not in the kitchen, I was pretty sure of that. Checked under the stairs, where Toby's things were packed away in boxes. Was pretty sure Mum wouldn't let Toby's ashes go over to Dad's studio.

We tiptoed upstairs, which was stupid, given the house was empty. I led Laura along the hallway and opened the door.

'Is this Toby's room?'

'Was. They cleared it out to sell the house.'

We both stood in the doorway, not wanting to go in.

'Where are you moving?'

'Dad wants us to go back to Tasmania.'

'Do you want to go?'

Right at that moment I didn't want to go anywhere. Standing next to Laura, gripping her hand, looking for Toby's ashes – it was the most alive I'd felt since he died. She turned her face up to mine and I kissed her. Was starting to get the hang of it. When we'd kissed before, in the forest, it was kind of soft, but today she kissed me hard, pulling me into her. Startled me at first, and then I responded.

She pulled away. 'Do you think they're in here?'

There was nothing of Toby in there. Shook my head. And then I knew. 'My parents' room.'

For my whole life my parents' bedroom had been a welcoming place, but as we walked in, I realised I hadn't been in there since Toby died. So many places in my home I'd stopped going to.

The bed was made, tight and hard, with cushions. The room was super tidy, apart from a few clothes over the armchair in the corner. The door to the bathroom stood open, and that mostly looked neat too. Like a hotel room. Mum must be keeping it tidy for inspections. I'd cleaned up my room when they asked and then forgotten to keep it that way. No one had said anything more about the house being for sale. Didn't even know if it still was.

The built-in wardrobe was the logical place for Toby's ashes. Slid the door open and looked in, thinking the box would be tucked up the top.

'Here,' Laura said.

She was crouched down by the bed. The grey plastic box was right under where Mum slept. I got down on my knees, reached under, slid it out. If Laura hadn't been there I would've pressed it against my chest. It was sealed with heavy grey tape. I scraped my fingers along the tape until I found the edge, picked at it.

'Let me?'

Her fingernails were longer than mine. She slid them under the edge of the tape and pulled it off with a loud rip. I prised the lid off, scared suddenly the whole lot would spill on me.

Don't know what I expected. Black and white ash, like you see in a fireplace? But the box was full of grey grit, like crushed shells. Felt a lump in my throat. Wanted to touch it, but was scared.

Laura reached past me and ran her fingers through the ashes. Fine grey dust rose up in a little cloud and she made a sound in her throat, like a half sob. I looked up. She was crying.

'At least you've got something of him,' she whispered.

'It's not him,' I said. I wanted to run outside and chuck it in the air and let it blow away. I hated it. How could Mum sleep so close to something that used to be Toby?

We both heard the noise at the same moment. The heavy thump of feet on the stairs, my dad's voice calling out.

'Hey, anyone home? Is that you, Jarr?'

Where did he come from? He was supposed to be in Sydney. I fumbled with the lid, desperate not to spill anything, but couldn't get it back on the box. I heard Dad stop outside my room, down the hall. 'Jarrah?'

Laura looked at me, wide-eyed. As I heard Dad start walking down the hall towards us, she grabbed my head and pulled me into a deep tongue kiss.

'Hello?' Dad's voice trailed off.

We pulled apart. Dad was standing in the doorway, staring at me and Laura in shock. He backed away and I heard his footsteps going down the stairs, slow and heavy.

'What the—?' I whispered to Laura.

She gestured to the box of ash. 'Better to get caught kissing, don't you reckon?'

I took a deep breath and my heart started to slow. She was right. Would've been worse for Dad to find us running our hands through Toby's ashes.

Faintly, outside, I heard the pool gate clang. Dad was going over to the studio. I got the lid back on, wrapped the tape around the box. Slid the whole lot back under the bed.

'You'd better go,' I said to Laura.

We crept downstairs and I slid the screen door open to let her out. She put her arms around my neck and hugged me hard. Kissed me quickly on the lips. She still had tears in her eyes. Turned away, down the stairs. Picked up the bike propped at the bottom and wheeled it across the lawn. Waved from the gate, and was gone.

The house was dead quiet, but I could feel Dad over there. He'd caught me kissing a girl in his bedroom. Plus wagging school. Was I in serious trouble? Or didn't this kind of stuff matter any more? I stood for a long time, waiting to see if he'd come back, wondering what to do.

Half an hour passed and he didn't appear. I picked up my phone.

<working today? wanna run?>

Tom texted back straight away. <not working run good. soon?>

<at my corner in 10>

I was changed and out there in four minutes, jogging on the spot and stretching my legs. Still didn't know why Laura was crying.

BRIDGET

Finn's back. You know it as soon as you pull into the driveway on Friday afternoon, before you see the light on in his studio. Before you come across the grass and spot him stretched out on the cane lounge on the verandah, asleep.

You missed him last night. The loneliness had a different quality. He's banished from your bed, but you still sense him hidden across in his studio, still sense you can rely on his presence.

You reach the verandah and stop. He stirs.

'Back early,' you say.

Finn rubs his eyes, eases himself onto his elbows. He looks dreadful. Lines carved into his face that you don't remember. He swings his legs over and gets to his feet.

'We need to talk.'

Your heart shrivels. Anything he wants to talk about can't be good. His legal advice. Your night away from the house. His night away from the house. Anything to do with Toby. There's nothing you can look forward to in this conversation.

'Is Jarrah home from school?' you ask.

He pauses, glances at his watch. 'He came and went out again, I think. I dozed off.'

'We need to keep a closer eye on him,' you say, following him inside. 'I'm worried about him.'

'I agree.' Finn sits on the lounge.

You hoped there'd be some preamble, some making of hot or cold drinks, something. You kick off your shoes, loosen some buttons and sit down.

You feel, rather than hear, that he's crying. The shake of his shoulders is an earthquake tremor that travels down the lounge, into the floor and up into you. As if the foundations of the house are shuddering. The legal news must have been bad. You're so close to reaching over with your hand and grasping his that it almost feels like you've done it.

When he speaks, his voice is choked.

'The buyers pulled out.'

You don't understand the words, and when you do, you don't understand the meaning. Is he talking about one of his sculptures? Is it something to do with Edmund? When you realise that he means the house, something akin to relief seeps into your body. You do reach over then and place your hand on his, and he turns his hand upwards and grips you like it's him who's drowning. It's terrifying, and you want to pull away from his downwards momentum. It takes all your strength to stay steady and not wrench your fingers out of his grasp.

'It was a crap price anyway,' you say.

He doesn't respond and your anger starts its familiar burn. The house sale is hardly the most important thing going on. He's been charged with manslaughter and you haven't even talked about it.

'Weren't you going to Sydney to get legal advice? What happened?'

You can feel him fighting for control, literally wrestling down the urge to sob, and you hope he wins. It's selfish, but you can't even manage your own pain, and the tidal wave of his will swamp you.

His shuddering recedes a little; he gains control. Withdraws his hand from yours, wipes his eyes on his arm, fishes in his pocket for a tissue and blows his nose. He balls the tissue up in his fist.

'I want you to hear me out.'

When you give a guarded nod, he continues. 'We can't stay here. It's ruining us.'

A clenching, down low in your belly. Did he even hear your question about legal advice? 'Hang on—'

'Edmund's offered us his home. He'll stay somewhere else. Jarrah can go to school, you can start looking for work. We can get away from here.'

It's not what you expected. 'In Sydney?'

'Just until we sell the house, or you find a job in Tasmania. Or I sell some pieces. I want us to pack what we need this weekend, leave the rest. We can be out of here by Sunday.'

The moment you felt softly towards him, the moments of missing him last night, are disappearing. 'This is hardly the most important thing we have to talk about, for Christ's sake. What did the barrister say?'

He shakes his head. 'We can talk about that later. This *is* the most important thing.'

'Have you thought of asking Jarrah and me how we feel about it?'

'I'm asking.'

Rage starts, low in your belly. 'Do you even know your son has a girlfriend?'

A strange expression crosses Finn's face. 'Yeah, I do.'

'Has it occurred to you he might not want to be dragged off to Sydney with two days' notice? And what about me? I just walk out of the job? Don't go back on Monday?'

'Yes.'

You're floundering. There's nothing to fight in these replies, nothing to grasp and shake. You change tack. 'What if we don't want to go?'

'We need to think about what's best for us as a family.'

'It's a bit late for that now,' you snap.

He looks up, shocked, and you know you've stepped over some line. You shut your mouth.

'Bridget,' he says softly. 'I'm begging you.'

Your head is shaking of its own accord. 'I can't leave Toby.' It's out of your mouth before you know it.

Finn looks at you, old and creased and confused. 'He's gone,' he says, as though you're a child.

You're wrong, you want to yell at him. *My son is out there in that pool.* Instead you challenge him. 'What if we won't come?'

Finn looks at you for a moment, then his eyes drop. His head sags into his hands. You expect him to begin sobbing but instead he becomes completely still.

You don't want to know the answer. You get up, walk quickly to the door and outside.

It's dusk, still hot, and there's no sign of Jarrah. You take a few breaths, and without thinking too much, you turn for the pool. Let yourself in the gate, close it softly behind you. Walk to one of the wooden chairs, drag it close to the edge and sit down, feeling the warm air lick the bare skin of your arms.

Nothing in your scientific training can support what you know without doubt: that Toby is somehow in the water. You don't want to know Finn's answer to your question. You don't want him to force a choice. You can't leave Toby. You won't.

FINN

Finn wanted to follow Bridget. Wanted to say: *Where were you all night?* Wanted to ask: *What's happening to us?*

Wanted to say: *I'm so fucking scared.*

Couldn't.

The garden gate clicked open and the boys came through, ruddy-cheeked, streaked with sweat. Tom said something to Jarrah, inaudible from where Finn was watching, and Jarrah turned his head and smiled. It was a smile that smote Finn. For a second his son was open, unguarded. It was a sweet smile, from a forgotten world.

They came up the steps, across the verandah; they were beautiful. Slender Jarrah, loose-limbed from running, moving easily, his boy's body maturing, hinting at what it would soon become. Tom, beside him, broad-shouldered, strong, in his young prime. Finn hadn't run or played sport in years. His belly was too big, his knees hurt, he was hairy, he was punch-drunk with pain, he'd become an old man too early.

Jarrah's face closed when he saw his father, his body visibly tightening.

Finn sat up and forced a smile that felt like a grimace. 'Hi, guys. Good run?'

Jarrah nodded.

'Hi, Mr Brennan,' Tom said. 'Yeah, Jarrah's thrashing me. You never said he was that fast.'

'Tom, call me Finn. Please. How about a beer?'

There was a hesitation and Finn willed Tom to say yes, to stay with them, to share the normality of his life, sprinkle it around them.

'Thanks,' Tom said, somehow getting it, 'Finn. That'd be great.'

Finn got to his feet and looked at Jarrah. 'Wanna try one?'

Jarrah blinked, and Finn had a sudden image of the scene in his bedroom, his son and the girl, kissing in that way of teenagers, all tongue and need.

'Sure,' Jarrah said, and Finn was certain the flush on his cheeks wasn't just from running.

'Your mother doesn't need to know everything.' Finn paused to make sure Jarrah knew what he was talking about. When he saw relief in the boy's eyes, he gestured. 'Sit down. I'll bring them out.'

In their old life, on such a Friday evening, the Brennan family would have headed out to the pool, plunged into its cooling embrace, laid around dripping on the deckchairs. Finn would have enjoyed watching Bridget in her swimming costume, would have wished his own belly were smaller, would have decided to eat less pizza. His sons would have played in the pool, Jarrah throwing Toby up and letting him fall into the water, snatching him out a few seconds after his head went under.

Finn shook his head. Way too dangerous. He opened the fridge, pulled out three longnecks. Corona wasn't a bad beer to start Jarrah on. He shook his head again. Best not to make any assumptions. He didn't think the kid was drinking, but then again he'd had no idea Jarrah was kissing girls – or more: at home during the day when he should have been at school, so what did Finn really know?

The boys had kicked off their shoes and socks and thrown them down on the grass. Finn sat down, handed over the beers.

'Cheers,' he said, and the three of them clinked and drank. He watched Jarrah out of the corner of his eye and saw the boy grimace slightly. Finn relaxed a little. Maybe it really was his first taste of beer. He wondered if Bridget was still sitting over by the pool, obscured by the thick palms. One small interaction at a time, that's what he could manage. He couldn't risk starting a discussion about offering their son alcohol. Better she stayed away, just now.

'Much work on?' he asked Tom. Wonderful, safe Tom.

'Been a bit quiet this week,' Tom said. 'But that's how it goes. Got a job on tomorrow.'

'You like the work?'

Tom nodded. 'Don't have to take it home.'

'You're good at it,' Finn said. 'Thought of an apprenticeship?'

Tom took a big swallow of beer. 'I dunno, Mr Bren— Finn. Mum'd like me to go to uni. We're doing the forms at the moment. I can probably get into teaching sport.'

'Do you want to?'

'Maybe.'

Finn turned to his son. 'What about you, Jarr? Any thoughts of late?'

Jarrah looked at him guardedly. 'No.'

He should have known that asking teenage boys about their future was a dead-end topic. Finn felt a wave of weariness. His muscles sank down into the chair and he took another mouthful of beer, trying to make it last.

'Hey, how's it going with your sculpture?' Tom asked. 'Jarrah says you were picked for a big show.'

Finn shrugged. 'Sculpture by the Quay. I missed it. I'm meant to be working on a couple of commissions.' He stopped. Gathered himself. 'Don't know if I can finish,' he confessed.

'D'you want a hand?' Tom asked as casually as if offering to mow the lawn.

Finn blinked. 'What d'you mean?'

'Well, you know,' Tom shrugged. 'Me and Jarrah could come over. Help you, like, lay it out, or weld stuff together, whatever.'

Finn felt a little flutter in his chest. He wouldn't call it hope. He wouldn't call it anything, he decided, lest he frighten it away with the weight of a name. 'We could give a try, I guess.'

'Great,' Tom said, as though this actually sounded fun. He got to his feet.

'Now?' Finn asked.

'Yeah, why not? I've got a couple of hours. We can make a start.'

Jarrah also stood and the two of them looked at him expectantly. Finn pushed himself up. 'Right. Let's go.'

Bridget was nowhere to be seen in the pool area. She must have slipped away while they were drinking beer. Finn led the boys through, opened the studio, and felt a wave of shame. It was disgusting. His life, in all its disaster, was laid out for everyone to see. But Tom seemed to take it in his stride.

'Can I make a bit of space?' he asked, and when Finn nodded, Tom instructed Jarrah to help him. They pushed the awful sofa bed into the corner and Tom tossed something over it. He shifted a few other hulking things to the perimeter and made an open space. Found a blue tarp, and after checking with Finn, spread it out on the floor.

'OK,' he said, hands on hips. 'What've you done so far?'

In a daze Finn went over to the bench. He'd rearranged his scraps with the components of *Dragon Sentry* so often, trying to turn it all into something else, that he'd lost it. He waved his hand at the scramble of metal. 'It's a bloody mess.'

'If you pass me pieces, we can lay it out down here,' Tom said.

Finn rummaged in the pile, struggled with a large, pitted flywheel that had been a centrepiece of the work. Tom stepped forwards, gestured to Jarrah. The two of them took hold of it and Finn disentangled it from the rest of the mess. When it came free, they laid it down in the centre of the tarp.

Finn felt another rush of shame that the boys should see not only his failure, but what he did in here even when it was working well. Playing with bits of scrap metal. It was nothing. Anyone could do it.

But Tom was looking at the pile of crap with interest. 'Next?'

Even Jarrah looked if not exactly interested, then not bored and not shut down, and God, that was something.

'The centre of it is a series of clockwork gears,' Finn said. 'They go on the top of the big flywheel.'

They continued. The piece started to take shape again, down there on the floor, and he only noticed the passing of time when the studio became too dark to see properly.

'Looking good,' Tom said, arms crossed. 'I can come back Sunday if you want?'

'Sunday?' Finn rubbed a kink in his shoulder. The weekend, when he'd planned to pack his bags, pack all their bags, get them out of this place, try to get them somewhere safe. Bridget wouldn't come and he wasn't brave enough to test her. He couldn't force them and he couldn't leave them.

'Thanks, Tom,' he said. 'That'd be great.'

*

The anonymous delivery of meals to the doorstep had dried up and the fridge was as disgusting as the studio. Worse. Finn pulled out some Tupperware thing from the back of the freezer, zapped it in the microwave until it was steaming, ladled it into bowls. It was unsuitable for the hot evening, but it was food, and he could put something on the table before calling up into the far reaches of the house: 'Dinner's ready.'

Jarrah and Bridget both emerged from whatever they had been doing up there on the second storey, where he almost never went now. Jarrah turned on the television as he came through the lounge, and by unspoken assent, all three of them took their plates and headed back in there. Dinner together at a table wasn't quite possible, but dinner together in front of the television could be tolerated. Finn willed himself to become absorbed in whatever was on, but it might as well have been pictures and sounds from another civilisation for all he could grasp it.

Bridget and Jarrah seemed content to stare at the glowing screen once they'd finished eating, so Finn collected the plates and took them through into the kitchen. He loaded the dishwasher and then stood with his hands on the sink, looking out the window into the darkness.

'Night, Dad.'

Finn turned. Jarrah was already withdrawing his head from the door, but at least the boy had voluntarily made the effort to speak.

'Night, Jarr,' Finn said hastily. 'Hey, thanks for today.'

'Yeah. You too.'

It was only a moment in which Jarrah paused and their eyes met, but it was something. Finn felt a stab inside him. He'd keep Jarrah's secret; it was the only line of trust connecting them. But it was the first time he'd hidden something about his son from Bridget and the tug of loyalties hurt.

Finn heard Jarrah climb the stairs. What had happened between Jarrah and that girl up there in what used to be Finn's bedroom?

In the other room Bridget switched off the television. Finn tensed, waiting. Then heard her footsteps on the stairs.

She wasn't even coming in to say good night.

He heard the faint overhead sounds of her getting ready for bed. The thumps, the soft thuds, the flush of the toilet, the creak of the bed as she got into it.

The house settled into silence. Finn reached across and flicked off the stove light, the kitchen's only illumination. Let the darkness fall around him, heavy on his shoulders. Let the silence lap at his earlobes and elbows. Let the steel of the sink cool his fingertips.

And let the memory of Toby come, from before. He could balance, for a moment, on that knife edge. Try to think of Toby without falling into the abyss, and without reliving what happened.

From the moment he could grasp things, Toby was fascinated by how they worked, and Finn knew that came from him. They both saw the world in a physical way, saw how its components fitted together, took pleasure in the arrangement of things to bring about a desired result.

It wasn't wood carving that interested Toby. It was the clockwork pieces. He wanted to watch, to touch, to hold. Finn had got into the habit of putting him on a floor on a mat with a pile of cogs and wheels and scrap metal in front of him. Totally unsuitable as toys, though he at least made sure everything was too big to swallow. Toby never tried to swallow them. He lay them out, rearranged them, banged them together. The interest came from Finn, but in Toby it went much further. It was a fascination, a drive. He would have lived a life centred on how things worked.

Finn stared, dry-eyed, into the dark, and rocked back and forth on the balls of his feet to let the pain know it hadn't won. His body thrummed. He'd come home wild with the energy of gathering Bridget and Jarrah and getting them out of there, the promise of doing something about the pain, even running from it, something.

The bed creaked above him, so faint he could barely hear it. He knew every creak and scrape it made, he knew how the timbers rubbed together, which joints needed tightening from time to time. How had it come to this, that he was afraid to set foot in the upstairs of his own house?

He pushed himself away from the sink. Very well, they wouldn't flee this weekend, but something had to change.

At the bottom of the stairs he found himself holding his breath, and taking the first step in a creep. He halted, took a deep breath straightened himself. Climbed the stairs like a normal person, not thumping but not creeping either. Walked down the hallway, past Jarrah's door, to the closed door of the master bedroom. Opened it.

Bridget's shape in the bed was unnaturally still. Finn stepped inside, shut the door. He pulled his T-shirt over his head, slid off his shorts. Walked across to his side, slid in, pulled up the sheet.

'I'm not sleeping away from you any more,' he said, low-voiced.

She said nothing. Didn't move. Didn't reach for him. He knew she wasn't asleep. It occurred to him that sleeping like this might be lonelier, in fact, than sleeping on the little couch across in the studio.

'Good night,' he whispered.

There was a slight stir, so subtle he might have imagined it. But nothing more. The dark lay heavily on him and he was so tired, so very tired. His body, feeling the familiarity of the bed, imagined itself safe, and he could feel sleep already coming upon him, feel his legs beginning to twitch, his breathing starting to slow. He'd intended to lie awake, to watch over her, but he was slipping, slipping.

When he jerked back into wakefulness he didn't know if minutes or hours had passed. He turned his head. Bridget's side of the bed was empty and Finn felt a rush of weariness. Coming back to their bed was pointless if it just drove Bridget to sleep somewhere else. Where could she have gone?

He got up. It was like moving through molasses. He put on his shorts, opened the door silently. The only place he could imagine she'd have gone was Toby's room, but when he crept down the hallway and peered in, the sterile little room was empty. Could she be sleeping on the couch downstairs?

The lounge room was empty, as was the kitchen. Finn stepped out onto the verandah. The car gleamed faintly in the driveway. She hadn't left him, then. Not yet.

Then he heard it. A ripple in the pool and a soft mammalian explosion of breath, like a porpoise. He shuddered, wondering if he was dreaming in the warm, surreal night, under a sliver of moon, the dark thick and full, the sound of the pool perfectly clear. What the hell was in there?

He crept to the gate, keeping to the shadows, and peered over. A little illumination from the streetlight spilled into the pool area and spread across the surface.

It was Bridget. She surfaced again, exhaling as though she'd held her breath as long as she could. Was she trying to hurt herself? Drown herself?

Faintly, in the dark, Finn saw her dive again. She stayed underwater so long he was about to wrench the gate open and dive after her, but he waited another moment and another moment and heard her surface.

He couldn't imagine ever going into that water again. Something was happening over there, in the water, with his wife that he couldn't understand. It was worse than sleeping separately. Now he knew just how far apart they actually were.

JARRAH

I hated Saturdays. Bad things threatened on the weekend. Too much time and not enough to do. Mum and Dad were weirdly polite with each other. I kind of wished they'd fight. Dad worked in his studio and Mum cleaned in a disorganised way, like she couldn't remember the bits she'd done already. I was so desperate I mowed the lawn without being asked.

No one was telling me anything and I was sick of it. By late afternoon I was walking back and forth in my bedroom. I couldn't stand it.

Texted Laura: <wanna do something?>

<working tonight>

Didn't know what to make of that. She didn't suggest catching up another time. Was she pissed off at me? Did she feel weird after Dad caught us kissing? Was she still upset about whatever it was?

Tom was coming over on Sunday to help with Dad's sculpture again, but Saturday was going to last forever. I sent Tom the same text. Took him an hour to reply, by which time I'd nearly given up.

<movie?>

I was out the front, jumping from one foot to the other, when he pulled up. Opened the ute door and got in before he could even turn off the engine.

'You said anything, right?' he said. 'Only, it's a surf movie. Didn't think you'd be into it.'

'I don't care,' I said. 'Let's go.'

He put the car into gear. 'How are your folks doing today?'

'Crap.'

'You?'

'Same.'

He didn't ask me anything else. Put the radio on loud and drove to Kingscliff. Took me into the tiniest cinema I've ever been in. I reckon there were about thirty seats in there. Ordered a beer for himself and a soft drink for me, and some chips. We sat down.

'You gotta have stuff to do,' he said. 'Or you go fucking crazy.'

I looked at my hands. 'I know.'

'I could teach you to surf if you want?'

'Nup.'

'Might feel different after the film.'

'Doubt it.'

The trailers started and the lights went down. I just wanted to watch something and forget everything else. It was one of those movies about riding big waves in Hawaii or somewhere. It was OK until they started on the underwater stuff. The guy training to hold his breath as long as possible. The way the waves held him down. Too much underwater. Too much blue.

I shut my eyes. Couldn't help wondering what it was like for Toby. Did it hurt? Was he outraged that no one came to help him?

A few minutes later Tom nudged me. 'Let's go.'

I followed him outside. We crossed the road, went past the surf club. It was still warm. The water was full of swimmers and kids surfing.

'Sorry,' I said. 'You can go back in if you want.'

Tom shook his head. 'Forget it. Bad choice. Let's just hang out for a while.'

We sat on the grass bank overlooking the beach. First time we'd just hung out without doing anything. I didn't know what to say. I fiddled with the grass for a while. Tom seemed happy watching the water. Maybe that was a surfie thing. To me it was just waves crashing – they all looked the same.

'Let's go for a walk,' Tom said. 'I already ran this morning, and surfed. Don't think I'm up for another run.'

I followed him down to the wet sand without a word and we set off to the south. In a few minutes we were away from the crowds. It was better, moving. I'd rather have run, but walking was OK. I liked being with Tom. He was steady. I felt calmer. I knew what was what.

'How are you going with that girl?' he asked.

My face got hot. 'Laura? I dunno.'

'Why aren't you out with her tonight?'

'She's working at the pizza place. Anyhow, I'm just her charity of the month, you know?'

He laughed. 'Girls don't hang around just because they feel sorry for you, Jarrah.'

'She's more interested in my dead brother than me.'

219

He didn't say anything. Watched the surfers for a while as we walked. I guessed he wanted to be out there, after all.

'You got a girlfriend?' I asked.

He shook his head. 'I'm kind of between girlfriends right now.' He glanced at me. 'I had girls interested in me after Dad died. But it didn't last long. People who haven't gone through it – they forget pretty fast.'

'It's not even three weeks,' I said.

'I know.'

We walked further. 'Where's your dad buried?' I asked after a while.

Tom swept his arm across the width of the beach. 'We threw his ashes in the ocean. He loved surfing.'

I stared at the water. It was easier to talk to Tom walking side by side, not looking at each other. 'Do you think they go somewhere?'

'Absolutely.'

'Like, heaven or something?' I snuck a glance at him.

'For my dad, surfing was heaven. I reckon he's there, in the water.'

'Do you think they can see us?'

Tom shook his head. 'Sometimes I think I can feel him when I'm surfing. But I could be making it up.'

He looked at me. 'What happened with Toby? Was he buried?'

I kicked the sand. 'He's under Mum's bed.'

It suddenly felt colder and shadows stretched the length of the beach. Tom stopped and turned.

'Why don't we drop in on your girlfriend for a pizza?' He grinned. 'I can check out what all the fuss is about.'

'Just don't steal her, OK?' I grinned back at him like everything was great. I broke into a slow jog back along the beach.

Tom groaned and then started jogging too, catching me up. 'You *are* keen.'

'You'll see why.'

But the truth was: I didn't really want him to meet her. I was happier just doing what we were doing. I didn't need anything more.

BRIDGET

Sandra has the hide to actually call you. It takes a moment to register when the number comes up on your mobile, and you stare, indecisive, at the screen. You long ago deleted her from your contacts, but hers is one of the few numbers you know off by heart.

She was your best friend. You met at some playgroup you joined when Jarrah was a baby. She left soon after, as her son started preschool. From that short crossing-over, a circumstantial friendship survived and became something more. You thought she was the friend you could trust with anything.

You'd said something to her, something you later regretted. You'd told her, one night over a few glasses of wine, what you could barely admit even to yourself – that you were the tiniest bit bored in your marriage, and even, perhaps, the tiniest bit embarrassed that Finn, your stay-at-home husband, lacked ambition and wasn't more successful. She'd rolled her eyes and told you she and Hans hadn't had sex in two years, and she'd taken to watching box sets of TV series most evenings because he bored her so much. She was thinking of enrolling in a Masters just for something to do. You'd laughed together and that was that.

Except it wasn't. It must have planted a seed in Sandra: the idea that she could fool around with your husband as a cure for her boredom. And he'd gone along with it. The two of them carrying on like they weren't betraying a friendship and a marriage. Like it was no big deal.

The phone stops ringing. You wait a minute until the notification pings through. She's left a message. You'll delete it without listening, of course.

How different might this whole thing be if she was still your best friend. You could have asked her advice about Finn, or told her you'd started to believe in ghosts and were, in all likelihood, going absolutely, slowly, mad. You could have asked her why, instead of weeping, you felt angry all the time. At Finn most of all.

Bridget, I know you don't want to speak to me. I just want to tell you I'm still here, and I'm thinking of you and ... um ... sending love, and if you need someone, just call.

You stab at the delete icon. You shouldn't have listened. What's the use? She betrayed you because she was bored. You won't forgive her. And now, after everything, you're a different person living in a different world. Sandra would hardly know who you've become.

It's Sunday and you're going crazy. Finn's out in the studio, Jarrah too, and that boy Tom has come to help, and it's the testosterone club out there and you've got nothing to do and nowhere to go and the house is closing in, pressing against your skin, crushing you.

When Meredith sends a text asking how you are, it's such a relief you nearly come to tears. You call and ask if she wants to meet for coffee. She hesitates, and at last suggests the truck stop on the highway. It's no crazier than anything else, and not far from your mother's nursing home anyway, and you agree. Leave a note on the table in case Finn wonders where you are, and head out.

The truck stop's crowded with people on the way to somewhere else. You drink a weak coffee and toy with raisin toast until she arrives. Looks around, spots you, makes her way across. She sits down, but doesn't take off her sunglasses.

She reaches across the table and clasps your hands. 'You've been on my mind constantly.'

'Thanks,' you say, for the want of something else. 'I suppose you saw the papers? Finn was charged.'

'I know. Are you OK?'

The words rush out of you. 'Finn wants us to go back to Hobart – he says he can't stay living here any more. I've lost track of Jarrah and I can't reach him. I'm scared about leaving. I don't know what to do.'

She lets go of your hand and sits back. 'I wanted to tell you in person, not on the phone. I can't support you any more. I shouldn't even be here today.'

Mid-rant, you try to collect yourself. 'What?'

'I found out yesterday. I'll be called as a witness in the case against Finn. So I can't speak to him any more, and probably not to you either.'

You struggle to understand. 'But – you're on our side. You said your foundation supports families in legal cases.'

She glances down. 'It's not about sides. We do support families during coronial inquests, but now Finn's been charged it's different. It's a criminal matter. Our foundation has been lobbying for years for a case like this to go through the courts to raise awareness. Do you know how many other families lost their toddlers in swimming pools last year?'

You shake your head.

'Sixteen. Sixteen families who lost their babies, mostly because someone was careless with a gate or a fence. Sixteen families destroyed.'

'But—'

'In my experience, when a child drowns, the mother always gets the blame, Bridget. But in this case, Finn modified the gates illegally, and now you're all paying the price.'

'Whoa!' You stand.

'Oh God,' she says. Slips off her glasses and puts her head in her hands. 'Let me explain.'

You hesitate, and sit again. She composes herself. Her eyes are red but she's kept the tears from falling. When she starts again, her voice is soft.

'If Finn's convicted, this case will help save lives. If he goes to jail, even more so. It will be in all the news, all over social media. People will hear about it, and they'll remember the message.'

Your head snaps up. 'Could he go to jail?'

'Haven't you had legal advice?'

You skipped off to Chen's instead of meeting the solicitor, you remember with a twinge of guilt as you shake your head. You haven't been paying attention.

'I'm not trying to hurt your family. I just want justice done and children protected. That's worth something, isn't it? If it even saves one child's life?'

There's no possible answer to that question. You look at her squarely. 'What happened to you, Meredith?'

She looks away, out the window. The forecourt buzzes. Cars come and go, people pump petrol, and beyond, vehicles roar on the highway, heading north, heading south, travelling. You wish you had somewhere to flee to.

At last she answers in a flat voice. 'I thought you might have guessed. My daughter drowned in the neighbour's pool. She wasn't quite two. My husband had taken her with him when he went over for a drink. Their gate was propped open.'

'How long ago?'

'Twenty-six years.'

'And whose fault was it?'

'Oh, no one could agree. My husband blamed the neighbours for leaving the gate open. The neighbours blamed him for not watching her. The coroner found it was an unfortunate accident.'

'But it wasn't your fault.'

She presses the tip of her car key into the top of her first finger, over and over. 'I should never have trusted him with her. But no one paid for it, Bridget. No one had to get up and account for what they'd done. And it didn't stop people wedging their pool gates open and children drowning. No one took any notice.'

'And you think Finn should pay?'

'They should all pay,' she snaps. 'Every one of them who left a gate open, or wedged it or tied it or—'

'Or looked away for a minute, like me,' you finish for her.

'You believed your pool was safely fenced,' she counters. 'It wasn't your fault.'

A best friend would have told you what she thought. If it was your fault, or Finn's, or no one's, or everyone's. You would have believed a best friend.

You stand. 'I'd better go.'

She looks up at you. 'It's not personal. If you didn't blame him yourself, Bridget, you'd be fighting for him right now. You wouldn't even be talking to me.'

'What happened to your husband?' you ask.

'Just what you'd expect.' She puts her sunglasses back on. 'Two more children with his new wife. All safely grown up now.'

FINN

When Finn pulled on a pair of trousers Monday morning, the button was tight around his waist. He placed a hand on his belly. Bridget was noticeably losing weight, but the opposite was happening for him. It was true: when things were bad he headed for the fridge. Eating helped, for a moment. Who cared if he was fatter?

Bridget had waited until they went to bed on Sunday night to tackle him about the charge. She'd had no idea he might go to jail, she said. Why hadn't he warned her? She was angry about that too. She needed the full story. She was coming with him the next day to see the solicitor. She'd take the morning off work.

It didn't help the sick feeling in his gut. He fell asleep anyway. It was wrong: Bridget awake and starving. Him asleep and overfed. But he couldn't help it. His stomach demanded food, and his brain shoved him into sleep when he lay down.

At ten am, the secretary ushered Finn and Bridget into Malcolm's office. Bridget took charge.

'Run us through it,' she said to Malcolm, forgoing the niceties. 'Assume we know nothing.'

Malcolm wasn't so confident this time. He seemed fidgety and nervous as he told them he'd consulted with their barrister.

'This case hinges on the prosecution demonstrating gross negligence,' he said. 'That means negligence to a level showing abandonment of moral and lawful standards. It's a very high standard of proof required from the prosecution and my opinion is they will struggle to make it stick.

'The first thing is the mention in the Local Court this Wednesday, which starts the process moving. It just takes a few minutes for the magistrate to set a date for a committal hearing. That's our first focus – getting the case dismissed at the committal. We're looking at maybe three to six months until that hearing. With any luck that will be the end of it.'

'If it's not?' Bridget asked.

'If it's not dismissed, it will go on to full trial in the District Court or Supreme Court. It could be eighteen months or two years before that happens.'

'What will it cost?'

'Well, you've got a barrister. If one or both of you is or are working, you probably won't qualify for legal aid. So for the committal – probably between thirty and fifty.'

Finn felt sick and Bridget physically slumped in the chair beside him. He wanted to reach for her hand, but didn't dare.

'Thirty and fifty thousand?' Bridget said. 'And what about a full trial?'

'Could be up to three hundred. I very much hope it won't come to that.'

Bridget took a sharp in-breath. 'Three hundred thousand? And he could still end up in jail?'

'It's possible. It depends on the judge. If he's found guilty – and that's a big if – he might get a good behaviour bond. He might get a suspended sentence. A jail term would be the worst case.'

'How long? Worst case?'

'You'll hear this mentioned, so I'll tell you now. The maximum penalty for manslaughter is twenty-five years. But that's not going to happen.'

He might as well have not been there, Finn thought, as they discussed his life. There was a long moment of silence.

'I know that's a lot to take in,' Malcolm said. 'Could we discuss some details of the day in question?'

Finn felt a twinge of fear. 'I don't want to put my wife through that again.' He turned to Bridget. 'You go on to work. I'll see you tonight.'

She hesitated.

'Please,' Finn said.

Bridget nodded. Made her farewells, left the room.

Malcolm picked up his coffee. 'Look, there's another thing. DI Evans has an axe to grind. She investigated a case a few years ago in Armidale where a child drowned in a neighbour's neglected pool. The thing was derelict, the fence had fallen down, the water was stagnant. The pool owner was charged with manslaughter, but it was thrown out at committal. I hope that's what will happen this time, but she'll be fighting hard. Let's run through your version of events again.'

Finn felt overwhelmed with weariness. 'Nothing's changed. It's just what I told the police. There's nothing to add.'

'Let me ask you some questions then. Who was responsible for Toby at the time he entered the pool area?'

'I was.'

'And where were you?'

Finn paused, his mind racing. 'In the studio.'

'And Toby was in the house with your wife?'

'Um … yes.'

'So she was responsible for him?'

'Look,' Finn said. 'It was incredibly traumatic. Neither of us can remember the exact details. I think Bridget thought I was watching Toby, and maybe I thought she was, I can't be certain now, but whatever, I went across to the studio and the gate malfunctioned and didn't close properly behind me.'

'Your original police statement says you'd been in the studio for fifteen or twenty minutes before Toby disappeared.'

Finn stared at the floor. 'Isn't the whole point of this trial that I was in the wrong by installing a mechanism for the gate that wasn't reliable?'

'The point of the trial is to determine exactly what happened and whether there was negligence involved,' Malcolm said. 'You must tell the truth.'

Finn stood up. 'I need to use the bathroom.' At the door he turned. 'Will I end up in jail?'

Malcolm shrugged. 'In my opinion – for what it's worth – the chance of your going to jail is about … oh, say, fifteen per cent. Those are odds very much worth fighting for.'

'We don't have three hundred thousand dollars.'

'Don't think about that now. You've got an excellent barrister and we'll push very hard to get this thrown out at the committal. If that doesn't happen, we'll make a new game plan. We'll have negotiating power, given your bereavement. This is just the first stage.'

Finn put his hand on the doorknob.

'While you're out there, think carefully,' Malcolm said. 'Your story doesn't add up. Bridget left Toby unsupervised for several minutes, didn't she?'

'No,' Finn said. 'That's not how it happened.'

He pushed the door shut behind him. The receptionist pointed the way to the toilets. Finn locked himself in a stall and wept in strangled silence.

JARRAH

'You just don't get it, Jarrah!'

I felt stupid. She was right. I didn't get it. She couldn't be crying for Toby. Had she been crying so hard because she was sorry for me?

The whole thing was getting weird. Expected all along I was going to be dropped. But she hadn't dropped me. She'd started acting like she was my girlfriend.

Laura had been waiting for me before school and she suggested we sneak off to the forest. When we sat down on the damp grass by the creek she started crying and I had no idea what she needed. Put my arm around her shoulder, but she held herself stiff underneath it. Wanted to take it away again, but I reckoned that'd make things worse, so I left it there and pretended it wasn't part of me. Did she want me to kiss her? Didn't feel like it but what did I know? Maybe she had her period or something. Didn't know much about that either, but knew it could make girls emotional.

'You only met Toby once.'

It was the wrong thing to say. She pulled away from me and I had to take my arm back or leave it hanging in the air.

I tried to backpedal. 'I mean, it's nice of you—'

'You don't know anything about nice!' she snapped.

'That's right, I'm just an idiot.'

She rolled her eyes. 'Oh fuck you.'

It shocked me. Not the word, but coming from her. She wasn't a swearer. The whole thing was turning to crap. All I'd done was ask her why she was crying and now we were stuck in some argument I didn't understand.

Did she like me? Today, no. Obviously. But she didn't just get up and walk away. She said fuck you, not fuck off. She wanted something from me, but I didn't know what it was. My guts were churning. Is that what love was meant to feel like? At least it meant I didn't think about Toby so much.

'I had an abortion. All right?'

That jolted me back. Didn't dare move.

'No one knows. I don't have any ashes or any grave; I can't even cry about it. You're lucky, Jazz. At least you can be sad.'

Lucky wasn't how I'd thought of myself lately, but tears were rolling down her face. Somehow knew it was the right moment to hold out my arm and she came close and leaned against me.

'When?' Safest thing I could think to ask.

'Start of the year. Lucky it was after my birthday, so didn't have to tell my parents. They thought I was staying over with a friend. I went to a clinic on the Gold Coast and stayed in a hotel after.'

A month ago I couldn't have imagined that. But it was something like what happened to me. You're suddenly not a kid any more. Your parents can't help you and you have to grow up fast. Doesn't mean you know much, but you know you've got to find a way through. Do things like tell your aunt on the phone that your brother has drowned, or work out how you can have an abortion without anyone finding out.

It all started to make sense. She didn't just pick me up to be the centre of attention. I'd got it wrong. She picked me up because maybe I'd understand her.

'What about the guy?' I asked.

'He doesn't know. We'd already broken up. He was a dick.'

She started crying again, softly. She was warm against me, and I had a feeling I hadn't had since … well, it was a feeling I got sometimes with Toby. Like a nearly overwhelming kind of love. I guess that was it. I squeezed her gently. I could feel she needed a big howling cry, but I didn't know if I could handle it. Might just set me off too. How could two people be so sad?

She lifted her face up to mine and I kissed her. Knew that was what she wanted, even covered with snot and tears, her mascara running. We kissed softly. When I drew back, a tear hung in her eyelashes. Wiped it off with my finger. I felt like I'd grown up about ten years.

'Do you wish you hadn't done it?'

'Wish I didn't have to do it. I hated it. When I woke up, I was already crying. Like, even through the anaesthetic, I knew what I'd done. I knew I'd killed it. I never want to do that again.'

She turned to me. 'Thing is, Jazz, I like sex. I really like it.'

I was a bit shocked. Not that she liked sex, but that she said it, just like that. She saw something in my face.

'Oh, I get it.' Her voice was bitter. 'Any girl who likes sex is a slut, right?'

'No!' I protested.

'I thought you were different. You've been through something. You're not a kid. And neither am I. Not like everyone else at school. They've got no idea.'

I'd never thought about Laura being an outsider before.

'I killed someone,' she said softly. 'Not that it was someone yet, but it would have been.'

She started to cry again. 'And you hear all these stories of women who have abortions when they're young and when they want to have babies later they can't get pregnant. Like they're getting payback.'

I put both arms around her and rocked her, and for once, I got it right. I knew what to do. She softened into me, like all the muscles of her body had kind of melted. Holding her like that, I knew the two of us could make everything all right. We could make a baby that would stop us being these broken people and let us know the world could be OK. We were teenagers but we weren't kids. We'd been through more than lots of adults. We could fix things.

Laura felt it too. She shifted her weight around and eased back, pulling me with her, so we were lying on the ground, and I was half on top of her. She put her hand on the back of my head, pulled me in.

I knew what she wanted. Her whole body was telling me, her arms, her legs, her mouth, her skin, all drawing me closer. She put my hand on her breast and pressed my fingers so I was squeezing and made a sound like a sob, but I knew it was a wanting sound. I could tell it wasn't just an idea she had, liking sex. It was strong in her.

She was breathing hard. So was I. She pulled my hand down and slid it into her underpants. I had the brief feeling of her

236

crisp hair. I thought I should stop there – wasn't there something about foreplay and girls needing a lot more time than boys to be ready for sex? It was all mysterious down there, I could feel heat and slipperiness, she was making that sound again. I hesitated and she took my hand, tilted her hips and pushed my first two fingers all the way inside her.

I'd never imagined I could make a girl feel the way Laura was feeling, clutching my arms, her body moving against mine, making that sound. It was incredible. I kissed her again, wetly and deeply, and I realised how fast this could happen, how it could go from sitting next to each other one moment to actually having sex, just like that. We were going to have sex. We were going to make a baby. We were going to make the world all right.

She reached down and put her hand on my penis, through my pants. That was a kid's word for it, but hell, I'd been a kid until a month ago. She squeezed and I felt a rush of feeling so strong that I gasped.

Then suddenly, nothing. I'd gone limp in her hand. Everything had disappeared.

She opened her eyes. 'Jarrah?'

It was all wrong. It wasn't going to bring Toby back. It wasn't going to bring her baby back. It wasn't even my brain thinking this. My body just switched off. Couldn't do it.

'What?'

I drew my fingers out of her. She gasped, like it hurt. I pulled her skirt down. 'I'm sorry.'

'You fucking bastard.' She scrambled to her feet.

'Laura—'

'No, fuck you, Jarrah Brennan! Fuck you and your dead brother and go to hell!'

It was like being hit in the face. She turned, scooped up her bag and was gone before I could move to stop her, crashing through the bush, setting off all the birds, disappearing. I knew she wasn't coming back.

I wanted to cry. I rolled over so my face was against the leaves and I said Toby's name, just once, clawing at the dirt so it jammed under my nails, hoping it would set me off. But my eyes stayed dry. What was wrong with me?

Time after Toby: twenty-one days.

BRIDGET

You've lost Toby. Nothing else should be shocking. But this morning's revelations have left you reeling. The possibility of Finn in jail. A legal bill that could swallow whatever home you might own. A nightmare that could drag on for the next two years.

Because of your late start, you arranged to meet Chen in the office. You walk in past the glances of your co-workers, who smile and nod, and you feel their relief at not having to see you daily. As you halt in your cubicle, you hear the murmur of conversation and a laugh across the room.

It's him; you know his voice. You glance across the open plan and spot him at the far end by the kitchen. He's talking to someone who has her back to you. He hasn't seen you, and you observe, with a sinking in your belly, the expression on his face. When the woman he's talking to says something and he laughs, easily and openly, you realise in a moment what it must cost him to buffer you from the world.

She's young. You can't recall her name; she's not in the same section as you and Chen. But she's unmarked by pain. She's whole. Not like you. She leans in close and he's still smiling at her and you wonder at the nature of his interest.

You have absolutely no right to be jealous. You repeat this fact to yourself and sit down to break your line of sight. You have no right. But it doesn't stop the burn of it in your veins, following the pain pathways seared into your being. As if pain is all you will ever feel now.

He comes to the door while you're rummaging, his face adjusted to the calm, accepting expression you'd thought natural on his features.

'Ready?' he asks gently.

You can't stand it. 'Look, I really need a day in the office. I've got emails banking up and a bit of research to do. Why don't we head out again tomorrow?'

He tilts his head slightly. Oh, he knows you all right. You turn your own head away from him and back to the fascination of the filing drawer, and you won't let him catch your eye.

'Sure,' he says at last. 'I could do with some admin time too.'

You scrabble, shuffle, crinkle.

'Everything OK?'

You nod, not trusting your voice. You won't cry.

'Do you want a coffee or something?'

'Maybe later.'

He stands watching you.

'Chen,' you say, 'go away.'

'You know I'd do anything for you, Bridget Brennan,' he says. 'You just have to ask.'

He doesn't wait for you to reply. He turns quickly and walks off. Damn him. Because you'd like to run after him, wrench him around, batter him or weep or hold him or fuck him or something.

There's only one place you can be where there's any peace, and there are many hours before you can get back to it.

*

You wait for Finn to fall asleep. Even through all this he can still do it. Within minutes his muscles start twitching and he's gone. You wait until his snores rip the air apart, and you slide out as softly and secretly as a woman going to her lover.

Finn's return to your bed wasn't negotiable, but you don't care much. Your being has narrowed its focus to these hours in the night when you lower yourself into the cool water. The more time you spend in there, the stronger the feeling gets. At first it was just a sense of Toby, a flash here and there, a feeling. Now, you're becoming convinced, there's something more. Like an essence of Toby is in that pool. Like – you can hardly believe you would even think this – your son is haunting the water.

It's not possible. You know that. So you decide to suspend disbelief. You disengage the part of your mind that would dismantle the sensation, and you immerse yourself in the dream of it.

Only it's not feeling like a dream.

You enter the water, slipping in silently in the dark, and you could swear Toby has run a small hand down your arm, or patted your cheek. You could swear to hearing his voice in the gurgles the water makes around your body. You could swear he's happy when you come into the water, and that he yearns for you when you leave.

The water lapping your body has travelled across the world for millennia. Falling as rain, evaporating, rising, condensing, falling again. Outside, in the air, your rage at Finn rises up. In the water that all drops away. In the water are love and grief; in the water are the world's sorrows. In the water you're in the womb again yourself, you remember your own foetal floating and then Toby floating inside you, and now you're floating inside him, your roles reversed. Images wash around you: reeds and plants, fish swimming, water that's clear, with a green light. Bubbles. Tranquillity. Microbes.

The pump clicks on with a jolt and the water gurgles and swirls, interrupting the silence. The system runs automatically at different points during the night to use off-peak electricity, and tonight its timing has coincided with your visit. The mechanical whirr grinds into the dreamy underwater world, disturbing it.

You surface, the moment broken. The throb of the pump means you can't hear Toby any more and you feel the grief of losing him again.

As you rise on the step, you return to gravity's pain. You trail your fingers in the water, saying good night. Then you step out, your toes reluctant to break the last contact with the water, and you towel yourself dry.

You detour to the pump house, grab the power cord and yank it from its socket. The pump splutters into silence, the water in the pumps gurgling back to rest. As a test, you return to the pool edge and lower a foot onto the step. Whatever trace of Toby you felt is gone, sucked away through the machine.

At the computer you swizzle the mouse until the screen lights up. Think for a moment. Type in a search term. And though you didn't know quite what you were looking for, what you wanted pops up. A picture of a swimming pool transformed into a pond. Reeds, water plants, fish. Clear, green-tinted water. Bubbles. Just like your underwater imagining.

According to the descriptions, it's not hard. Turn off the pumps, wait for the water to go green, introduce plants and fish, let them establish a new balance. You could still swim in it. Some local councils are apparently helping people transform their unused swimming pools into natural ponds. Beautification, economy and a backyard ecosystem. It takes a few weeks. You could do it. You could bring it back to life.

FINN

Finn clenched his jaw and willed his hands to stop shaking. Lowered the mask over his eyes, steadied the torch, applied it to the join and squeezed the trigger. The mask snapped to black as molten metal spat and splashed in eerie electric green. The dreaded replay of images that welding always prompted was just beginning when a sharp sting and the smell of burning made him jump back, dropping the torch.

The weather was too hot for full protective gear and a piece of hot slag had hit and rolled down his bare arm, searing a path. As Finn pushed back the mask, the metal lump fell to the floor and he grimaced at the stink of burned hair. He'd have a streak of blister now, and his concentration was shot.

His concentration was non-existent anyway. Finn peered at the weld line. He could barely remember why he was trying to join those two pieces of metal. He rubbed his eyes, breathed in and out a few times. Fought down the livid images by focusing on his burned arm.

Somehow, with Tom's help, he'd finished the first commission and sent it off. What remained of *Dragon Sentry* was now gone from his life. This new piece was the commission for the barrister, in lieu of the first raft of legal bills. He needed this one, and more, to pay those costs and have any chance of getting his family out of here. And, irrationally, it felt like if he got the sculpture done, he'd ward off the risk of jail.

He heard the pool gate click. Tom had promised to help again. It wasn't that he needed help, but it felt like nothing bad could happen if Tom were there, and Finn was less likely to regress into memories. Tom, sensing this somehow, had set himself the task of sorting Finn's scrap metal by size and type, the bigger pieces into crates, the smaller into a wooden type-drawer Finn had found at a long-ago garage sale. It was a slow, steady job Tom was obviously spinning out. Finn was grateful.

'Hello, Finn?' a woman's voice called.

Finn stepped to the door. Tom was walking across the pool area, followed by his mother, Angela. She smiled as they drew close.

'Good news,' she said. 'I wanted to tell you in person.'

As Finn peeled the safety mask off, Angela nudged Tom. 'Go put some coffee on while I talk to Finn.'

She waited until Tom reached the far gate. 'There's been another offer. A good one.' She named a figure not far below the price Finn and Bridget had paid.

'But ...' Finn couldn't take it in. 'When did they see it?'

'Didn't need to,' she said. 'Investors. It fits their formula and they're happy with the building report. But they're hard-nosed. They'll buy if you exchange today and waive the cooling-off period. So you need to be sure.'

Finn's legs felt weak. 'Can we sit?'

Angela followed him through the pool area and onto the verandah. Finn lowered himself to the couch and waved her to a chair.

Angela sat. 'I hope this isn't too much pressure. You haven't changed your mind, have you?'

Finn shook his head. 'Christ, no.'

'Good. They haven't asked for any special conditions, just vacant possession, but I won't be able to hold them longer than today.'

'We can do it,' Finn said, his mind starting to race. Could he find them a house in Tasmania before the trial? They could rent, he supposed, but something in him wanted to anchor the family while they recovered. Renting a home was just setting up something they knew they'd leave. No, they needed to buy something. Especially if he was going to end up in jail; he needed to know they were settled and safe.

He remembered, suddenly, how it had felt to find the purple house the previous summer. A home full of colour and promise, like life opening up in new directions.

'Tom will miss you,' she said. 'He and Jarrah have become good friends.'

Finn saw the car pull up outside, heard the familiar sound of its door. Bridget, home at lunchtime on a weekday for some unfathomable reason. The moment of relief he'd felt at Angela's news disappeared. He didn't want to break the news to Bridget in front of someone else.

Bridget walked into the garden, glanced up and visibly started at seeing them.

'Perfect timing,' Angela called out, standing.

Finn waited until Bridget was on the verandah. 'We have another buyer. Almost the full price.'

Bridget literally whitened as he watched.

246

'They're serious,' Angela said. 'The only thing is, you'll need to act today.'

'Right,' Bridget said.

Angela gathered her bag. 'I'll leave you two to discuss it. The contract is with your solicitor ready to sign. You'll need to do it by – oh, say, three pm – so the exchange can go through.'

She called through to Tom and he came out of the kitchen, handing over Finn's coffee, then joining his mother to walk across the lawn, out to the free world where people laughed and life went on.

'Bridget.'

Her face was turned away from him. 'I don't know how much more I can take.'

Desperation rose in Finn. 'We've got to go somewhere safe.'

'Is this what you think Jarrah wants?'

'He wants to leave this house. He told me. Anyhow, just look at him – he won't even go into the pool area. He can't live like that. None of us can. And anyway, he needs us to be the parents and make the decision. He's still a boy.'

'What if you go to jail?'

'All the more reason to go back. You and Jarrah can be somewhere familiar if the worst happens. My family will help. Anyhow, we won't know for ages. We can't wait here all that time.'

It seemed to Finn that Bridget shuddered. 'I don't know if I can stand the Brennans' help, Finn. And what about my mother?'

'We'll move her back too. She doesn't know where she is. She won't even know she's been shifted after a few days.'

'I just ...' She wrapped her arms around herself.

Finn fought down panic. 'You heard her. The deal's only on the table today. If we take it we could afford to buy back into Hobart.'

'Or pay your legal fees.'

He reached out and took Bridget by the shoulders, forcing himself not to shake her. 'This isn't about my fucking legal fees! This house is destroying us!'

She stared at him, eyes wide and shocked. He wondered if he'd frightened her, but there was no fear on her face. Just a vast distance. Like he was holding a stranger.

He dropped his hands. 'I don't know you any more.'

Her face crumpled and she buried it in her hands. Finn almost staggered with the pity that washed through him. He took a deep breath. Reached out again, gently this time. She let him fold her into his chest.

'We can get through this,' he said, his mouth against her hair.

'What sort of people are they?' she asked.

'They're investors. I don't know much about them, and I don't want to. At least they're not trying to screw us.'

He felt her shift against him and lift her head. She laid it on his shoulder, her face looking in the direction of the pool. He didn't dare move. How long since she'd come to him?

Then she took a shuddering breath in his arms and drew back. 'All right.'

'All right we can sell?

She nodded. 'As long as we can settle after Jarrah's school term finishes.'

Finn stared at her, hardly believing it. Relief started to wash through him. Was she coming back? Was it possible?

He glanced at his watch. They still had a couple of hours, but he couldn't risk her changing her mind. 'We should go and sign.'

'What about Jarrah?'

'We'll tell Jarrah tonight. We'll involve him in whatever comes next, but you and I are making this decision.'

'Investors won't care about the house,' she said, picking up her bag.

'Not the way we did,' Finn said. 'Maybe that's for the best.' He put a careful, gentle hand to the small of her back, a light touch, encouraging her to move. 'Shall we go?'

She took a step, and another. And allowed him to take her hand.

JARRAH

'Hey, Jarrah!' Tom was parked across the road from the school, elbow out the window. I dodged the cars, the parents, the squalls and squeals of the afternoon pick-up, and made it over in one piece.

'Thought you might want a run?'

Wanted to bury myself in a hole in the ground, but a run would do. Went around the car and got in. 'Got no shoes.'

'What about the beach? We can run barefoot.'

I hated the beach, but Tom was already pulling out, and really I didn't care much where we went. I slid down in my seat while he drove. I'd gone back to school eventually, after Laura left me in the dirt. Snuck into a bathroom, washed my face, waited for the next break and joined my class like I'd been there all along.

But I felt shit. What was wrong with me? I wasn't normal. Any boy would be over the moon at having sex with Laura Fieldman. Not me. I'd chucked it all away. No wonder I was such a loser.

'Heard some news,' Tom said.

'Mm?' Wasn't really concentrating.

'About your place. Looks like it's sold. Another buyer came through.'

'*Another* buyer?'

He glanced across. 'They don't tell you much, do they?' Rolled his eyes. 'Mum'll kill me, but I can't stand it. The place was sold once, but the buyers pulled out at the last minute, after your dad was arrested. Another lot have made an offer. Your mum didn't look so happy about the news.'

'How do you know?'

'I was there today when my mum told them.'

Turned away and stared out the window, hardly seeing what was passing. What was Mum even doing home on a workday? They hadn't said a word about selling the house. No one had ever come and looked at it, not when I was around. Christ, what else were they keeping secret? Even Tom knew more than me. Maybe they were going to break the news to me all at once. *We've sold the house, darling, and we're getting a divorce.* Where was I going to end up? Didn't want to go back to Tassie. After today, didn't want to stay in Murwillumbah either.

'You kept quiet,' I said bitterly.

'Yeah. Sorry.'

He was so bloody calm. Never got worked up about anything.

'What's up with you?' he asked.

'Totally blew it today with Laura. She'll never talk to me again.'

'Can't be that bad?'

'It's fucking worse. She hates my guts.'

'And how do you feel about her?'

That stopped me. Mostly I was so amazed she liked me, I never thought how I felt.

'I dunno.'

Tom braked to make a right. What was my problem with Laura? She was pretty, she liked me, she wanted to have sex with me. What was wrong with me? It was all fucked. That was the only word for it. Fucked, fucked, fucked.

'What about your last girlfriend?' I asked Tom as he turned on to the beach road. 'Why'd you break up?'

'Kristy?' he said. 'Dunno really. It started OK but in the end we both lost interest.'

'Doesn't sound so bad. Anyone break your heart?'

He drummed his fingers on the wheel, then reached over and turned the radio up. It was a dumb question. Wished I'd kept my mouth shut. Sometimes it was like Tom was my age. Sometimes he was like an adult.

'Don't worry, I know about a broken heart,' he said over the music. 'You?'

I felt a lump in my throat. Shook my head. Toby was the only one who broke my heart.

Tom turned into the road that ran along Kingscliff Beach, passed the entry and headed south. Drove a few minutes past the houses and into the scrub. Parked on a patch of sand.

'It's a nor-easter,' Tom said. 'If we run into the wind, we'll have it behind us on the way back.'

The sky was overcast and the wind roared down the beach, throwing up spray from the big waves rolling in. I hoped Tom didn't want us to swim – there wasn't anyone around and the waves looked scary. We stretched for a few minutes. That was always boring and I didn't know if it made any difference, but Tom did it and I followed.

'You ready?' he asked.

I nodded and we set off, him leading the way down the dune

through the soft sand. It was tough going until we reached the edge of the water, where the sand was hard and we could run side by side. I'd been getting fitter. Could match his stride, easy.

First time I'd run on the beach. We'd run through the suburbs, parks and ovals and along little tracks in the patches of bush on the edges of town where it was steamy and hot. Murwillumbah was a hilly, shut-in town. When you could see the sky, you always saw that big mountain.

The beach was empty. No one. Not even a speck on the horizon, not in this weather. The air was hazy with salt. Didn't have to watch for uneven ground and tree roots. The sand felt damp and cool under my feet, sinking a bit under each step. Got into a rhythm and the wind blew my thoughts back behind me and I felt like I could run forever. Tom seemed to be in the same groove, pounding beside me, breathing steadily.

Running usually settled me. Could get in that zone where nothing mattered. Even on a bad day, could kind of leave things behind.

Except today was a really bad day and I started thinking about Toby and couldn't stop. Remembered the last time I was on the beach with him and how I'd ignored him and snapped at him and made him cry. And then the moment when we got home and he hugged me, even though I'd been mean to him. Even back then when he was alive, it was nearly more than I could stand.

Sped up, breaking the rhythm, leaving Tom behind. Didn't matter how fast I ran, I couldn't go faster than these thoughts. Toby came right along too. I went into a sprint.

In my mind I'd pretended Toby was mine. Was I crazy? I didn't want to have sex with Laura Fieldman – but I wanted to be a father to my own brother? Didn't make any sense. Ages ago I'd had this daydream that something happened to Mum and Dad and I was left alone with Toby. Just him and me. After a while he forgot about Mum and Dad, and I was everything. I was the centre of his universe and he was the centre of mine. We didn't need anyone else. Couldn't tell anyone that daydream. So weird. Don't reckon even girls my age would daydream about having a kid. Boys wouldn't.

My breath was tearing at me by then, a stitch stabbing my side. I stumbled, caught myself, slowed to a jog. Tom pounded up at high speed, overtook me, slowed and stopped. He bent over, hands on his hips, gasping. I stopped next to him.

'Not fair,' he panted. 'Too much head start.'

Didn't answer. My breath rushed in and out, in and out so hard it hurt. Tom straightened up and looked at me.

'Christ, Jarrah, is it that bad?'

That was it. Started to cry. Wanted to cry down there in the bush on my own after Laura had walked off and couldn't. Now couldn't bloody stop. Blubbing like a kid with Tom, making sounds I had no control of. Felt Tom's arm around my shoulder, easy, like he wasn't scared of making an arse of himself, doing or saying the wrong thing. Just saw I was hurting and wanted to help, and did it without thinking, and I never knew how to be natural like that. I was scared: the crying was getting out of control.

'It's OK, Jarrah.'

Something in his voice told me it really was OK to fall apart, and I kind of crumpled with my face on his shoulder. Wanted to hang on to him, like it was me drowning. Forced myself not to grab him and hang on. I was OK until he patted my back. Lifted my head and his face was closer than I expected.

Had no control. Kind of lunged at him. Somehow, without planning it, I was kissing him.

It took about two seconds for my brain to realise what was going on. Threw myself back from him, my mouth off his mouth, my body away from his, oh fuck, what had I done? He stared at me, wide-eyed, and I wanted to die with shame. Swung around and ran away from him fast as I could, breath still heaving. I'd fucked everything up. I was a total fucking disaster.

The wind shoved me down the beach and I didn't care if I ran till I dropped dead.

BRIDGET

It's done and signed. The sale will be settled in six weeks, a few days after the end of the school year. You've given in and taken the rational course, and you carefully hold the devastation of this choice at bay.

Finn suggests dinner together so you can break the news to Jarrah and plan your next steps. But as you wait on the verandah, Finn nursing a beer and you a glass of wine, dusk falls. Jarrah is nowhere and not answering his phone.

'Is he often this late? Should we start worrying?' you ask.

'He is often this late,' Finn says carefully. 'Now he's got a girlfriend. And he runs with Tom in the afternoons. He's almost never home straight after school.'

'Can you call Tom?'

Finn pulls his mobile from his pocket, squints at the screen, presses slowly with his big fingers. He greets Tom and there's a long pause as he listens.

'Hang on. You left him where?'

You have to put the glass down because your hand starts to shake. You grip the front of the chair, sink your fingers into the cushion, strain your ears to make out what Tom, in his tinny voice, is saying. You can't afford to lose another son.

'Christ.' Finn gets up fast, stabs at the phone. 'They had an argument or something. Tom's driving around looking for Jarrah, but he can't find him. Over on the bloody beach.'

Acid scrapes the back of your throat. In a moment you're back, kneeling on the edge of the pool, Finn standing in the water on the step so your faces are level, Toby lying face up on your lap, limbs slack. As though asleep, except for his terrible, open eyes.

'I'll get in the car,' Finn says. 'You stay here in case he comes home.'

'But how will you know where to look?'

'I can't just sit here.'

He goes for the keys. You check the sky. It'll be dark soon. Jarrah's nearly sixteen but he's a kid. He's not street-smart. Anything in the dangerous world could snatch him and smash him.

Finn is coming back out the door when the gate clicks and you both turn. Jarrah crosses the lawn barefoot, in unfamiliar shorts and T-shirt, his tread heavy, his head down. You try to restart your breathing so it's something resembling normal. Finn puts a warning hand on your arm before you can speak.

'Jarr. We were getting worried.' His voice artificially casual.

'Sorry.' Jarrah's is low and flat.

'Where've you been?'

'Running.'

'Everything OK?'

'Yep.'

Jarrah's face is chalky. He hasn't been running, not in the last half hour. You want to speak, but Finn tightens his grip, feeling it in you. Does he think hiding your worry is a good thing? He must, and so you bite your lip.

257

'We're going out to dinner,' Finn says. 'Want to shower and get dressed?'

'Got homework,' Jarrah says in that same flat voice.

'We've got important things to talk about.'

'Can't we do it here?'

Finn sighs and his body sags. 'Yeah, I guess we can do it here. I'll call in a takeaway.'

If Jarrah says *whatever* you'll scream, but he just nods. He comes up the steps, past you and inside. His legs are covered in sand. In a moment he's disappeared.

'I'll let Tom know.' Finn types a text so laboriously you want to snatch the phone from him and do it yourself. Instead you sink back down onto the chair, shaking with the sickening aftershock of adrenaline. Jarrah's safe, but you've never seen him look so shut down. Not even after Toby.

Finn's phone pings and he glances at it. 'Tom says thanks for letting him know.'

'Wonder how Jarrah got back here from the coast.'

'He's home,' Finn says. 'I think we should leave it alone. He's got enough going on, Bridget.'

You want to snap at him: *How do you know?* Not just in anger, but as a genuine question. How does he know what's happening to your son? You have no idea how to enter Jarrah's world, how to ask him a question, how to manage the fact that he's not a child any more, but not an adult either. It was all so simple before when the biggest problem was his crush on that girl at school. A crush you were pretty sure had no chance of going anywhere.

You don't want to leave it alone. 'What could they be fighting about?'

He shrugs. 'They're boys. Could be anything.'

'Tom's not a boy.'

'He's only nineteen.'

'He drives, drinks, votes and works, Finn. He's an adult. Maybe he's not a good influence.'

'Oh for God's sake!'

At the anger in his voice you jump.

Finn visibly controls himself. 'Jarrah needs a friend. Leave it alone.'

Your glass is empty and it's an excuse to walk away from him. 'You'd better call the takeaway,' you say over your shoulder. In the kitchen you pour a large second glass of white and down half of it. Maybe that will stop your hands shaking. Maybe that will let you sit down to a family dinner like you could be normal again.

Standing in the kitchen, hearing Finn ordering pad thai, red duck curry, spring rolls, jasmine rice, your head spins. The rush of fear that something had happened to Jarrah has set off memories stamped in your cells. You want something to hold onto, one stable thing, and you've just signed away your home. Right now, all you have is hoping that when you creep outside tonight, in the dark, and lower yourself into the water, Toby will still be there.

'Bridget?'

Finn has come into the room behind you. You can't answer him. You're shaking so hard you can barely stand.

You feel his hand on your shoulder, the other one at your waist. 'Please,' he whispers, 'let's stick together on this.'

You begin to break. 'All right.'

He wraps his arms around you. You lean back into him, let him absorb your body's shuddering, and to your surprise you feel something. Some inkling of kindness. Maybe you can do this.

FINN

Finn wanted to do it properly. Not plastic takeaway containers on the table; not tonight. He decanted the food into china bowls and laid them out. Bridget set the table with placemats and napkins, lit candles. Once, their shoulders brushed in passing and she didn't pull away from him. He allowed himself to feel a moment of hope.

He had to call Jarrah twice before the boy padded downstairs in clean clothes, his hair slicked down over his blank face.

No television. No devices. The three of them sitting in the soft light as dusk fell outside. The warm smell of curry and coriander and jasmine rice, the hint of sesame oil in the stir-fried noodles. Finn felt a wild urge to fold down his head, shut his eyes and pray out loud. He hadn't said grace before a meal since he was a boy. But this was a night to ask for help, even if only in his own mind.

They busied themselves with serving, passing the dishes hand to hand. Outside the wind picked up, tossing the palm leaves and ripping through the old gum on the street by the gate. It wasn't a familiar wind; Finn didn't know it like he knew the salty south winds of Hobart, carrying their hint of ice. But it was a wind that whispered of summer, a wind he sensed might blow for days.

'Jarrah. I know it's a bit sudden. We've sold the house.'

Jarrah swallowed his mouthful. 'Yeah, Tom told me.'

'Oh.' Finn's insides sank at the shut-off tone of Jarrah's voice. 'I'm sorry. We thought you had enough to deal with. And the offer came very suddenly today. We had to decide straight away.'

Jarrah shovelled in another mouthful.

'We don't belong here,' Finn said. 'We need to be with family and friends.'

They both looked at Jarrah, who glanced up, then dropped his eyes.

'We want to decide the next step together,' Bridget said. 'The three of us.'

Jarrah shrugged and shovelled in another mouthful.

'I promise things will be better once we get home,' Finn said.

'How the hell can you promise that?' For a second the adult Jarrah blazed out of the boy's eyes, all violence and anger.

Finn was shoved back in his chair with the force. 'I ...' he managed.

Jarrah scraped back his chair and started to rise. Finn rose too, reached out his hand, stopped before touching the boy.

'Wait. Please.'

They stood in a frozen tableau for a moment, then Jarrah subsided. Sat again, rested his elbows on the table and hunched over his meal.

'Let's just eat together,' Finn said. He gestured. 'Look at this beautiful food. Eat!'

But it was no good, he knew. The food was now heavy and greasy in his mouth, the taste overblown and garish. The three of them chewed methodically.

'If it's Hobart that's the problem, we could go somewhere else,' Finn said.

'I thought you were going to jail?' Jarrah said.

Finn lost his hunger suddenly. They were falling to pieces. What hope did he have of trying to hold them together? For a moment he saw the scene from outside his body. The three of them hunched over the scattered, messy plates. Jarrah, set, adult, closed off. Bridget, silent and struggling. Himself, desperately feeling them slip from his grasp.

And somewhere, floating around beyond them, Toby. A wisp. A hint. The thing that kept them all together.

'We don't know that,' Bridget said. 'It's only a small chance, and even if it happens, it won't be for – oh, one or two years. You don't have to worry about it at the moment.'

'Two years?' Jarrah looked shocked.

'You might be finished school by the time the case gets heard, for all we know,' Bridget said. 'It doesn't affect this decision.'

'Why does it take two years?'

Finn sighed. 'That's just the process. It's crazy. I go to court for the first mention tomorrow. That's just a few minutes, entering a plea, setting a date. Then there's a thing called a committal hearing in a few months. That's when they decide if the case will go ahead. It might all be over then, but if not, then—'

'I get it!' Jarrah interrupted. He turned to Bridget. 'Do you really want to go back?'

Finn saw Bridget's face working. She didn't want to go, still. At night she left him and went into the water and he had no idea why. It frightened him.

'Your dad wants to go,' Bridget said finally. 'We need to stick together. What do *you* want?'

'You didn't answer my question.'

'I want us to do what's right for everyone.'

'Well, let me know when you've made up your minds.'

'We're asking you,' Finn said. 'Tell us what you want.'

Jarrah shoved his chair back again and stood. 'I don't want anything,' he snapped. His voice rose. 'You don't know anything! You don't know *fucking anything!*'

Before Finn could react Jarrah stormed out of the room, thundered up the stairs and slammed his bedroom door so hard that the house shook.

Finn dropped his face into his hands. They'd lost Toby and now they were losing their other boy. The Jarrah he'd known was disappearing. The Jarrah he'd known never swore at his parents.

'Now what?' Bridget said. 'What do we do now?'

Finn rubbed his eyes and looked up. 'I have no fucking idea.'

BRIDGET

You and Finn go to bed in silence. You hate how far away Jarrah has gone, and your inability to reach him. You hate being so helpless. You hate the thought of leaving.

Perhaps, in the pool, you might find an answer. Or at least a reprieve. Ignoring Finn, who's lying wakeful and silent an arm's length away, you rise and tiptoe downstairs and out to the pool, drop your robe, lower your feet into the water. The afternoon's wind howls through the evening. If anything it's picked up, blowing away the clouds, leaving a haze across the stars. It roars across the pool, rippling the surface, turning your skin to goose bumps.

You lower yourself, gasping at the slow creep of water up your thighs. You take a breath and drop into it, and the feeling floods you. You and Toby, submerged, entwined, one.

Away from this, during work hours, you doubt the experience and you doubt your sanity. But in here there's no doubt at all. It's true and you're floating in it. In here, you can almost love Finn. Or at least remember loving him.

Images, memories, dreams wash around you. You remember first meeting Finn, dragged to some gallery opening by your artistic friends and watching him across the room, burly even then, back when he was young and lighter and had more hair. There was always something of the village blacksmith about him. Those craggy hands you wanted to be cupped in. The slow smile. The broad chest to measure yourself against. When you started to sleep together, your mind-whirring insomnia vanished. He brought you to your body, and to rest, and you slept like a dog, deep and twitching.

You remember, as though Toby is somehow putting thoughts into your head, sex with Finn one night down in Tassie. Jarrah was safely asleep. You shut the lounge-room door, turned off the light, lay down with him on the rug by the fire and fucked in the flicker of flame and heat, the skin facing away from the fire chilled by the cool air. You were both hot for it that night; you fucked like teenagers. He cupped his hand around your mouth so you didn't wake Jarrah and you cried out into his palm as he pierced you, as he moulded you, as you fitted around him, as you came shuddering and hard.

You feel a flicker of Toby laughter and understand. You made him that night. You'd never believed those women who knew they'd conceived while having sex. It wasn't physically possible – it took longer than that for sperm to join egg. But now you know Toby's conception.

You roll onto your back and float in the inky water. The house creaks in the wind and leaves flutter into the pool. Water laps at your hairline, reaching into your ears when you tilt your head back, muffling the wind. Underwater sounds bloom.

Don't think.

If your scientist's brain gets a grip, you'll reason Toby out of existence. It's dangerous to analyse. Safer to breathe, to close your eyes, to feel him. You submerge, feeling the water close

265

over your head, letting in the underwater world again. The wash and whoosh of it against your eardrums, the sound of oceans and tides, the pull of the moon.

You open your eyes and look up. Above you, the trees toss wildly against the sky. The sound of the wind has followed you underwater and you can't rid yourself of it. It blows louder and louder and louder.

JARRAH

An hour or two after I'd stormed out of the kitchen, Dad tapped on the bedroom door and said my name softly. Paused. Went away when I didn't answer. A bit later I heard the faint sound of my phone pinging out in the hall. Got up and silently opened the door. My schoolbag was resting against the wall. Tom must have dropped it off, I guess, and Dad had put it there. I brought it in, shut the door again, got back into bed, put the covers back over my head. The only safe place in the world. I couldn't face people again. Not Tom, not my parents, not Laura.

Shame. Shame. Shame.

And Toby was gone: Toby, the only one who could have helped me through this. Without him we were falling apart. Mum going one way, Dad going the other, me in the middle without a clue. Every option was siding with one of them against the other. Every option blew someone's life away. Stay – and be ashamed every single day. Go – and end up right back where I was in Tasmania. Or try to make a new start somewhere different, all over again, without Toby. I couldn't do it. Murwillumbah had been my new start and I'd fucked it up. No way out now.

Every time I remembered that moment on the beach my insides shrivelled. Didn't even know how it happened. One moment I'd been crying, the next trying to kiss Tom. There was no way he could mistake it. Christ.

If Toby had been alive, I could have crept down the hallway into his room. He would have patted my face, asked me to *weed it*. He wouldn't have cared how fucked up I was.

Except.

Toby should care. Because all the things they said were true. I was a fucking faggot. The moment I forgot everything and lunged for Tom's lips was the first time I'd ever let myself go. And look what happened. As soon as I lost control, I was gay.

That wouldn't even be so bad – I could maybe even cope with being gay – if it wasn't for Toby. Because what did it mean about how I loved him?

Groaned again and rolled into a tighter ball. I thought loving Toby was pure. The best thing in my life. Now I didn't even have that to hang on to. Like losing him all over again. No way through this. I couldn't even cry.

The idea slipped into my head so easily, like it had always been there. There *was* a way out. Get it over with. Go and find Toby. If there was anything afterwards, then he'd be there, wouldn't he? Maybe he'd forgive me. And if there wasn't … well, I wouldn't know about it anyhow.

The more I thought about it, the better the idea was. I knew Mum and Dad were pretending to be united. Without me, they could just go their own ways. They could deal with two years of court. I'd be with Toby. Laura would be sorry she'd told me to fuck off. Maybe Tom would understand I'd made a mistake and I was sorry.

Didn't have too many options for how, but that never stopped anyone who was serious. Just needed something to put around my neck, strong enough to take my weight, and something else to tie it to, right? The old gum tree out the front had strong branches and any bit of cloth that was long enough would do.

Down the corridor, Mum and Dad were pretending to be asleep. But even if they were awake, they wouldn't hear me. The wind that had nearly swept me off the beach and blasted me with sand was even stronger now, its roar drowning out the night.

Scrabbled around in the dark cupboard. Track pants. Grey soft cotton. Made in China, I guess. Not made to last, but they'd last for this. One leg around my neck. The other around the branch. Important thing was not to think too much about it, or I'd be too scared.

We'd all got good at creeping around the house in the night. Didn't make a sound opening my door, getting down the stairs on the balls of my feet. Lifted the screen door slightly so it slid without a sound.

Outside, the monsters snarled and the gum tree beyond the gate thrashed in the wind and the whole night roared at me: Do it, do it, do it.

Grass underfoot. My breath coming in and out, in and out. Dark, but the streetlight down the road showed me the way. Bright stars up there. I hesitated and remembered the afternoon, and shame shoved me across the grass, shame pushed open the front gate, shame knotted a loop in the tracksuit pants and put it over my head so it settled around my neck.

Soft. Like a promise this wouldn't hurt.

The bark had peeled off the trunk in long ribbons and crackled under my feet. Above me the trunk was smooth and white. Not warm, not cold, under my hand. Put my cheek against it for a moment, then reached up, grabbed the first branch, boosted myself. When my arms felt weak I thought again of the afternoon. The shame roared inside me. Hooked my legs over, hauled myself up and lay on the branch, trembling.

The branch swayed and I grabbed it with both hands to keep my balance. Had to do it right now. Lay down along the branch, wedged my thighs on either side, gripped it, found the other end of the tracksuit leg. It was harder to tie it on than I thought, in the dark and with the tree moving and my hands starting to shake. I couldn't see much anyhow and stupid tears were running down my face and my nose was running. I was such a cry-baby.

Toby?

I wanted to be with him so bad, even if I was all fucked up. Maybe it wouldn't matter there. All I had to do was get the knot tight, push myself off the branch and we'd be together. Where the monsters were roaring and we would be kings.

FINN

Wind buffeted the house, as if trying to pound it to the ground
It reminded Finn of those Hobart nights when the winds of
the Roaring Forties came up from the Southern Ocean and
smashed against the windows and even their brick cottage
trembled under the onslaught. Perhaps a cyclone was coming. It
would be a relief if something external tore through their lives,
flattened the house, flooded the town, flung them out.

She was gone from the bed again. He got up and crossed to
the window. Kneeled and rested his chin on the windowsill.

Ripples on the pool's surface. He peered, trying to make out
her shape. What did she do in there? How could she bear it?

'Are you coming to bed?' he asked, too softly for her to hear
him.

The wind roared and whirled around him. He closed his
eyes and murmured, 'Just come to bed, Bridget.'

A muffled splintering, cracking sound reached him over the
wind and his eyes flew open.

What was it? A loud noise far away or a soft noise close by?
Below, Bridget surfaced.

'What was that?' he yelled, loud enough to reach her.

Her face turned up to him, a glimmer in the dark. 'I don't know.'

Finn pushed himself to his feet in a single move. He'd sworn never to ignore a strange noise again. He turned and headed out of the room towards the stairs. As he reached the top he glanced towards Jarrah's room. The door was shut. It hadn't woken him, then. But the unaccountable urgency shoved him down the stairs and he broke into a run. Slid the verandah door open to find Bridget running from the pool, a towel flung around her.

She grabbed his arm, pointing. 'Over there?'

Outside the gate Finn could see an odd, flickering light that filled him with a formless panic. He sprinted across the lawn, wrenched the gate open, skidded to a halt. Tried to understand what he was seeing as Bridget ran up behind him.

A huge branch of the gum had come down, its leaves obscuring the grass verge. Through the leaves, the light flickered. He could hear something, maddeningly indistinct.

'Who's there?' Finn tried to shove his way through.

'Help!' he heard.

Bridget caught her breath. 'Oh Jesus, Finn. Oh Jesus.'

By the glancing, flickering light of an iPhone: branches and leaves everywhere, a bent back. A head of hair. Too many limbs. Or not enough limbs.

Tom's bent back. Tom's panicked voice, hoarse: 'I can't get it off him.'

'What the fuck is going on?'

Because it couldn't be true, what he was seeing in snatches of light. Jarrah's ashen face, the choking sounds coming from him, and Tom struggling with something around Jarrah's neck. Finn fell to his knees beside them.

'Loosen it, loosen it!' Tom urged.

Somehow he and Tom got the two sides of the knot and prised it loose. Jarrah took a wretched, rasping in-breath over the wind. Then exhaled with a keen of agony.

Behind Finn, Bridget cried out. 'His leg!'

Finn glanced to his left, and shuddered. A glimpse of bone and blood, crushed under the heavy fallen branch. He spun back to her, met her eyes. She nodded, turned and ran.

Tom was pulling the fabric out from under Jarrah's neck. Jarrah cried out again, and Finn found his hand, and grabbed it.

'It's all right. You'll be all right.'

'I was worried,' Tom panted. 'I texted him to come and talk. I was waiting over the road. But he climbed the tree and ...'

He looked up and extended what had been around Jarrah's neck in Finn's direction. It told Finn he'd nearly lost his second son; that if Tom hadn't been out there on watch, or the branch hadn't snapped, a second unimaginable nightmare would have engulfed him.

'What the hell did you fight about?'

'I don't know! He had a bad day with his girlfriend. I think they broke up.' Tom looked ready to run.

Jarrah groaned again and writhed. Finn couldn't tell if he was fully conscious.

'I can't ...' Tom pushed himself to his feet. 'I'm sorry.' He scooped up the phone, backed away and turned and ran, leaving Finn in the dark.

Over the wind Finn heard Bridget shoving her way through the branches to reach them again. 'They're coming,' she called.

Above the wind, the wail of a siren rose.

BRIDGET

You force yourself to face this. You hold Jarrah's hand and watch as Finn and the paramedics lift the fallen branch off his leg. You see the jagged ends of his tibia piercing the skin, the sickening crush and angle making your head swim. You keep hold of him as they lift him to the stretcher and he cries out. You feel his grip slacken as the nitrous oxide kicks in. You don't know how conscious he was, or is. You squeeze into the ambulance next to him, understanding distantly that Finn will follow somehow. You won't let Jarrah go to the hospital without you. Not this time. Not this son.

'He'll be all right,' one of the paramedics says, as the ambulance pulls out. They're not the same ones who came for Toby, thank God. She's trying to comfort you, and you nod as though agreeing. But how can Jarrah possibly be all right? How have you got it all so wrong? The broken leg is just the surface. Jarrah's deeper wounds have been turning septic, poisoning him. You didn't notice. It might yet be too late to save him.

Oh God, teenagers and their loose grip on life! No fear when they should have fear, and too willing to give life up. Don't they know how precious it is? If losing Toby has taught Jarrah anything, shouldn't it be that?

The siren wails through the dark wind-lashed streets. You remember, from when the police drove you after the ambulance carrying Toby, that the hospital is only a few blocks away from the house. Rounding a corner rouses Jarrah and he opens his eyes, gazing at you without focus.

'Mum?'

'I'm here, darling.' You bite your lip to stop yourself telling him everything is all right. 'We're nearly at the hospital, Jarr. Not much longer.'

His lips move. He's trying to tell you something and you lean close. 'I changed my mind, Mum. I was trying to get down.'

'Don't worry, Jarrah.'

'But really. I couldn't get the stupid knot undone. The wind ...'

His eyes close and you swallow hard. He's too out of it to see that you're crying.

'Are we nearly there yet, Mum?'

'Nearly there,' you murmur.

'Is Toby asleep?'

Oh God. He's more out of it than you knew. You murmur something comforting and his head rolls to the side.

You let your gaze burn into him, as if you can read his heart, trace the lines that led him out to the tree in the dark to break his own neck. Your heart's been so dark and raging you haven't been able to see into anyone else's. You've refused to see Jarrah's agony.

You bend close and whisper. 'I'm sorry.'

The ambulance halts outside Emergency. Murwillumbah Hospital, a place seared into your being. When you ran in here just three weeks ago, you'd still dreamed some miracle would happen when Toby reached medical care. As you follow the paramedics pushing Jarrah's gurney into the hospital, the smell of antiseptic hits and the memories come hard.

You repeat to yourself: He's alive. He's alive.

FINN

Finn edged his chair close to the side of Jarrah's bed. Bridget was on the other side holding their son's hand as he slept. Finn couldn't. Couldn't bear it. Could hardly breathe. Their lives were holding together by the slimmest of threads.

Jarrah would recover, the surgeon had assured them. Six weeks on crutches for the fractured leg, but no other serious injuries. The mark on his neck was milder than the bruises coming out on other parts of his body, and so far, no one seemed to have realised its significance.

The hospital hummed with activity. Chatter from the nurses and the orderlies, phones ringing, incessant beeping, voices. Finn let it wash over him, concentrating on Jarrah's sleeping face.

A voice intruded: Meredith, peering around the curtain.

'My God, what's going on? I just saw Jarrah was admitted.'

Finn forced himself to turn and face her. 'A branch fell on him in the storm.'

Her eyes narrowed. She was wired for suspicion, Finn thought. He shot Bridget a warning look.

'Jarrah was mucking around in our big tree with his friend Tom last night. Crazy boys. Like to push the limits.'

Bridget looked at him, confused. Meredith studied Jarrah for so long with her horrible, knowing eyes that Finn wanted to stand and block him from her sight. He couldn't tell any more if the mark on Jarrah's neck stood out or not.

'Is there anything I can do?' Meredith asked.

Finn shook his head. 'We just need some privacy.'

'Of course,' she said. 'I'm sorry.' Her gaze lingered on Jarrah for too long before she withdrew.

Finn got up and walked to the window. The storm was still blowing itself out, the wind gusty but no longer ferocious. Grey clouds scudded across the sky and drops pearled on the glass. He forced his mind to work, to lay out the evidence.

If anyone there – even Meredith as a volunteer – suspected Jarrah tried to commit suicide, it would be mandatory for them to report it and unleash the system upon them. The world where institutions took your children away wasn't one Finn had inhabited – but he felt its chill breath on his neck. What if they judged that he and Bridget had neglected Jarrah? What if they tried to take him away? Meredith would be a witness against Finn at the hearing, and here before her eyes was more evidence of his failure. Another son endangered. The court case might not be the worst thing facing them.

A nurse bustled into the room, startling him. 'Time for Jarrah's obs.'

Finn put his hand on Bridget's shoulder and leaned close. 'Can we talk?'

She followed him out of the room, down the squeaky-floored hall, into a small lounge where a television murmured in the corner. Finn checked the corridor; they were alone. When Bridget sat, he crouched down in front of her.

'It was an accident,' he whispered. 'Both the boys were mucking around in the tree and it broke.'

'But—'

'If anyone thinks … they might take him away. Look at us. We look like bloody dangerous parents. Meredith was suspicious straight away.'

Bridget's forehead creased. 'But – they'll ask Jarrah – and Tom – surely?'

'I'll call Tom now. You talk to Jarrah as soon as he wakes up, before that bloody Meredith can get to him.'

Her eyes scanned the room. 'Christ, Finn. Really? It seems crazy.'

He leaned in close. 'As soon as Jarrah's discharged we'll take him away. We'll get out of here. Go somewhere. Anywhere.'

'But …' Bridget took a deep, shuddering breath and shook her head. 'For God's sake. Look at us. We can't make any decisions right now.'

Finn groaned and rocked back on his heels.

'I'll go on leave,' Bridget said. 'As of right now. I'll stay home and look after Jarrah until the house settles. I'm not deciding anything else.'

The nurse who'd been seeing to Jarrah walked briskly past and Bridget half-rose. Finn grabbed her arm. 'It was an accident.'

'I've got to get back to him.'

Finn held her tighter. 'Are we agreed?'

She hesitated, then nodded. 'All right.'

'The story's the same for everyone. Not even family can know.'

'Tell me you're not just worried about how this looks in court?' She glanced at her watch.

Fury rose in Finn. 'I'm just trying to protect—'

But Bridget interrupted him. 'Isn't your court thing this morning? It's nearly ten.'

Finn felt sick. 'Shit. It starts at ten.'

She pulled free. 'I'll stay with Jarrah. It's just the mention, isn't it? You'll have to get changed, though. You look like a wreck.'

He was wearing muddy shorts and a tattered T-shirt he'd flung on the night before, as he raced to the car.

'You'll have to go on your own,' she said. 'We can't have him waking up alone. Will you be all right?'

'Yes,' Finn said. He had to be. No choice.

'We're not taking off. We need some stability.'

Finn watched her turn away and hurry up the hall almost at a run. She thought he was worried on his own behalf. She hadn't even started thinking it through. The decision hit him with the force of a revelation. It was his to make and his only.

BRIDGET

Jarrah's plastered leg lies outside the blanket, neat and straight and clean, all the pieces put back together again. He looks asleep, still deathly pale, the fine skin around his eyes still dark.

You take up your position by the bed, but don't reach for his hand. Until today, you've not examined Jarrah closely for a long time. He's had the teenage way of sliding out of your gaze, hiding himself. He must have hidden so much from you. Is it only since Toby died? Or for longer?

He's been shaving. His skin is still fine, but the wisps of hair appearing on his chin have been razored. He has a few pimples, little ones, but not many. His hair is longer than you realised – you haven't been paying attention to things like haircuts. His left arm, flung outside the sheet, is showing muscles you haven't seen before. He's turning from a boy into a young man, a metamorphosis that's sudden and shocking and beautiful. You've been oblivious to it.

He stirs slightly and you move back so that when he opens his eyes you're not looming in his face.

'Mum.' His voice a croak.

'Darling, I'm here.'

He tries to move and winces. 'Is it bad?'

Patching his smashed leg took three hours and he must still be awash with drugs. You try to smile. 'You won't be jogging for a while. Your leg is broken. Apart from that you're fine. You were lucky, Jarrah. *We* were lucky. Thank God.'

He's silent for a few minutes, downcast. Then, in a half-whisper: 'Does everyone know?'

You wait until he glances up and shake your head. 'Only Dad, me and Tom. We told the hospital you and Tom were both mucking around in the tree and the weight broke the branch.'

He looks afraid. 'Why? What'll happen to me?'

Why did you even agree to this? Is Finn being paranoid? It's too late now, you're in and you'll have to stick with it.

'Nothing. It's just better to keep it simple. You might be asked a few questions. You can say you don't remember. And then we'll take you home and look after you, Jarr. I won't leave you alone, I promise.'

He seems slightly reassured by that. Turns to look out the window.

'Would you like me to tell Laura?'

He closes his eyes wearily. 'No.'

'Sure. Nothing you're not ready for.'

He seems to be drifting and you resist the urge to keep talking. If you're never going to leave him alone, you'll have to be OK with silence.

When you're sure he's asleep you step outside again, back to that little room off the corridor, and dial.

'Chen.'

'What is it?'

You'd forgotten how well he can read you, even with just a word. 'Jarrah's in hospital with a broken leg.'

'Oh, Bridget. Hell. I'll come over.'

'Don't. I'm going on leave. Can you tell Rob I won't be in? I'll call him in a day or so.'

His worried voice: 'What can I do?'

You're so raw you've forgotten how to phrase things. 'Just stay away. I can't deal with it, I can't—'

'I only want to help.'

'It's too dangerous.'

'I'm your friend,' he says. As if it hasn't all been about something else.

'I've got to go.'

'Don't cut me off,' he says.

It would be better to refuse, to make the break clean. It'll just make it harder, having the door still open. But you're not quite ready to close it yet. 'I'll be in touch. Don't call me.'

You pocket the phone and walk back towards Jarrah's ward. You're in a state of hyper-awareness that started when you saw him lying on the ground in the torchlight and hasn't stopped. If anything, as the sleepless hours have passed, it's intensified.

This could tear what remains of you into pieces that can never be put together again – or be what pulls you through. Jarrah's given you purpose with this. He's given you a reason to get up and try to assemble yourself into something like a person each day. A real job.

FINN

Was it an offence, being late for a court mention? He had no idea. But he couldn't go straight to court, not half dressed, smeared with mud and covered in scrapes. He drove slowly home, blinking through half-shut eyes. A council team was parked out the front, chainsaws blazing, reducing the fallen branch to manageable chunks and feeding them into the chipper. He circled around them to the gate. The smell of shredded timber, something he normally loved, cut the air like hospital disinfectant.

He changed, splashed his face, stared at himself in the mirror. The empty house scared him even more now. The place was attacking them. It was after ten-thirty. He grabbed wallet, keys, phone. Got into the car. Checked the address. Started the engine. Knew he was too strung out to drive. Got out, called a taxi.

At the courthouse he went through the security check and upstairs. The foyer of the Local Court was full of people. Children, adults, toddlers, old people – some as out of place as he, some clearly in their natural habitat. He looked around, disoriented.

'Finn!' Malcolm came striding over to him. 'Where were you? Why didn't you answer the phone? I've stalled them, so we're all right for now, but you could lose your bail like this.'

'Can we talk?'

'Sure.' Malcolm gestured to a nearby meeting room.

It was a relief to shut the door on it all, slump into a seat and say it out loud. 'I want to plead guilty.'

Malcolm stared at him, shocked, then visibly shook himself. 'Hold on. Let's go back a step. Firstly, negligence in this case is a matter of opinion and must be proved to an extremely high level. I really doubt they can do it. Secondly, you and your family have gone through enough. You don't need a criminal record and a jail term to add to it. There's a good chance it will all be over at the committal hearing in a few months, if you can just be patient.'

Only someone who hadn't lost a child accidentally could suggest that it would all be over if he were proved innocent, Finn thought. 'But if I do plead guilty, won't it speed things up?'

'Yes,' Malcolm conceded.

Finn forced himself to concentrate. 'Talk me through it.'

'Christ.' Malcolm rubbed his face. 'You should consult your barrister. If you plead guilty now, you'll waive a committal hearing. The magistrate will probably refer you straight to the next sitting of the Supreme Court for sentencing.'

'How long?'

'Depends on the sitting schedule.' Malcolm pulled out his iPad. 'You could possibly get into the next Lismore circuit or go to Sydney.' He scrolled down the screen then looked up at Finn. 'It'd be quick, at least. They're sitting in Lismore on the seventeenth of November. Less than two weeks. You could get into that hearing, potentially, and Justice Kelly is a good choice for this case.'

'What else?'

285

'It's true you would get a twenty-five per cent reduction in whatever sentence is imposed. That goes for anyone who pleads guilty straight off. Acknowledging guilt does impact on the type of sentence too: you are more likely to avoid a custodial sentence. But there'll still be evidence heard so the judge can make up his or her mind. We'd have to build a case for why you shouldn't get a custodial sentence. Things like the wellbeing of your surviving son would play a part. The judge will still want to hear an account of what happened, and there'll still be cross-examination of witnesses. All that will still happen, Finn. And you'll be a convicted criminal.'

'I could still be a convicted criminal if it goes to trial. I could still go to jail if it goes to trial. And it might cost all the money we have. I don't want to put my family through it. I don't want my son on the stand. What will it cost if I plead guilty?'

'Nothing like a trial. Say thirty thousand.'

Finn shrugged and sat back in his chair. 'So then my wife can buy a house back in Hobart. My family has somewhere to live if I'm in jail.'

'You realise if you get a custodial sentence, you go straight from the hearing to jail? You'd have to be prepared. Have all your affairs in order. And I really think you should refer this to your barrister.'

'I'm ready,' Finn said. He looked past Malcolm, out the window. In the weird, normal world that he seemed to have lost, it was another almost-summer brilliant sky-blue Tuesday.

'I've made up my mind. When do we go in?'

*

Afterwards he had to tell someone. Found a quiet spot outside the courthouse and rang. Edmund's phone went straight to voicemail, but Conor picked up. Finn tried to explain, realising how incoherent he sounded as he stumbled through the agreed explanation of Jarrah's accident and his guilty plea in court.

'I don't understand.' Conor sounded dazed. 'I thought these things took years.'

'They can. That's why I've done it. There's a sitting in two weeks when I'll be sentenced and that's it. Done.'

'But but are you saying you might go to jail? In two weeks?'

'It's possible. But at least we'll know the outcome.'

'And you don't want to fight?'

'I can't.'

'But this sounds like terrible timing for Jarrah. Is he going to be all right? If it's the money, the family can help, we can—'

'Jesus, Conor,' Finn snapped. 'It's hard enough, all right? I've done it.'

'I wish you'd spoken to me first.'

'Why?'

'Dad's not in a good way. We thought it was the shock over Toby, but he isn't recovering. He's not himself any more.'

'Christ. How am I going to tell him this?'

'I don't think you can. He won't handle it. He's so confused, I don't think he'd understand.'

Finn felt disembodied with exhaustion. 'But I'm coming down. I've got to see him before court.'

Conor was silent for a moment. 'Yes,' he said at last. 'You'd better.'

JARRAH

Dad was asleep in the chair by the bed when I woke up properly. I'd slept on and off all through the day and it was dark outside. The clock on the wall said nearly eleven.

His head was hanging to one side, looking really uncomfortable. When did he get so old?

'Dad,' I whispered. It took three goes before he started and woke.

'What is it?'

'Why don't you go home?'

'I'm fine here,' he said, moving his neck from side to side.

'Nothing's gonna happen, Dad. I'm OK.'

He gave me a weird, lopsided kind of smile. 'I can't risk it, Jarr.'

It hit me then, what it had meant to them. I was sorry. And glad the branch broke.

'How you feeling?' he asked.

'Better. You?'

'OK. Try to sleep, eh?'

I lay still, listening to his breathing. It didn't change and I figured he was wide awake.

'Dad?'

'Mm?'

Maybe because it was dark and I didn't have to look at him, or maybe because we were in the hospital, but I really wanted to know about the day Toby drowned. I was alive, and I wanted to know everything.

'When are we moving?' I asked instead.

I heard his breath catch. 'Don't worry about that. You'll finish the term first. I'm going down to see Pop for a few days. He's not well. We won't make any other decisions for a while.'

'Are you going to take Toby's ashes?'

A long pause. 'No. We'll scatter his ashes together when it feels right.'

'Dad?'

'Mm?'

'What happened?'

He knew what I meant. He was silent for so long I thought he wasn't going to answer. At last he wriggled a bit and started.

'I was working. I should have helped your mother get ready, but she insisted I get cracking, and you know that was the whole point of Toby going to child care. I was over there, welding. Couldn't hear much with that going on. And I had my back to the pool and the safety mask on.'

'And?'

'Heard your mother. I realised it was something bad. I ran out. She was on the step in the pool, holding Toby. Carrying him out.'

We were both silent. I could hear in his choked voice how hard it was to say it, and it wasn't any easier for me to hear it. I was ready to tell him not to go on, but he started again.

'She'd gone to the bathroom. Left him alone reading on the kitchen floor. Just a few minutes. If the gate had been working properly, it wouldn't have mattered.'

'What was wrong with the gate?'

He shifted around again, rubbed his neck. '*Owl* malfunctioned. Didn't shut the gate properly behind me when I went through to the studio. I didn't notice it. If I'd been paying attention … That's why they charged me, Jarrah. It was my fault. I should never have changed the gate system.'

His voice was trembling. No wonder. He blamed himself for the whole thing.

'Thanks for telling me,' I said.

'It's OK. You know, Jarr, you can ask me anything. I'll do my best to answer.'

I lay there for a long time trying to get up the courage and I think he was starting to doze off by the time I did.

'Are you and Mum divorcing?'

'Absolutely not,' he said in the dark. 'Don't even think it, Jarrah.'

I closed my eyes. Still kind of drugged, spiralling down towards sleep, being dragged there in spite of everything.

Just before I dropped off, I realised what was nagging at me. I didn't know why, but I didn't believe him, about him and Mum. And if he'd lied about that, what else was he lying about?

PART THREE

FINN

Finn turned up his collar against the cold and leaned over the railing. Below, oily rainbows pooled on the water's surface and the seagulls shrieked and swooped around him as a nearby child threw chips for them to snatch. He'd nearly forgotten how Hobart could make a joke of summer, obliterating its heat with a glacial roar of wind and rain.

His leather jacket smelled mouldy, and he felt alone, alone, alone like he'd never been in his life, sick with his losses and the way they joined together, streams in a watershed rushing to the lowest point, creating a torrent after a storm, washing out and ruining everything in its path.

The big orange Antarctic ship was in port, her stack steaming as she prepared to sail south. Hobart knew what ships were coming in and out. People watched the *Aurora Australis* leave for the long journey to the ice three or four times in the summer season, and they kept an eye out for her return, that long hoot of the horn as she manoeuvred into the dock. He'd grown up with the sound, known those ships since he was a kid. Hobart was in his bones; Hobart held his roots. He'd thought. But he'd got back to confront everything his brother had kept from him.

Conor had picked him up at the airport a week ago and tried to convince him to go for dinner or a drink, but Finn demanded to be taken straight to his father's house. It was so familiar. The crooked path planted with lavender and rosemary and the cold-climate scent they gave off. The odd height of the two steps up to the door. The bricks, when he'd become accustomed to the weatherboards up north. The old pale-blue lino inside. The dear familiarity of it tightened his throat. Until he saw his father.

When the Brennans left Hobart, Toby's poppa had been an active eighty-five. White-haired, big-boned like all the males of the family, leathery-skinned. He'd had a daily routine of walking, bowls, lunch at the club, mass on Sundays, flowers on his wife's grave, the children and the grandchildren. Signs of slowing down, but still living. Someone who showed little resemblance to the empty-eyed man now slouched in the armchair in the late-afternoon dark of the lounge room.

'Dad?'

The head turned slowly to find him. 'Finn, boy.'

Finn stepped forwards onto the rug, crouched down so his face was near his father's. Reached for his father's hand and took it. Couldn't speak. At once the little boy reaching for his father and the man who knew there was no safety there.

Tears began rolling from his father's eyes in a steady stream. 'I can't ...' He stopped, fumbled, produced a handkerchief. 'I didn't believe them. But it's true, isn't it?'

Finn nodded. In the face of his father's tears, he remained dry-eyed. He felt Conor's hand on his shoulder.

John gulped. 'I wanted to come. I'm so sorry.'

'I know.'

Finn tried to re-form his world, again. He'd lost a son. And now, in some indefinable way, he'd lost a father too.

John lifted his head and looked out the window. A vagueness had come over him. 'Sometimes it's very hard to understand God's will,' he murmured.

Finn hadn't been to mass since he was a kid, but without a particular reason to doubt it, he'd assumed some kind of benign God existed. He knew now – though he'd never tell his father – there was no God. He felt himself sag.

Helen arrived shortly afterwards. Finn hadn't seen her since it happened either, and they hugged hard. She drew back, tearful.

'You and Conor go out,' she said. 'Your dad can't take too much at once. I'll do his dinner.'

The second shock came at the pub, over steak and chips and a cold ale.

'I've moved out,' Conor said. 'Stayed in the pub a couple of days, thinking it would blow over, and been at Dad's since then. Didn't seem worth getting somewhere to live until I knew how he would pull up. Helen's been a huge help, I'll give her that.'

'But – what happened?'

'She says she's been unhappy for years, but she waited until the kids were through school and out of the house.'

'You had no idea?'

'Well, you know. I thought it was just being middle aged. Our sex life was pretty non-existent and in the evenings we didn't have much to say to each other. But I thought after the kids were gone we'd do something else. Travel around Australia or something. I guess I didn't take enough notice. And then, when Toby died, she said that made her re-evaluate everything. She said life was short. Like we don't all know it.'

'I don't know if Bridget and I will make it,' Finn said.

Conor shook his head. 'You've got to. It's too awful otherwise.'

'She doesn't want to come back here. She wants to stay where he died, like she's closer to him.'

'Maybe this time apart will do you good.'

'Or maybe I'll end up in jail and it'll be a relief for her.'

'So fucking unfair. It makes me want to …' Conor trailed off. 'You think life is OK but everything can go to shit in a second.'

They both drank too much. There seemed no reason not to. Their father's place was in darkness when they got home. Finn curled into an old quilt on an air mattress on the floor and floated into disembodied sleep.

The next morning, searching for coffee, he bumped into friends in Salamanca Place and the pity on their faces was too much. They didn't know what to say. Stumbled through awkward commiserations and invited him around for a meal, without conviction. He broke off the conversation as fast as he could.

What had all those old friendships been? Would any of them survive if he and Bridget split? Or were they based on the ease of a family unit?

He could barely cope with his own family either. He drove up to Deloraine to visit Mary and her girlfriend Edie, spent two nights with Carmel and her husband Graeme. He'd left Hobart less than a year back, but in that time his family had grown shockingly old. Finn himself was the much younger youngest son, like Toby had been. There were eight years between him and Conor, his next brother up. But all his siblings had aged and his father was ancient. Was it losing Toby that now hung the years so heavily on them? And if that was it, why didn't he feel closer to his brothers and sisters in his grief? He'd dreamed of coming home to find family again, of having them hold his pain, but sorrow had done strange things with the bonds between them, stretched and twisted them into unrecognisable shapes.

Whatever comfort he'd dreamed of finding, it wasn't there. But coming back to Hobart meant he was at last separate from Bridget's pain. Whatever he felt, it was his own. It might take him over and take him down, it might be merciless, but it was his. Toby soaked his days and nights. Toby throbbed in the empty air, filled the silence, expanded to take in every inch of the room. Toby demanding to be heard, Toby demanding to be remembered. Toby demanding more.

How could life make sense again? All those dead children, the ones who died every day, every minute, from bad water and war and disease and beatings and starvation and malaria, the ones who died in orphanages, the ones caught in violence – domestic, racial, national, international. Now he knew what each death meant, how could he live?

Here, in Australia, according to online reports, sixteen children had drowned in the past year like Toby had, and eighteen the year before that. Sixteen sets of parents who'd looked away for a few wrong moments, who'd dragged the limp bodies of their offspring from the water, who'd pushed at their small chests and blown into their slack mouths, who'd begged whatever god they believed in to bring their child back. All those families out there somehow lived on with this unliveable grief and guilt. How did they do it?

The world without Toby in it was a grey, grim, hard-edged place, its beauty bitter, its sorrows manifest.

In a way it was a relief to be away even from Jarrah. The prospect of jail was starting to draw him. He'd have time to stay still and allow his memories to bubble to the surface. The short sweep of Toby's life, his smell and heft, the dreams of his future, the wonder of who he was, and who he might have become. In there, he could be immersed in Toby, undisturbed. The prospect was terrifying. And also inviting.

A gull shrieked so close to Finn's head that he started and turned, and there she was, at the far end of the dock walking towards him, her fair hair whipping across her face and out behind, her cream trench coat buckled at the waist. She moved lightly, soft on her feet, not carrying the weight that burdened everyone in Finn's world, compressing their spines, curving their shoulders, heavying their tread.

She'd heard he was back, and she'd sent him a message and he'd sworn he wouldn't do this, wouldn't see her, wouldn't ask for trouble, wouldn't give Bridget one more reason to doubt him. But as Sandra walked towards him and the features of her face started to become clear, he didn't need to see the expression there. He could feel it in the set of her body. She didn't blame him. She didn't hate him.

Inside him, inside some terrible place where metal tangled and fizzed and melted and re-formed, something started to ease, and he felt a rush of desire in his groin. Before she even reached him, before she even put out her hand to take his, Finn started to cry for the first time since he'd stepped onto the island's soil.

JARRAH

Watching TV was like eating lollies. At the start you thought you could go on forever, but after a while you felt sick.

Mum set up the sofa bed for me in the lounge room when I came home from hospital so I didn't have to get up the stairs. It was nearly a week later but I was still woozy and kind of wobbly on the crutches. Everything was weird. She was home all day. Dad was gone. Toby was gone. Everything about the family was upside down. It was too much to think about. So I slept a lot and watched TV. I didn't even care about being on full display, spread out on the sofa bed in the lounge room.

Mum was watching me. She tried not to be obvious about it, but she'd stay up in the kitchen reading after I turned the light off. Sometimes in the night I'd wake to see her sitting up, or resting her head on her arms, asleep at the table. A few times she crept in and slept on the other lounge. She was always up when I woke in the morning. I didn't know how to tell her it was OK. I wasn't going to try it again.

It was nearly summer. The TV droned on and I kicked the sheet on and off, and turned the fan up and down, and flicked the channels and dozed. All my bones felt heavy. Crutching to the kitchen left me wiped out. My skin itched under the plaster. My leg didn't hurt, but it gave weird little stabs and aches.

When I stopped sleeping so much, Mum asked me about going back to school, but as soon as she did, I felt tired again. I didn't want to go back. She said she'd talk to the teacher about sending over some work so I didn't get too far behind, and I kind of agreed.

The next afternoon when Mum was in the kitchen someone arrived. They talked at the door and from that distance the voice was familiar, though I couldn't hear it. Next thing, Mum came into the room.

'Jarrah, Laura's brought over some schoolwork,' she said. 'I'll make you guys some afternoon tea, hey?'

Mum disappeared at the speed of light and there was Laura, red-eyed, looking everywhere except at me.

'Hey, Laura.'

'Hey.'

'Wanna sit down?'

She came closer and perched on the couch opposite and finally looked at me. 'I only just heard today, Jazz. I can't believe it. I feel so terrible.'

I struggled to remember what Laura and I had said to each other. It felt so long ago. 'It's not your fault.'

'But we had that fight. Then you just didn't come to school. I didn't know what happened.'

I opened my mouth to say it wasn't anything to do with her, and then closed it again. Took a breath. I was getting better at thinking before I spoke. Plus we'd agreed on the story, Mum and me.

'It was a stupid accident. Just fooling around. Fell out of the tree and the branch fell on me.'

She looked at me directly. 'And the mark on your neck?'

'A bruise,' I said. 'I hit it on the tree when I was falling.'

Her look didn't waver. 'I said something like that once to Mum about a love bite. She even believed me.'

Mum came bustling in with two milkshakes on a tray and a plate of biscuits, like we were five years old. She put them down on the table and scuttled out again as Laura was thanking her. It would have nearly been funny, if it wasn't. Laura got up, grabbed one of the milkshakes and perched on the side of the sofa bed next to me. 'I wish I'd never said that about your brother. I didn't mean it.'

She'd told me to take my dead brother and go to hell, I remembered.

'I was a dickhead that day. It's OK.'

She was quiet for a moment, then scrabbled in her bag and pulled out a bunch of books and papers. 'Addison gave me some maths for you. You coming back to school soon?'

'I dunno. Guess so.'

Maybe I could do it. Make up with her and try again. If I was staying, being Laura's boyfriend was a good idea. And I did like her. I'd thought I loved her. Whatever that meant. Maybe I still could. Except it looked like we'd be leaving by Christmas.

She put the maths stuff down on the floor and before I could gather my thoughts she leaned in close.

Something made me press myself back against the pillow. 'Laura ...'

She pulled back. 'What?'

'I'm sorry. It's not you ...'

Her lip started trembling and she turned away. 'Yeah, right. Thought you were different.'

I knew I sounded like a bad movie, but I didn't know any better way to say it. 'I think I *am* different. That's the point.'

Her face shut down. I reached out and took her hand. 'I never thought you'd even notice me.'

'You think I just felt sorry for you?'

'Um. Sort of, at the start.'

She pulled her wrist free. 'So if you're *different*, Jarrah, why didn't you just say so? I feel like an idiot.'

'Shh.' I made a face in the direction of the kitchen.

'It's not the end of the world, being gay. It's no big deal. '

'Shh! You don't get it.'

'So tell me.'

'I would if I could. I don't know what I am. I just – I can't explain it.'

'Is it about your brother?'

I kept my gaze down and fiddled with the corner of the sheet. 'I dunno. Maybe. It's all sort of mixed up.'

Laura stood and slung her schoolbag over her shoulder. 'Glad I could help you work out you're gay. I guess.' Her voice was bitter.

'I'm sorry.' I reached out, trying to catch her hand, but she stayed out of my reach. 'I like you. I really do.'

She picked up the milkshake and finished it, wiped her mouth across her hand. 'Missing your brother doesn't have to mean you're gay. It just means you loved him.'

She reached out and touched the back of my hand, then headed for the door. I nearly called out for her to come back. I hoped like crazy she was right. I wanted to grab her hand again and pull her down for that kiss. Maybe it would be different this time. But I didn't say anything, and then she was gone and it was too late.

A few minutes later Mum put her head around the door. 'Did you make up?'

I felt exhausted again. 'We're just friends, Mum.'

'It's a pity. She seems like a nice girl. Maybe you just need some time.'

'Mm.'

She went to say something, stopped herself. Started again. 'Are you OK?'

'Yeah.' I picked up the remote and turned on the TV so she didn't ask me anything else. She stood there for a while, then collected the tray and glasses and went back to the kitchen.

I stared at the stupid screen, not watching. What kind of fucking idiot was I, telling Laura to go? The dream girl who, unbelievably, wanted to be my girlfriend and I was just letting her walk out. No, I was actually pushing her away and I didn't even know why.

Only that now when she wanted to kiss me I wanted to run. When did that even happen?

For a second I remembered what happened with Tom. If I was gay, wouldn't I be happy to remember that? But every time I thought of it, I just felt shame. I wriggled and changed the channel. There was one thing I knew for sure. It was better if we never saw each other again. I forced myself to think about something else. Something that wasn't Laura or Tom.

For the first time I wasn't too sleepy to remember what Dad had told me about the day Toby drowned. I didn't want to picture that day, but now it had found its way into my brain and started playing over and over.

I looked out the sliding doors into the garden. I was thinking about Laura and Tom and Toby. And then I remembered something.

BRIDGET

You wait until Jarrah is deep in some space-war movie before you give in. You text Chen from the kitchen around the time he'd be finishing work.

<could you come over?>

It's been over a week since you said goodbye, but he responds like he's been waiting for it, the text pinging back in moments. Within twenty minutes his car pulls up outside and he's at the door.

'What?' he asks, as if you've never pushed him away.

You shake your head and gesture towards the lounge room, where Jarrah's sprawled under a sheet, a fan flapping cool air on his skin. The intergalactic battle is at full pitch on the TV but you know the way children's hearing can pierce through a babble of noise and zero in on exactly what you don't want them knowing. You doubt Jarrah has lost the ability.

Chen is familiar and lovely and concerned, and you long for his arms around you so hard that you feel weak with it and you have to physically restrain yourself. You won't even kiss him on the cheek or shake hands; any contact is too dangerous. Oh God, you are so alone.

A week ago, without warning you, Finn pleaded guilty to the charge of manslaughter by negligence. He had no answer to your incredulity, claiming the choice was his to make. The next day he got on a plane to visit his father, leaving you alone to care for Jarrah, with twelve days to plan out how your lives would look if he went to jail. He hasn't told you when he'll be back. The two of you have barely spoken – though he calls Jarrah daily.

You've spent seven of those days hovering over your son, refusing to allow yourself to call Chen, and creating a disaster out there in the garden. Today you're desperate.

'Is there somewhere we can talk?' Chen asks.

You nod. 'I want to show you something.' You raise your voice and call to Jarrah over the laser guns, tell him you'll be outside. You hear a faint 'Sure, Mum,' in response.

You open the pool gate, hold it for Chen, lead him through. It takes him a moment to notice, then he stops dead.

The pool is opaque, a livid green. It happened fast in the subtropical heat, once you pulled the plug on the pump and chlorinator, let the machinery die away into blessed silence. 'What the …'

You try to explain. 'I'm changing it into a pond. They say you put in plants and fish and the system balances up. I just didn't think it would be this green. I can't bear it …' Your voice trembles and you trail off.

You're desperate for the water to be clear again. You knew it would be hard to forego your swims, but you didn't know how you'd ache for them, how the nights would be unbearably empty. You can't bring yourself to even dip your hands in the vivid green water, and so another part of Toby has been lost to you.

Chen crouches by the pool and peers into it. When he stands again, he's pale. It's seeing at close quarters where Toby drowned, you realise.

But he shakes it off. 'I can see a few wrigglers. That's a good sign. Start of an ecosystem. What now?'

You pull the crumpled printout from your pocket. 'They say once you've got wrigglers you can introduce plants and fish. Then the water should clear.'

'Have you got plants?'

'The nursery's got water plants, I checked it out—but I don't want to leave him to pick them up.'

He looks at you with deep, sympathetic eyes. 'What happened, Bridget?'

You can't stand the look of pity on his face. You shake your head. 'Don't.' Then you sweep out an arm. 'I've got a list. Could you collect them?'

Being a plant courier probably isn't what he expected. The nursery might well have delivered; you didn't check. The truth is you wanted to see him. You wanted another adult. You are grateful for Jarrah's presence beyond anything you've known before, but he is, still, your teenage son.

'You could help me get them in there. If you've got time.'

'Sure.' He starts moving, still pale and seemingly keen to get away from the green water. You lead him from the pool area back to his car. As he turns the key you lean down to the window.

'Why don't you bring back a bottle of wine too?'

He smiles a small relieved smile. 'I'd like that.'

He reverses the car around and drives off. You hurry back inside to check on Jarrah.

JARRAH

Time after Toby: thirty-two days. When I heard a man's voice I shifted around on the sofa bed so I could see into the kitchen. Mum's friend from work was there with her. For the first time I wondered about him. What was he doing at our place? He'd been around at the start, cooking meals and helping out, but I hadn't seen him lately. There was something weird about him coming over while Dad was in Hobart.

As they headed outside, I told myself it was probably fine. Maybe Mum hadn't really settled into Murwillumbah, like me. Maybe she didn't have any friends either. What happened to us meant people either came close or ran away. Maybe all their new friends had run away. Maybe she was as lonely as I was.

She came back in after a while and sat on the couch watching telly with me. For some reason I suddenly noticed how thin she'd got. It was like I hadn't seen anything lately. I hadn't noticed she was thin and pale and lonely. I saw new lines around her eyes and what looked like streaks of grey in her hair. Dad was fat and old and a mess. I wondered how he was going in Hobart. He called every night, but he didn't say much. Just asked how I was and about the TV programs I'd been watching. He said it was cold down there.

After a while Chen appeared at the door holding a box of plants and Mum stood up.

'There are more in the car,' he said. 'I'll bring them in.'

'What are they for?' I asked after he'd gone out.

Mum blinked. 'A little project outside.'

My brain was literally going to melt and run on the floor if I didn't get up. 'Can I have a look?'

She hesitated.

'Or do you want to be alone with your boyfriend?' It was out of my mouth before I thought.

She looked at me like she was shocked. 'Don't be stupid, Jarrah.'

The pause before she said it made me think I might be right, but I'd shocked myself too, saying it out loud. 'Sorry.'

She gave me a weak smile. 'It's OK, Jarr. It's a weird time. The plants are for the pool. I'm turning it into a natural pond. It doesn't look so great at the moment. But it'll get better.'

'I wouldn't mind seeing,' I said. It wasn't really true. I hated anything to do with the pool. But I was so, so sick of lying down. I levered myself off the sofa, balanced on the crutches and followed her outside. Chen was carrying another box of plants into the pool area, holding the gate open with his shoulder. Mum took it and gestured for me to go through.

I swung into the pool area and saw it: the whole pool a thick, gluggy green like a bowl of slime. I came to a dead stop, and had to swallow hard. It was the most disgusting thing I'd ever seen.

'That's gross.'

'It won't stay like this,' she said. 'In a week or two the water will clear up. It'll be full of plants and fish. Like a real pond. It'll be alive, won't it, Chen?'

'Absolutely,' Chen said, putting down the box.

'I'm going back in,' I said.

'I'll come with you.' Mum started towards me.

I shook my head. 'Just do your plant thing.'

She hesitated. 'Jarrah—'

'I'm not going to kill myself, OK?' I snapped. 'You don't have to watch me every second.'

Mum stepped back and Chen looked shocked. Good. I manoeuvred my crutches and Mum opened the gate to let me through. Felt like she wanted to say something, but didn't know what.

'Does Dad know what you're doing?'

'What?'

'The pool. Does he know?'

She let the latch drop so the gate was locked between us. 'This will turn the pool into something useful, Jarrah. A living system.'

'But we won't even be here, will we?'

I made my way inside, flopped back on the sofa bed and watched something so mind-numbing on TV that it put me to sleep. One of those weird hot-afternoon dozes when you don't know if you're dreaming or awake. I thought I heard my phone ping. I was sure for a moment Dad was in the room, and once I thought I heard an echo of Toby, as if he were up in his room asking someone to read to him. Then I knew I was dreaming, even in the dream, and tossed and turned until I woke up.

It was cooler and the light had changed. I could hear low voices and the clink of glasses and the thud-thud-thud of chopping from the kitchen. I pulled the sheet up over me and Mum poked her head around the corner.

'You've been asleep again.'

I grunted.

'Chen's cooking. Dinner'll be ready shortly.' She stepped into the room, holding a glass of wine. 'What are you watching?'

'Nothing.' I found the remote and flicked it off. 'Hasn't he got his own family?'

'He's been a good friend to me,' she said, lowering her voice. 'I don't have anyone else, Jarrah. Let me have one friend.'

I fiddled with the sheet and wouldn't meet her eyes.

'Do you want to invite someone for dinner? Maybe Tom? Laura?'

'Nope.'

We sat in silence for a while.

'Go and talk to your friend,' I said at last. 'I'll come in a bit.'

She smoothed her hands over her dress, nodded. 'Jarrah, it's best you don't say anything more about your accident, OK?'

'Why? Is it embarrassing you?' I knew I sounded nasty, but she flinched when I said that.

'We don't want anyone to take you away,' she whispered.

I had no idea what she was talking about, but I could see she was upset. I felt sorry then. Tried a smile. 'It's OK, Mum.'

'Is it?' She looked relieved. 'We need to be OK, Jarr. We really do.'

I nodded and she went out. I looked at my phone to see if there really was a message or if I'd dreamed it. Even though I didn't want to think about Tom I checked my messages. He'd come around the night it happened, hadn't he? I still didn't know what for. I hoped he was coming to say it was OK, what I'd done, and we could forget about it. Tom was a nice guy. It was the sort of thing he'd do.

311

There was no message on my phone. There'd been nothing from Tom since that night. Trying to kill myself had pushed things too far. Two really big stupid mistakes in one day that left no doubt what kind of person I was. Too much for him. Couldn't blame him, really.

From the kitchen I smelled garlic frying. I hadn't smelled cooking for … it felt like forever. We'd eaten so many casseroles and so much takeaway. When Dad cooked, he always used lots of garlic. He knew he was a crap cook. He told Mum garlic was a substitute ingredient for talent. They used to laugh about it.

I got out of bed and up onto my crutches. I didn't like that guy.

BRIDGET

He throws together a meal from what's cluttering up the fridge and old stuff in the pantry: pasta with tomatoes and a few herbs he yanks from the garden, some forgotten cheese, capers, bacon, stock cubes. It tastes like something from a restaurant, at least compared to Finn's cooking.

Jarrah stumps into the kitchen and slouches down, sullen and unfriendly, but even he softens a little as you eat, as if Chen's kindness overflows, washing over you all like the good food and the wine. It makes you warm. It lets you forget for as much as a few minutes at a time.

Jarrah's eyelids droop again at the end of dinner. You're worried at how tired he is; you hope it's still the surgery aftermath. You send him back to bed, and when he's settled in the lounge room you press a kiss to his forehead and switch off the light.

Back in the kitchen Chen is quietly stacking the dishwasher. You wipe down the benches and, without asking, empty the rest of the wine into your glasses.

'Let's go outside,' you whisper.

Without words you agree that the couch on the verandah is too close to where Jarrah has just bedded down. Chen leads the

313

way down the steps onto the lawn, crosses to the patch of light furthest from the house. Sits.

'We'll get eaten by mozzies,' you whisper.

He shrugs and you sit. Not too close. Not too far off either. You can't be sure if you're out of sight of the lounge room, though you think it probable. Hopefully Jarrah has fallen asleep fast, the way he usually does.

'How's the survey going?' you ask.

'I've got a graduate helping now. We'll finish the fieldwork this week. It'll take a couple of months to analyse and write it up. But … you know how it goes with these projects.'

'How?'

His smile is sad. 'I've never seen a report stop a highway from going where it wants. Bureaucrats don't understand the subtlety of genetically distinct populations. Koalas are being culled in parts of Victoria because there are too many of them, so why worry about the ones here dying out? How many koalas do you need, after all?'

You once cared about the koalas too, but in truth you now wonder the same thing. What will it matter if this small local population, hanging on by a thread, doesn't survive? Perhaps it's better to let them go rather than building koala crossings, overpasses and underpasses, trying to protect tiny patches of habitat, creating little oases that become traps surrounded by human development.

It's better to dwell on these questions than to look at the shape of Chen's shoulders. That's one thing you mustn't do. Dwell on the way his slender bones lean slightly towards you, the way his leg folds up under his arm with a flexibility Finn could never manage.

He slaps away a mosquito. 'Are you going to tell me about Jarrah?'

You point at the gum tree towering overhead. 'The branch broke when he was climbing.'

'Bridget, it's me.'

You take a deep breath. 'He says he changed his mind about hanging himself and was trying to get down from the tree.' Recounting it to someone else, your voice begins to break. 'But he already had something around his neck, and the branch broke and fell on him and I nearly lost him.'

'Oh, Bridget.'

You gulp a cold mouthful, wipe your mouth on the back of your hand. Repeat the mantra that gets you through the days: he's alive. You have one son still alive.

Chen is looking at you with soft eyes. 'I wish you'd let me help.'

'You've done so much already.' You choose a stock phrase to keep him at a distance.

'I wish I could take the pain away.'

A bat lands in the tree with a leathery flap of wings, shaking the leaves and squealing, and you're grateful for the cover because you nearly say, 'There is.' It would take the pain away, you know it. Perhaps only for the duration, perhaps only for a matter of minutes, but those minutes would be something.

You could take him to your bed. Make sure Jarrah is asleep, make sure no one will find out. You could take Chen to the studio, rather than risk doing such a thing in the house. Hell, you'll be leaving the house soon enough. It may even be that Finn never comes back here – not if he goes to jail.

Chen's skin is so smooth you want to run your hands down his hairless arms. You imagine feeling his small firm biceps, cupping the back of his neck and pulling him towards you. Your breath comes faster. You stare at the grass, because if you look at him, meet his gaze, you'll fall.

The crickets start up in a sudden chorus and a frog croaks invisibly nearby and bats overhead call out and the first prickle of stars begins. You can feel the wine thrumming but you can't blame it. The desire would be there without the wine, you know it. The desire for just one thing that isn't laden with grief or fear or fury.

You don't know how long you sit there, neither of you moving, but it's dark by the time you lift your hand from the grass. You feel the glass tumble gently to one side, the rest of the wine soaking into the lawn. You raise your hand and extend it towards him. Your fingertips find the cloth of his T-shirt and slowly, slowly, you press your hand until your palm is where you've longed to place it, over the centre of his chest. His heart thuds against the spread of your fingers.

FINN

Finn's breath came hard in his chest, rasping in and out. Sweat dripped down his forehead. He sucked in another lungful, paused momentarily, braced himself. Looked up.

Mount Wellington's summit was ahead, not far, he knew. The clouds had sunk down to hang from the mountain's shoulders. Sandra was up ahead too, out of sight, and he wondered how he'd become so unfit since moving north. It was too damned hot to exercise there. In Hobart he could walk out the back door and hike the lower levels of Mount Wellington's slopes and be back in a few hours. Any North Coast walk was a hot, sweaty exercise, peppered with ticks, mosquitoes and leeches.

He shifted his pack, gulped water, set off again. It was shameful for her to beat him to the top by too much. Shameful to arrive sweaty and red-faced and gasping too.

Around the bend she was sitting on a rock, waiting.

'Nearly there, buster,' she said, pushing up to her feet in a fluid movement. 'Race you.'

'It's only gentlemanly,' Finn panted, 'to let you win.'

She smiled and set out ahead of him. He didn't mind. Sandra looked pretty good from behind, much better than he did. It was definitely his preference for their walking order. The sight

317

of her bare calves gave him something to focus on. Something other than remembering the last time he climbed the mountain, with Toby in his backpack, when Toby was still small enough to be toted around.

His chest was really hurting by the time they made it to the top. They emerged into the car park, strode across the tarmac, scrambled up a shortcut. Avoiding the main tourist lookout, they headed in silent assent to the spot where locals waited to see if the clouds would part for them.

No sign of it today. The clouds swirled damply across the view, and Finn felt his sweat begin to chill. Sandra pulled a couple of nut bars from her pack and tossed him one.

'Let's give it a while,' she said. 'You never know.'

She was cheerful and he liked that. No one else dared be cheerful around him.

Something had happened in the ten days since he'd come south. The dream of coming home had fallen apart, but it wasn't just that. It was being apart from Bridget and Jarrah, being alone.

Seeing Sandra, that first time, had crystallised it. He'd wanted to snatch her up, crush her to him, bury himself in her. A feeling so much stronger than their previous flirtation, savage in its intensity. He wanted them to go, that moment, run together into some new world, leave their spouses, their children, all of it. Wanted to throw himself into the heat of it, cauterise his wounds with desire's burn.

She'd responded in kind. Held him hard, let him sob raggedly, kissed his head and said his name. In that moment he could have done it.

But a squall had blown in across the water and they'd escaped its stinging rain in a nearby pub, and the warmth and the smell of beer and the act of ordering food had killed the moment so thoroughly that Finn doubted he'd really felt it, or seen it in her, and the pain claimed him again, snatched him back from any hope of reprieve, and soon they were eating hot chips across the table from each other and the moment was gone.

And by the time they'd ordered their second drinks she'd dispelled any lingering doubt. 'It won't ever happen with us, Finn. It was a flirtation that went too far. But I never would have done it.'

It was so ridiculous that Finn had found himself laughing. 'Right. Well, thanks for breaking it gently. Maybe you could have told Bridget that.'

'Of course I told her, but it was too late. We crossed her boundary of betrayal. It was different with Hans. He knows what happened. I had to tell him why we couldn't come to the funeral. He's OK.'

'OK?' Finn asked, incredulous.

'Well, not thrilled obviously. But he understood. We moved on.'

'Just like that?'

Finn had been chewing over that ever since. For him, the attraction had set off a domino cascade of disaster. Sandra and Hans had simply moved on. It was hard to comprehend.

The clouds swirled and lightened around him, and Finn glimpsed for a second the harbour far below before they closed in again. Sandra finished her nut bar and tucked the wrapper in her pocket.

'Do you think she'll ever forgive me?'

Finn sighed. 'I don't think forgiveness is her strong suit.'

'Does she blame you for Toby?'

Finn didn't know where to start. The question of blame, the question of paying for it, the question of guilt, the question of the gate, the question of forgiveness, all so tangled together.

'It was my fault. You've read the papers.'

'It was an accident.'

'Not according to the law.'

'It's almost like you *want* to go to jail.'

'I almost think I do.'

'Finn!' She pushed herself up off the rock. 'That is fucking crazy!' She came over, put both hands on his shoulders. 'You're not still carrying some stupid guilt about you and me, are you?'

He shook his head.

'Then what? What makes Bridget such a saint and you so evil?'

Finn stared back at her, feeling the heat come to his cheeks under her gaze. He wavered. So alone in this choice. So many secrets. He could tell Sandra. It might help.

'If it was Bridget's fault, could you forgive her?'

'Yes.'

'Then give her the chance to forgive you.'

Finn shrugged, confused. 'I don't know what you mean.'

She looked around. 'I don't think the clouds are going to clear and it's getting on. Should we head down?'

Finn exhaled. The moment was gone. He wouldn't tell.

'Could you give me a few minutes on my own?'

She stepped back, shouldered her pack and strode off. The mist swallowed her in moments as if she'd never been there.

The truth was, Finn had no idea how Toby got into the pool. He hardly knew what he was doing any more, except that he had to stick to the path he was on, take everything that came

320

with it. Pay the price, carry out the penance, and hope that somehow, at the end of it, Bridget might still be there.

Was that what Sandra meant? That in taking the blame for Bridget, he'd given her the harder task – of having to forgive him?

It was too much of a head-fuck; he couldn't make sense of it. He had to trust his first impulse, the deep knowing that he had to carry this for her, and it was better for her never to forgive him than never to forgive herself. He had to remember that one thing and stick to it, stand up and plead guilt, knowing it was the best chance of saving them. Or at least of saving her.

The solicitor had sent down a pile of paperwork and he'd signed various parts of it. In the normal course of events his wife would have taken the power of attorney, but Malcolm had warned him against it and advised appointing Conor instead. He'd had some strong words to say about the house sale, suggesting that the money went into a trust in case anything happened while he was inside. 'Anything' presumably meaning Bridget leaving Finn, something Malcolm clearly considered a strong possibility.

Finn looked around to make sure he was alone, then eased his backpack to the front and opened it. Unzipped an inner pocket and drew out a small wooden box. Something he'd carved years ago from a single piece of Tasmanian Huon pine and assembled without nail or glue, using only dovetail joints and fine timber pegs.

It might have been, he knew, his greatest betrayal yet, but he couldn't come back to Tasmania without bringing something of Toby with him. It could have been a toy or piece of clothing, those were the things he'd thought of, but when the moment came, the only thing that would do was a handful of ashes from the box under the bed. Some tiny part of his son to put to rest, there at home. Was it some kind of sacrilege, separating the ashes of Toby?

He took out his penknife, kneeled, scraped a shallow hole in the soil beside the rock. He eased the lid off the box and looked down.

He was crossing some line, taking some irrevocable step. He tilted the box, saw the ashes shift and begin to slide. Had a sudden image of Jarrah's face and the way his older son had looked at Toby sometimes.

Stopped himself. Righted the box. Snatched up the lid and pressed it back on. He wouldn't do it, not alone and in secret like this. Not without Jarrah and Bridget. He wouldn't split his grief from theirs.

The things no one knew. He'd told no one about almost losing Jarrah too, and remembering that night flooded his body with adrenaline. It had been bad enough saying goodbye in hospital. He'd known Jarrah was being discharged the following day, that everything was set up at home, that Bridget would be there. Known he had to go to Tasmania and see his father. But leaving Jarrah had been torment. In the end he'd done it the coward's way, kissing the boy's forehead while he slept and writing him a note. Every cell in his body screaming its protest as he walked away, down that long squeaky corridor stinking of antiseptic and death.

He couldn't go home to Murwillumbah before the case. He only had it in him to leave Jarrah once.

He slid the box into his shirt pocket, feeling it bump against his skin as he put his pack back on. He'd keep it with him, hold Toby close.

JARRAH

Mum had to go out for shopping and stuff and I guess she thought I was better, because she left me alone, promising to be back soon. As soon as the car pulled out, I crutched outside, opened the gate, let myself into the pool area.

It was still pretty bad. I could kind of see the new plants in there, some with their leaves sticking out, some down low. Every now and then there was a little movement on the surface and ripples spread out. Those poor fish, I reckoned, trying to swim through the slime. But Mum promised it would be better in a few days.

I lowered myself onto one of the pool chairs and laid down the crutches beside me. It smelled mouldy but I ignored it. Sat in the pool area for the first time. I'd walked through here a few times when I had to, but never just sat and looked at where Toby had died.

The last time we'd swum together was the day before Toby drowned. Dad had come out of the studio kind of happy, saying the sculpture was going well and he could have a break. Mum and me were playing with Toby, helping him swim a few strokes between us. He could dog-paddle the short distance from one of us to the other. I guess I thought that meant he could swim.

Dad watched us from the deckchair, and I remember looking up at him and he had this big goofy grin on his face, like life was so fucking fantastic, and I guess it was, right then, though I didn't know it.

It was his fault, he said. Dad's invention left the gate open and Toby got through the gate. Mum left Toby alone for a minute. Dad had his back turned. Mum found Toby in the pool. Dad was arrested. I couldn't make sense of any of it.

I shut my eyes. It was hot. My leg sweated under the plaster. I could smell my underarms and I thought I could smell the water, the green soup it had turned into. It was creepy. You couldn't see into it. There could be a dead body down there and you wouldn't know.

I still couldn't picture what Toby looked like dead.

One of those moments hit. It was like a huge wave, coming out of nowhere and slamming into me. I held on to the chair with both hands and clenched my teeth together, and when that didn't work I screwed my face up. A whimper came out of me. I was alive, and I guess I was glad, but it didn't mean I'd ever get over Toby.

After a while I kind of got control again. I let go of the chair. Wiped my face on my T-shirt. Wished it wasn't so hot.

I could never remember if I'd said goodbye to Toby on the morning he died. Maybe trying to remember it in a different place would help. I shut my eyes. I'd been about to go to school and Mum had told me to put on deodorant and I'd gone back to the bathroom. I tried to watch it like a movie in my head. I could see myself reading to Toby, flipping through the pages. I picked him up and put him into the highchair. Buckled the little belt that held him in there. Mum came in from her swim and asked me about how to make breakfast. I ate breakfast. Then there was a blank. Deodorant. Blank again, and then I was walking across the grass towards the shed to get my bike. As I wheeled it out Dad was pushing the bin to the gutter for the garbage collection, and he came back in the gate before I went out. Clapped me on the shoulder to say goodbye, and I remember hoping he wouldn't kiss me, like he sometimes did in public, forgetting I was nearly sixteen. I pushed the bike through the gate and closed it.

Something nagged at me.

Again. I turned as I closed the gate behind me and saw Dad heading to the studio. Because he'd put the garbage out, he wasn't near the pool gate. He was headed to the back door of the studio, the one he hardly ever used.

Walked through it again like it was a film set. Heard the parrots making a racket, remembered it was hot and sunny, just like now. Heard the click click click of the bike. I'd been thinking about those boys in the year above me, the ones from the pizza parlour, and working out how I was going to avoid them at school, and what I was going to do if I couldn't avoid them, and thinking there was a good chance I'd be called Little Mummy all over school and that would be the end of my invisibility. That's what I was thinking. And Dad was walking to the back door of the studio, and back in the house Mum was finishing breakfast with wet hair, and the gate clicked behind me and I put my foot on the pedal and pushed off, swinging my leg over the bike and leaving that world behind me forever.

I think maybe I got it, finally. What Dad was doing.

BRIDGET

You don't like Malcolm. It's not personal. Or maybe it is, maybe you wouldn't have liked him even meeting him at a party or as a colleague. There's something about him – some whiff of profiting from the misfortune of others, something you can't quite put your finger on.

Plus he's always catching you on the back foot.

'Let's get the small matters out of the way first,' he says. 'The house sale. You need to have some agreement about what happens to the money if your husband does end up with a custodial sentence. You both need your interests protected. You may want to consider appointing your own solicitor.'

He doesn't like you either, you surmise. 'I'll consider it. But I'm here to talk about the case.'

He closes the house sale folder with exaggerated patience and you bite the jagged place inside your lower lip that keeps you calm. He opens the next, much bigger folder.

'I feel your husband rushed into the decision to plead guilty. Did you discuss it?'

'No. He decided the morning after our son's accident. There was no chance to discuss it.'

'Do you agree with his decision?'

326

'It doesn't matter what I think, does it? It's done.'

'Your attitude matters. You'll still need to give evidence in the sentencing hearing in Lismore next Tuesday – I suppose Finn told you that? You should argue that you son needs his father. It all contributes to the judge's decision about a sentence. All helps keep him out of jail.'

It's been calmer since Finn left for Hobart. Without him around, your fury has abated. You and Jarrah coexist in an orbit of loss, but somehow, you think, you're managing. You focus on Jarrah and your pond. The truth is, you don't want Finn to come back, not just now. Jail might not be the worst outcome. Though you can't tell this to his solicitor. And it makes you not only a bad wife, but a bad mother, because of course a boy needs his father.

You give yourself a jolt, sit up straighter. There's no one in the world, with the possible exception of Meredith and DI Evans, who thinks Finn should be in jail. You'll have to help him with this.

'We should go through your police statement,' Malcolm says. 'You'll be cross-examined and we can discuss our strategies and predict what questions they might ask. It would help to get evidence from your son. Finn says he doesn't want him in court, though I've advised him it could be helpful. If he's not going to give evidence, we should get that psychological assessment. Can you organise that? We can give you a list of court-approved psychologists.'

'Tick,' you say, though you can't imagine how this will fit with concealing Jarrah's suicide attempt.

He takes his glasses off. 'I'm going to presume we're all on the same side here, trying to keep your husband out of jail. You can sort out any differences much more easily afterwards, if he's a free man.'

'Differences?' you say.

'I'm very sorry for your loss, Mrs Brennan,' he says, closing the file. 'Don't think I'm not. I can barely imagine what you've gone through. But I have a good idea of what's coming up. A lot of people pin their hopes on court. They think someone will be punished, and they think they'll have closure. But it's not like that. Don't think court will make anything better.'

*

'You smell,' your mother says, waving her hand in front of her nose.

'It's the cakes, silly.' You open the paper bag, slide out the cardboard box. 'Chocolate brownies. Fresh. Your favourite.'

She checks out your offering suspiciously. 'Who's that for?'

'One for you, one for me, one for—'

'Toby.'

'Jarrah,' you say at the same moment, speaking over the top of her.

'Toby loves his chocolate.'

'It's too rich for him. He can have a banana. But don't tell him, OK?'

These conversations with your mother should be devastating, but you find a strange comfort in them. For a moment you can almost pretend none of it's happened and Toby is at home with Finn, ready to throw a tantrum over a chocolate brownie.

You cut one of the brownies in half and hand it to her in a napkin. She sinks her teeth in, closing her eyes in pleasure, chews noisily, bites again. While she's occupied, you slide the remainder into the bag and put it out of her sight. She tends to forget she's eaten and wants more. When she finishes, you take the napkin and wipe the chocolate from the corner of her mouth.

'Something still smells,' she says.

'I can't smell anything.'

'Fish. I can smell fish.'

You busy yourself, carrying the napkin over to the bin and taking your time to pop the lid and drop it in and look out the window into the garden. You put your hands into the pool before you came here. Hoping for some development in the ecosystem. Hoping for Toby. It's true, your hands smelled fishy afterwards, but you scrubbed them. Surely that's not it?

'Have I seen Toby lately?'

The question takes you by surprise and you turn. You have no idea, at any given moment, if a question is coming from an opening of lucidity or the fog. This one sounds lucid and she's looking at you steadily.

'Not for a while,' you say softly.

'I miss him.' Tears form in her eyes.

Your own tears threaten and you're sick of lying to her, sickened by pretence. 'He's gone, Mum.'

You have the sense of her in there somewhere, peering out through the thickets that have formed in her mind, catching sight of you in the world for once, knowing you, hearing you.

'Don't say that!' she cries and presses her hands to her mouth.

You're already regretting the words, wishing you could snatch them back, hoping they'll find no purchase in her tangled brain, nothing to catch them and hold them.

'He's gone with Finn to Hobart,' you say, forcing a smile. 'To visit the family. I'll bring him in when they get home.'

'Can we go to Hobart too?'

'Do you want to go back?'

She nods vigorously.

'Sure.' You're under control again and you move to her side, rest your hand on her thin shoulder.

'I'm packed,' she says. 'Let's go now.'

'OK,' you say and squeeze her shoulder. 'I'll go and bring the car around. Wait here.'

It's simplest this way, you've learned. You step out of her room. Use the toilet, wash your hands, flinch at your gaunt face in the mirror. Only days until Finn's sentence hearing and it still seems unreal.

'You should start preparing yourself,' he said last night when you answered the phone. 'I'll organise Tom to help you pack up the house if it's needed. Malcolm's drawn up some things you need to sign. I've asked Conor to be my power of attorney.'

That, more than anything, said how far apart you were. He didn't trust you.

'Shouldn't we talk before the hearing?' you said. 'About strategy or something?'

'Nothing's changed. Just tell your story and we'll let the judge decide what's right. And make sure Jarrah's not there.'

'When are you coming back?'

He hesitated. 'I'll stay in Sydney the night before and fly up early on the trial day.'

'You're not even going to see Jarrah?'

'It's too damned hard, Bridget. I'll just see you in there on the day, OK?'

You hung up, not understanding any of it.

You envy your mother for her ability to live in the present, relatively unaffected by past and future. You run your fingers through your hair and step out of the toilet. The sun slants into the hallway window and onto the patterned carpet. You wait another few moments, breathing deeply. Head up, back in the door, as if arriving.

'Hi, Mum.'

'Why, hello dear,' she says. 'Lovely to see you.' Then wrinkles her brow. 'What's that smell?'

JARRAH

Time after Toby: thirty-four days. Dad said it was best this way. It wouldn't be hanging over us for the next two years. He said it'd be hard no matter when it happened and it was best to get it over with.

'But won't I see you before court?' I asked.

He didn't answer for a while. 'Jarrah, I miss you more than you can imagine,' he said at last. 'I hope you'll understand. I can't come back early. It's too hard. The three of us will have coffee before the court case. Then Eddie is going to take you home and wait with you. OK?'

'But …' I didn't understand. 'Is that when we'll say goodbye?'

'I think this is best for all of us. And it might go well, and then I'll be home.'

'But Dad, I remembered something.'

'It doesn't matter, Jarrah,' he snapped, so fast I was shocked.

'But you didn't go through—'

'It doesn't matter!' His voice rose. 'This case is about one thing only, Jarrah, and that's how I modified the gate and that contributed to Toby drowning. That's it.' He took a deep breath. 'Now, try not to think about it, OK? I don't want you worrying about it. It's nothing to do with you.'

I thought I was on to something and the disappointment rushed over me. 'Nothing to do with me if you don't come home for two years!'

'Stop,' he said, and his voice was weirdly calm. 'I don't want you there. I don't want you to hear it all again. You can't change the outcome.'

I wanted to hang up on him, but I forced myself not to.

'When you do something wrong, you've got to pay for it. And this will do some good. It might stop someone else out there from putting some stupid thing on their pool gate or forgetting to close it. It might save some kid's life.'

'You sound like that Meredith woman.'

'Yeah, well.'

'So you won't even come up the night before?'

I heard a sound in his throat before he answered. 'If I do that I'll never be able to walk into court.'

'I don't get you.'

'You will, one day.'

'But in the meantime you can't be bothered to see us?'

I suppose I was hoping he'd snap, but he just didn't react. He was quiet for a minute and then he said, 'Jarrah, I love you more than any other thing on this whole planet, all right? It seems hard, but I'm trying to do the right thing for all of us. Can you trust me?'

I stared out into the night. All I could feel was him leaving. 'I don't know, Dad,' I said.

FINN

The worlds he now inhabited that he'd known so little of before. The hospital. The police. The courts. This morning, in a hungry jostle outside the court building, the media. And perhaps, from this day onwards, jail.

The day: jagged, disconnected, unreal.

Flying in – the view from the banking plane – that mountain, the warning, at the head of its winding river valley.

Meeting Bridget and Jarrah in a café around the corner from the courthouse. Like two strangers. He was already shutting down, moving away from them, preparing.

The cameras and microphones shoved at him outside the courthouse, questions shouted at him, and Edmund trying to clear a path for them to get inside.

The faces of the people waiting for it to begin. Some familiar. Angela and Tom. Bridget's workmate, who looked away. Meredith, who wouldn't look away. Some of the police he remembered. Strangers staring, or carefully not staring.

Waiting in the small conference room at the side of the court's entrance. Realising Bridget would have to stay outside the courtroom until she was called as a witness.

Being led into the court and across to the dock. Understanding

334

he would sit on that exposed seat for the entire proceedings, unless standing to answer questions or when the judge entered or left. The architecture of blame and scrutiny.

Seeing Jarrah levering his way into the front row and sitting down next to Conor and Edmund, his face a blur of defiance and entreaty.

Three knocks on the wood to signify the judge was ready. The all-rise and the bowing, the vivid red robe and the grey wig, the white collar and ruffle, her considered gaze upon him. The Crown Prosecutor, the learned friend, the low voices, the lack of windows, the fear permeating the carpet and the chair and the wooden bench in front of him. The whole human world, and every possible deed within it, held inside that room. The guilty and not guilty feet that had stood where his were waiting. The lives decided. The 'How say you?'

The legalese, more intimate than he'd imagined. The standing. The deep breath. The oath.

'Tell us the circumstances of that morning.'

His walk through the gate, his preoccupation, his failure to check the device had closed the gate behind him. The lie, early and strong. And he was back there, in the studio. The acrid smell of ozone burning the insides of his nostrils. The stink of his trade, the metallic taste of it. He was working with welding torch and hands, he was creating that piece, assembling it, watching it grow, watching something emerge from a pile of junk and his own imagination. He'd lost that, forgotten the feeling, and there it was in his memory, the strange joy of art, now the armature of truth upon which his story hung.

'And when did you realise something was wrong?'

He was absorbed in the pleasure of welding, the sound ringing in his ears, the glow and spit of the slag, the safety mask blacking out the world. The last perfect moment. Then the faint noise, the muffled sound he couldn't identify that made the hairs on his arms stand on end. The noise of something wrong, the noise that called to him with its distant desperation. And as he flicked off the torch and lifted his mask, it roared into his hearing. A howl that burned its way down inside him.

'What did you do?'

Turned around into a new, maleficent world. Tore off the mask, ran − tripping, scrambling, propelled − and wrenched open the sliding door. Hurtled headlong into the pool and fought the water like an enemy to get to her. Fought the water, which had rendered his living son into this limp, lolling thing.

Inarticulate animal sounds of horror.

A gap in his memory that he couldn't fill in.

Next, Toby lying on the ground. Bridget kneeling over him, her fingers exhuming foam from his mouth. Her frantic demand, pointing: *The instructions!*

They were nailed to the fence. Faded, unread. He ran to them, placed both hands on the plastic, leaned in, tried to focus.

Clear the airways.

'Take your time, Mr Brennan. We have time. You read out the instructions to your wife and then what happened?'

WHAT NEXT? Bridget had screamed at him.

He had tried to focus. The words and pictures shifted and moved and he couldn't hold on to them. Tried to instruct Bridget without shrieking.

Tilt the head back and open the mouth. Couldn't say *Toby's mouth.*

Cover the victim's nose and mouth with your mouth and give five slow, gentle breaths, one breath every three seconds.

He turned. Bridget's mouth was over Toby's. She raised her head and bellowed at him.

FOR GOD'S SAKE HELP ME, FINN!

BRIDGET

Chen wants to wait outside with you, but you refuse and send him into the courtroom. It's wrong to take his comfort on this day.

The crowd has filed into the court and the waiting area is almost empty. Just a couple of other witnesses, standing alone, fingering phones or trying to read. You don't know who they are. Don't care. Retreat into yourself to wait.

You wish Jarrah hadn't waited until last night to talk.

You'd been sitting outside after dinner, the stink of the mosquito coil curling in your nostrils, watching the last of the light fade from the sky. It surprised you when Jarrah joined you instead of watching TV or something. You'd put it down to the case, the imminent prospect of Finn going to jail. You were glad of the company.

'Tell me again how Toby got in there,' he'd said. 'I'll hear it tomorrow anyway.'

'No you won't. You're not coming,' you'd replied, on automatic.

Jarrah had worked himself to his feet and crutched over to the verandah railing. He leaned on it and looked out.

'Do you still not get it?' He turned back to you, so adult you hardly recognised him. 'I have the right to come. You can't stop me.'

Your eyes locked together for a long moment and you exhaled and surrendered.

'Your father went through the pool gate and didn't notice it malfunctioned and stayed open behind him,' you explained. 'I left Toby alone for a few minutes while I went to the bathroom. He got into the pool area and fell in.'

'But Toby could swim. We swam with him the day before. How long before you found him?'

You got up, crossed to the railing, and put your hand on Jarrah's arm. 'He was out of my sight for, I don't know, maybe four or five minutes. Part of that time I was searching the house for him because I looked out and saw the gate was shut. Meredith told me a toddler can drown in sixty seconds, even one you think can swim.'

You were both quiet, imagining that.

Then Jarrah said: 'I don't understand how the gate was shut when you looked.'

You let go of him. 'The police spent hours examining the pool and the fence and I've gone over it and over it trying to work it out. Toby must have gone through the open gate and bumped it, so it started working again and shut behind him. I can't think of anything else that makes sense.'

'How long after I left?'

You knew you'd have to relive the day in court the next day anyway, so you forced your mind back. You'd kissed Jarrah goodbye, sent him back for deodorant. Finished Toby's breakfast, lifted him out of the chair. You'd gone to the bathroom.

'It wasn't long, Jarrah. Maybe fifteen minutes.'

He hesitated. 'Do you remember if I said goodbye to Toby?'

That simple question, enough to break your heart again. It was in your power to give him that at least.

'Don't lie to me,' he warned.

You turned. It was nearly dark, but you could still see his eyes, fixed on yours. He frightened you sometimes, the way he was suddenly adult. What he seemed to know about you.

'I can't remember,' you said. 'I'm sorry.'

The silence went on so long you thought the conversation must be over. You were loath to go to bed, not expecting any sleep, but it seemed like time. You began to stir.

'I don't think Dad went through the gate.'

You swivelled. 'What?'

'You know when I left? He was putting the bins out on the street. He came back in through the gate when I went out and he went around to the back door of the studio.'

'I don't understand. Did he tell you this?'

'No, I saw it. I saw him go round the back.'

'But – that can't be right. He told me he went through the pool gate. He told everyone. On the day it happened.'

'I know,' Jarrah said.

'Did you ask him?'

'He told me I remembered it wrong. But I don't think I did.'

The two of you stood in silence until he leaned over to kiss you on the forehead and wished you good night.

You sank onto the cane lounge and sat in the dark a long time, unmoving. When at last you heard a soft teenage snore from inside the lounge room you got up. Walked on the balls of your feet down the length of the verandah. Raised the noiseless, squeakless, reliable new latch and opened the gate. Closed it behind you and heard the click as the latch dropped unerringly in the cup.

The explosion of primitive life in the pond had scared you at first, but over the past few days it finally settled, and you'd switched the automatic light back on. The plants and fish cast rippling shadows on the sides, but you could see right through to the bottom again.

You'd thought about swimming, for the first time, but when the moment came to put your feet in you baulked. Something stopped you from even running your fingers through the water. You sat, instead, on a deckchair by the pool and leaned forwards, watching the fish darting in and out of the plants. Silver perch, firetail gudgeons, Pacific blue-eyes: small Australian fish suitable for seeding an ecosystem without causing environmental havoc. The green light glinted off their scales and eyes.

It had become beautiful. It had turned into what you imagined. A living, breathing system. Life-supporting. Benign.

You had swum, the morning Toby drowned. You'd gone out while Finn was making coffee and breaststroked a couple of laps. Towelled yourself dry, leaned over the gate and pulled down the lever that operated *Owl Sentry*. You'd passed through the gate, preoccupied and focused on getting back indoors. You'd trusted the mechanism to shut the gate.

No, even that was untrue. You hadn't given it a thought. You had no memory of hearing it close or of not hearing it. Your thoughts had thrust forward to the things that needed to be done, and it hadn't occurred to you to glance backwards.

Perhaps Jarrah was right. Perhaps Finn didn't walk through the gate at all. Perhaps you were the only one to open it that morning.

You shook your head, pressed your hands to your temples. Did it matter? The issue was the gate not being safe. The issue was that terrible, fallible device you smashed.

'They'll ask,' Malcolm had said, 'about the nature of the modification. How many times it played up, if you or Finn were aware of it, or if he ignored it. They need to establish an extreme level of negligence.'

You had, you slowly realised, only Finn's word to say that the thing had malfunctioned at all. Finn's word and the elimination of other probabilities. The absence of any other theory.

Why would he say that? The question Jarrah hadn't answered. The question you couldn't answer. Or had you known the answer all along and been unable to face it?

'Mrs Brennan?' Finn's solicitor has to say your name twice to get your attention.

You start and push yourself to your feet.

'They're ready for you.'

You push your hair back, tug your jacket. Glance at him until he nods, then follow him to the door.

'Bow your head to the judge when you enter,' he says and sweeps in, trailing his robes, nodding gracefully. You follow, repeat the move awkwardly, look up.

To your right, Finn sitting alone in the dock. Above the judge's head, a massive and elaborate coat of arms: crown, lion, unicorn, rose, harp, flourishes, Latin words decorating an elaborate ribbon. You'd never noticed – or considered – such things before, or the obscure but powerful weight of tradition and authority they confer.

This is real.

FINN

She was sworn in and took her seat on the stand. Close to the judge's right hand, far from Finn, the accused. Another design feature cementing might and right.

His barrister, Jack Ferguson, stood. 'Mrs Brennan, tell me what happened the day your son died.'

Bridget shuddered and began. 'He was on the kitchen floor reading his favourite book and I left him to go to the bathroom.'

Finn squeezed his eyes shut. Just a short retelling, that's all. A confirmation of what he'd said. He willed her to keep it simple.

'I was away from Toby for perhaps five minutes,' Bridget was saying. 'In that time he left the kitchen and somehow entered the pool area.'

'What happened when you realised he was missing?'

'I went outside to look and saw the pool gate was shut, so I didn't think he could be in the pool area. I couldn't see him in the garden. I was calling him. I ran upstairs and looked in his bedroom. Then I ran along the hall and looked in our bedroom. You can see the pool from our window. That's when I saw he'd fallen in. He was face-down in the water. Not moving.'

'What did you do?'

The room was silent. Finn had to open his eyes. Bridget was crying. She looked across at him and swallowed.

'I knew I had to get him out, and had to get Finn. I ran downstairs and outside into the pool area. I started screaming for Finn. He was working in his studio. I knew it would be hard for him to hear me. I ran into the water to get Toby, and I kept yelling for Finn and eventually he heard me and came out. We got Toby out of the water and put him on the ground, and I told Finn to read out the instructions for resuscitation.'

'Had you ever done rescue breathing before?'

Bridget nodded. 'I trained in first aid when I had my first child. Fifteen years ago. I'd done it in the training. Never on a person.'

Finn sank back into the day. Peering at the sign, his hands on either side of the dancing words, the dreadful pictures he'd never noticed before, trying to read ahead. Bridget's screams for help echoed around him, sounds stretching and distorting like he was hearing underwater. Parrots squawking in a tree above his head, their racket piercing. This was beyond them, beyond any printed instruction. He was running to phone the ambulance in curious slow motion, nightmare steps, his legs refusing to work properly. Stabbing at the zeros with his thick fingers, somehow making himself understood. The voice on the line telling him to go back outside giving further instructions for him to relay to Bridget.

Kneeling. Bridget gasping and breathing into Toby, breathing for both of them, for all of them. Toby's small hand, limp, outflung.

The tinny voice in his ear: *You need to stop rescue breathing and begin chest compressions. Put the heel of your hand on his breastbone. You're going to do thirty quick compressions, counting aloud.*

Dropping the phone. Taking Bridget's shoulder and pulling her back. Toby's blue lips. Placing his hand on Toby's chest. Its chill.

'What else happened before the ambulance arrived?'

Finn remembered it then, the impression that agony must have driven from his mind. His palm flat on Toby's chest, he felt Toby hurtle out of his small body in a rush. The full force of him punched into Finn, and he felt, for an instant, that he could hold his son, stop him from leaving.

Before the thought was finished Toby was gone, leaving a turmoil of emotion. Confusion. Fear. And, weirdly, joy. A rush of excitement, as their boy leaped into the universe – unconstrained, free.

And then the first paramedic trying to wrench the gate open, and the look on his young face and the way he tried to hide it and the little groan of despair that escaped him and how Finn leaped for *Owl Sentry*'s lever and the paramedic ran to Toby and the second paramedic followed and Finn pulled Bridget out of the way and held her as she keened and wailed and he knew it was too late and too late and too late.

'How do you think Toby got into the pool area?'

Bridget took so long to answer that Finn opened his eyes again, just as Ferguson prompted: 'Mrs Brennan?'

'I don't think we'll ever know. The gate was closed when I got to the pool. Perhaps the device malfunctioned earlier when I had a swim and didn't shut properly. Perhaps Toby found some way to set off the device himself. He was a child you couldn't hold back. When he wanted to go somewhere or do something, he found a way to do it. My husband blames himself. But we don't know what happened, or even if the gate *was* open. All I

345

know for certain is that I walked out of the room and left Toby unsupervised.'

Finn blinked. Looked at Jarrah, who dropped his head. Looked at Bridget. For the first time she was really looking back at him.

JARRAH

It was like a great big held in breath was let out when the judge finally spoke. *A suspended sentence of fifteen months*, she said, and then read out a whole lot of legal stuff that went on forever. I didn't follow it all, but I got the idea. Dad wasn't going to jail. She finally finished, stacked her papers, stood up, nodded her head. Everyone got to their feet as she walked out, and people started turning to each other and talking. Some were smiling. The legal people shook hands. Conor hugged me and Edmund patted me on the back.

Tom was sitting up the back with his mother. They must have come in after me; hadn't known they were there. I kept my head down, stayed in my seat and avoided looking their way. Dad caught my eye and smiled as he stepped out of the dock, and I smiled back, but with the crutches I was stuck in my row and I nodded for him to go outside. By the time I got out there, Mum and Dad were hugging. I didn't want to interrupt that, but Dad looked up and called me to come over. I stumped across to them and he opened his arms and pulled me in so all three of us were hugging. Dad's face was wet and I was crying too. He felt so big and real and warm and I realised how much I'd missed him, and I wanted to bawl like a kid, and had to control myself.

People were melting away. Chen must have gone; I'd seen him leave the court in front of me and he wasn't anywhere outside. I couldn't see Meredith either, and Conor and Edmund kept their distance. Then Dad looked up from our hug as we were sniffling and starting to loosen our grip on each other, and he caught sight of Tom and his mother and waved them over. I saw Tom hesitate.

'We just wanted to see that you were all right,' his mother said to us. 'We're so pleased.'

'Thank you,' Dad said. 'We appreciate the support. Don't be a stranger, Tom. Come by for a beer, eh?'

'Sure,' Tom said, not meeting my eyes.

They walked off. I was pretty sure he wouldn't come for a beer. Didn't know if I was sad or relieved. Still squirmed whenever I thought about that moment. But seeing Tom was kind of like seeing Dad again. Hadn't realised how much I missed him.

The hug was over, though Dad still had his arm around Mum's shoulders.

'Let's go home,' she said.

I saw Dad baulk. He'd been away from where Toby died and he didn't want to go back, I realised.

'It'll be OK,' Mum said. 'We can make some decisions now.'

The TV cameras and the journalists were out the front, interviewing Meredith, but I couldn't hear what she was saying. She finished and walked off without coming over to us. Then Dad's barrister spoke to the cameras while we stood in the background. Edmund drove us home, with Conor in the front and the three of us squashed into the back seat and my crutches across our laps. Mum and Dad held hands like teenagers.

When we pulled up out the front, I realised there was nothing to show what had happened. Everything looked normal. It looked just like the other houses on the street.

'Off you go,' Edmund said. 'Conor and I are going to check out the coast.'

'You don't want to come in?' Dad asked.

Edmund looked back at the three of us and smiled. 'Not today. We'll see you tomorrow.'

Mum reached over and the sound of the car door handle was loud as she pulled it and the door cracked open. I opened my door, swivelled to the side, arranged my crutches so I could lever myself out of the car.

Edmund drove off while we were still standing there, the three of us close together. I didn't feel so happy suddenly. Dad didn't know what Mum had done to the pool. What would he think?

Dad's feet seemed rooted to the ground, like he couldn't move to walk to the gate and go inside.

'I feel like I've already left here,' he said.

Mum took his hand. I knew she was thinking that what she'd done to the pool would make things better, and even I knew what a dumb idea that was, but I couldn't say anything.

'You still sleeping in the lounge room?' Dad asked me, stalling for time.

I nodded. I probably could have got upstairs on my crutches by now, but I'd got used to being down. I could flick on the telly if I woke up during the night and it wasn't as hot as upstairs. I kind of liked it. Upstairs felt like my old life. Too many things up there reminded me of Toby.

349

'Guess we'd better not stand out here all afternoon,' Dad said.

I let them go first. You could tell a lot by how people held hands. I thought they were maybe going to be OK.

It was thirty-six days after Toby.

BRIDGET

You can't settle on any feeling, not yet. Not while a fragile connection has tendrilled unexpectedly between you. And you won't speak of it, not of the gate and who went in or out, or didn't. Not yet, not today.

Now that Finn is about to see what you've done to the pool, you're afraid. As chlorine evaporated and algae colonised the water, thank God it eventually turned clear. Now you can see down through leaves and fronds to where the fish dart and flash, and fallen leaves swirl their way to the bottom and sunlight makes patterns of it all.

You feel his unease at returning to the house and you know not to take him there, not straight away. Lead him instead to what has become your outdoor seating area, the gathering of old chairs on the verandah outside the lounge room. From that spot you can see the pool fence, but only obliquely, and you've become used to facing away from it.

'Beer?' you ask, as Finn lowers himself to the couch.

He takes a deep breath. 'Yes.' Looks up at you with the trace of a smile. 'And bring one for Jarrah too, eh?'

You look at Jarrah with an eyebrow raised and he gives a sheepish half-grin and your protest about the effects of alcohol on a young brain die away, and you want it too, the three of you sharing this moment almost like equals, together, and drinking the same thing symbolises it.

You take three Coronas from the fridge, pop the lids, slice a fresh lime and crush the slices into the long necks. Before heading back outside you look around the kitchen. It's not that Chen would have left evidence, and anyway, what if he had? But you sense something changing. Something's shifted between you and Finn; something new is about to start. You don't know what it is. You don't know if you're terrified or relieved at the idea. You feel shaken and too light, blown about, unsettled. You have made some kind of choice and you don't know any more how to make such choices, or how to know if any choice is right or wrong.

The kitchen is still and bright, the afternoon sun slanting into the rear window and pooling on the floor. That's the last time you saw him alive, sitting in that very spot, his whole being focused on the book lying spread open on the floor in front of him. The story of a boy who wouldn't be contained and his journey to a wild and distant land.

The feeling threatens to rise and take you by the throat and you swallow hard and clasp the cold necks of the beers and turn away. You won't give in to it. After dark you'll take Finn to the pool and you'll bring him into Toby's world and find, for those moments, comfort.

FINN

It was a night to get drunk. He'd only done it once since Toby had died. Afraid that drinking too much would take him beyond the comfort of alcohol and into the dark. But now he and Bridget were both on their fourth beer, finished off over home-delivered Japanese as dusk fell around them and the mosquitoes whined and the crickets chirped and the bats squealed high overhead. Bridget put on music, something soft and easy, for perhaps the first time, or at least the first time Finn could remember, since Toby's death. She'd chosen well: music you could lean into and feel safe with.

'I'm gonna watch some telly,' Jarrah said after dinner.

Back when, Bridget would have asked him to clear the table and stack the dishwasher. But back then he hadn't sounded so adult, so much like he understood both their need to be alone together and their fear of it. Like he knew that sitting not too far off he'd be a comfort to them, while the television and the wall in between would give them privacy too.

She stood and came around beside his chair. He felt the warmth of her body alongside his, and with it a wave of longing that hurt his throat, ran down and hurt his chest and his gut and his bowel. No difference between longing and pain. All the same.

'I've got something to show you,' she whispered. 'Come?'

She took his hand. The comfort of that was almost as deep as the pain. The comfort of her touch and the feeling that she was there behind it, present, with him for the first time since Toby died.

He would have followed her anywhere, but when she led him to the pool gate and reached up with her left hand to unlatch it he recoiled instinctively.

'Where are we going?'

The clutch of her hand said he would be safe, but he didn't want to go in there and his body pulled back of its own accord.

'Trust me,' she said.

I never stopped trusting you, he wanted to say, but instead gripped her hand harder, steeled himself, followed. Then stopped dead. The water was pale translucent green, full of moving shapes. He pulled back, horrified. What was in there?

'It's plants,' she said, anchoring him with her hand. 'Fish. It's alive now.'

'What?' He couldn't understand.

'The pumps are gone. The chemicals are gone. It's a living pond.'

His breath shuddered in his chest. 'Christ.' He wanted to run from the water and its awful, flickering life.

'Come closer.' She drew him forwards, led him to the edge, shifted his body so that he lowered himself to sitting. He gasped when the water first touched his feet and wanted to fight her, but she held him there and slowly, slowly lowered his feet to the first step, and the water came around his ankles and up his shins and he hated it.

She sat next to him, lowered her own feet until they were next to his on the step, white in the green flickering, the shadows of the plants playing across their skin.

'He's here,' she said.

Finn's chest tightened. That day in court he thought she'd come to some place he could understand, some place he recognised. Had he been wrong?

She put a finger on his lips. 'Shh. I want you to feel it.'

She shrugged off her shirt and bra. Stood on the step and pulled off her shorts and underpants. Stepped down to the next step, the water coming midway up her thighs. Held out her hand to him. She meant to immerse herself, he saw. Had she forgotten their son drowned in that water?

'Trust me, remember?' She extended her hand further. Took his.

There was no choice. Not if he wanted to keep her. He stood. Let go of her hand and began to unbutton his shirt. Felt his body shaking.

JARRAH

Didn't look straight away when the phone pinged. Gave it five minutes. A little window when I could hope. When I could imagine it was him and everything was OK. Imagine I'd never done such a stupid, stupid thing.

And then it *was* him.

<run?>

In spite of myself I smiled. <beat you to the corner>

<u r on. Come out?>

He must be out the front. If he wasn't kidding around. That wiped the smile off my face. How was I going to play this? And how was he? Did the text have another message? *Let's go on like it never happened?*

Well, I could do that. He was probably going off to uni. God knew where we were going. If he could forget it, so could I. Or act like I could.

I got up quietly. Left the television on. Manoeuvred through the screen door. Mum and Dad must have been in the pool area. I could see the light flickering between the bars of the fence, but couldn't hear anything. Felt like none of my business, whatever was going on over there. I levered myself down the steps and across the damp grass. Fumbled with the garden gate, opened it, went through. Looked around. If he'd been kidding, I was going to feel so stupid.

'Need to warm up?'

He was there, under the tree, in his running gear. As I went closer I could smell his sweat, mixed in with the smell of gum leaves. It reminded me of that night.

It might have reminded him too, because he said, 'Can you walk? I need to warm down; I'll go slow.'

I was glad to get away from the tree. I was pretty fast on the crutches now and I swung along the road and Tom jogged on the grass verge. Paced from one streetlight to the next, pools of light in the dark. It was hot. I started sweating.

At the end of our street was a small park with an exercise point. We stopped and Tom started doing back presses. I positioned myself under the bar, dropped my crutches and reached up. It was too high. I wasn't going to ask him to lift me up for chin-ups. I bent down and got my crutches again, leaned on them.

'Good to have your dad home?'

'Yeah,' I said. 'Real good.'

The fact of his dad's absence sat between us, but I didn't know what to say about it.

'Did you get back with Laura?' he asked.

I nearly said yes. I nearly said no. I opened my mouth not quite knowing what answer I'd give, then closed it again. Took a breath. Sitting there with Tom in the night, I knew what the real answer was.

Toby would have given it. Toby wouldn't have cared what someone else thought.

'I won't get back with her,' I said. And then I tried it out. 'I reckon maybe girls aren't for me.'

He didn't say anything for a while. Did another round of press-ups. 'So you're gay,' he said finally. Not quite a question.

I remembered how Toby had lunged for everything he wanted, and how I'd felt when I'd done that with Tom. For one single second it was more right than anything in my life before. Nothing that happened with Laura even came close. Toby, I reckoned, would have loved me anyway, knowing this about me. It wouldn't have frightened him.

'Guess I won't know for sure until it happens.'

I could feel Tom's fear, rippling the air. Strangely, mine was gone. I didn't care now that he knew. I'd lost his friendship already. Anything now was a bonus.

'Look, if you're thinking I—'

I interrupted him. 'Don't worry. That was a mistake. I don't think—'

'Because I'm not.'

'I know. And anyhow, you're not that hot.'

He snorted. 'Thanks.'

I nearly grinned, in the dark. I could make a joke. That was something.

'I won't be a dickhead about it,' he said.

'Really?'

'Look,' he said. Stopped. 'Thought it was better if I stayed away. Last thing you needed in the middle of everything.'

'Yeah, right. Thanks.'

'Your parents trusted me. You're under age, Jarrah! What if someone found out – with all this other stuff going on?'

'I'm eight weeks under age. Guess you just didn't want to get into trouble?'

'Fuck it! That wasn't it!'

'Whatever.'

He started on another round of press-ups and I looked out across the park. I could feel it coming, big and fast and unstoppable, one of those moments where I missed Toby so bad that it was like being torn apart.

I was always going to be alone. Even when I'd been kissing Laura, even when we'd nearly been having sex, I'd felt alone. Now I even felt alone with Tom. Maybe we could be friends, but I didn't know if I'd ever have that feeling back, the one I used to have when we ran together. The two of us, side by side, step by step, everything OK.

All of a sudden I'd had enough. I didn't want the feeling to hit when I was still sitting there with Tom.

'I'd better get back. Didn't tell Mum and Dad I was coming out. I'll see you round.'

He started to say something but I was turning away, not wanting to hear it, wanting to get away from him, and it was dark and the stupid crutch slipped and I stumbled. Couldn't save myself, not with the leg in plaster. Went down. Not hard.

It wasn't the first time I'd tumbled. It was no big deal. I could get myself up, though it would take a bit. But I'd dropped the crutch and it was out of reach.

'Hey.' He reached his hand down and without thinking, I reached up and took it.

He hauled me to my feet, dropped my hand like it was hot, reached down for the crutch, passed it to me.

'Thanks,' I said, tucking it under my arm.

He didn't move. We were close together and there was something about his stillness that wasn't still at all. I could feel the movement of his breath, stirring the air around me.

'Oh Christ, Jarrah,' he said, close to my ear.

And the world changed.

BRIDGET

When Finn is naked you take both his hands in yours. You can feel him shaking, a deep shudder as you draw him down to the next step and the water rises to his thighs, and then to the next, and it rises to his waist and he moans.

The hot night air presses down and the pool – the pond, you remind yourself – is deliciously cool, and you long to sink into it and find Toby. Alone, you'd let your body go limp and drop into it, but you have to bring Finn with you, step by step, you have to introduce him to this world and let him know it's safe. You can't let go of him or he'll fall into horror.

'I've felt him here,' you whisper, stepping onto the bottom of the pool and gently pulling him with you. You can feel the unaccustomed brush of trailing plants, the scatter of leaves under your feet. Finn twitches and startles at every touch and you bring him close so your skins are touching.

'I came out every night and swam with him,' you whisper. 'But the pumps and the chemicals were destroying him. So I got rid of them and made a place where he could be.'

You can see Finn's face in the light coming up from the pool and you know he's thinking you have finally lost your grip. He's afraid of you, but you're so sick of being alone now. You don't want to lose him again.

'Come under,' you whisper.

You both inhale deeply, you lock gazes with him, pull his hand down and let yourself drop below the surface.

The water closes over your head and you open your eyes. *Toby?* You send the thought out. *I'm here!*

Finn is on the other end of your hand, big and warm and alive even in the cool water; perhaps that's why you can't feel Toby. Finn goes up for air but you wait until your lungs start to burn before you surface. You still can't feel him.

'I'm letting you go, just for a minute,' you whisper. 'I'll find him. You'll be OK.'

You start to see pity on his face and you inhale and lower yourself before the hint of it can solidify, and you propel your body, reaching out with both hands, stretching for him.

Toby?

All around you the pool throbs with life. You can sense the fish darting and gliding around the stems of the plants. You can sense the slow, soft scrape of the snails. The water smells of leaves and fish and frogs instead of chlorine.

But no Toby.

You surface, breathe, dive again. Propel yourself to the deep end of the pool, twisting between the plants, sending the fish into a scatter. Nothing.

Your head breaks the surface again.

'Bridget,' Finn says softly, from the shallow end.

'He was here!' you cry. 'He was!'

He glides through the water towards you and reaches to slide a hand down your body, leaving it on your haunch. You can see on his face what it's cost him to swim just that far in this water.

You twist away from him, submerge, breaststroke your way back towards the steps, reaching, reaching. You heard Toby's laugh here. You didn't dream it. Where is he? The whole pool is alive now, just for him.

And he is dead.

You know it, suddenly, deep in your cells. Like you have never known it since the day he drowned.

Finn comes beside you, standing neck-deep in the water, reaches his arms out and wraps them around you, lifting you so you wrap your arms and legs around him, and you wail into his ear, a wail that should terrify any human being, but he's not terrified. His arms tighten as if he would squeeze you into him.

'He's gone.'

'I know,' Finn murmurs, his voice deep and alive.

The pond is not your healing, you realise, as Finn rocks you in the water and the ripples lap at your neck. It's the beginning of your grief breaking upon you. You thought you were ready to climb from the hole, but you haven't even been into the hole yet. Not until today, not until you allowed Finn to be not guilty.

'I'm with you,' he whispers. 'As long as it takes. We just have to forgive ourselves.'

'Never,' you say.

'One day. One day you will.'

You don't believe him. You can't lose something as wondrous as Toby and go on. You must live with being unforgiven as long as you have breath in your body.

'I forgive us,' Finn says.

He gathers you up all over again, as if there were any more of you to gather, and in that living, breathing water that Toby has left forever, melded to Finn, you begin to weep, and of all the weeping this is the first that's reached down into the pain of it, and the first time you've let him come with you. You can feel in his body that he's not afraid, not of this, that he's speaking the truth and he will stay, and in the midst of it you remember Chen, remember the night you put your hand on his chest, and knowing that you took your hand away again makes this somehow more bearable.

You can leave here, you realise.

Finn's body is stirring under yours, your legs are already gripped around his waist and it's simply another wave washing into you when he slides inside and you open yourself and take him in.

EPILOGUE

The boy comes into the night like he owns it, like he is, in fact, God, and has conjured this up: this crescent moon cutting the sky, this bat tonguing the nectar from the eucalyptus blossom, cocking its head to watch with dark eyes and wrapping a leathery wing around its body. This cool slap of water on skin, this warm scent of dew and grass, this scuttle and creep and pursuit of creatures, the shiver that turns the school of fish in a new direction.

He remembers this place. He remembers stepping out into a morning after night rain, and from everywhere rising the scent of soil opening, of grass reaching down to its roots.

He remembers that morning, when he considered his kingdom. *Today, where and what?* He remembers placing a bare foot down and, beneath his sole, the ground damp and alive. He remembers the water calling him, and wanting with his whole being to answer that call. He remembers the fence rearing up in front of him and the invitation and reach of its cool bars in his hands, as he shook and pulled.

He remembers the exhilaration of discovering the grip of fingers and leverage of foot and swing of weight that let him, for the first time, hoist himself up and up and up, let him climb out of his world and over those bars, fly over the top of the fence, king of his world.

This time nothing slows him. He moves from air to water without effort, expanding to lap at the edges, becoming liquid, becoming container and contained, containing everything, the fish, the plants, the skating insects, the leaves beginning to rot, the algae, the two human bodies, the ripples around them, the salty taste of their faces, the arch of a neck, the grip of fingers, the breath. He knows these bodies. He remembers them. He remembers the accident of cells colliding, the moments in which everything changes, the instant in which life divides into before and after.

And then she comes into the world like she owns it – like she is, in fact, God and has conjured this up, this world waiting to take her. She pours herself into liquid, she follows the call, she finds the world and embeds herself into it, ecstatic. She splits into two, into four, into eight, into thirty-two. She knows these bodies, wrapped together in the water. She belongs to them.

She is weightless. She is floating. She is at the centre of the universe.

AUTHOR'S NOTE

It took more than forty years to write this book. Forty years to understand my own sister's death and how it shaped my life, and nearly two to write a fictional story about a family facing a tragedy in some ways like mine.

When I was twelve, my two-year-old sister wandered through an unsecured pool gate. She fell into our backyard pool and drowned.

That event has rippled through my life since 1976, affecting me in known and unknown ways. I wrote about it, aged twenty-eight, in my first attempt at a novel – a piece of thinly disguised autobiography that didn't make it to the bookshelves.

It wasn't until 2014 – as my late sister's fortieth birthday approached – that *Sixty Seconds* leapt into my consciousness, sure of its time and demanding to be written. I finally had the maturity as a writer and a person to make a true creative response to my sister's death.

On the day of her birthday, my father, one of my sisters and my brother gathered around that little headstone in the babies' section of the cemetery where she's buried. There was so much sorrow still with us, but incredible love too. We shared that moment, acknowledging the power of this loss in our lives, acknowledging grief and pain, and acknowledging that this had helped make us who we are.

In the midst of horrific events it's so difficult to understand them, or make sense of them, or believe that you'll ever experience happiness again. They feel so cruel and random and senseless. There's a great deal of self-torturing about the seconds of inattention that lead to accidents. They can cause a lifetime of guilt.

I came to understand that this event had changed my life and my family's lives – dramatically, tragically, powerfully. I also came to see some meaning and beauty in it.

This is a book about going through traumatic experiences and coming to learn they are part of life. It's not my story, nor my family's story. I'm not telling anyone how they should go through grief or that it's good for them. From the perspective of forty years down the track, I'm writing a story in which three people – Finn, Bridget and Jarrah – take the first steps in making sense of tragedy in their lives.

ACKNOWLEDGEMENTS

A number of people helped me navigate the complex terrain of this novel.

Solicitor Adam van Kempen advised me about the legal aspects of my initial idea. Magistrate David Heilpern expanded on that advice, walked me through the background of a relevant case that was being heard at the time, and gave comments on the manuscript.

Shaunagh Cassidy and Warren Dick gave me a police perspective on attending a drowning. Katherine Plint, founder of Hannah's Foundation (which supports families through drowning and near-drowning tragedies), was an eloquent source of information and experience.

Metalwork sculptor Daniel Clemmets set me straight about the mechanics of welding.

Even with such strong advice, I have probably made some mistakes – and they are mine alone.

Special thanks to my aunt Carol Birrell, who was a wise and encouraging companion through the writing of this book, including during our month as joint writers-in-residence of the Island Institute in Sitka, Alaska.

My writers' group provided ongoing advice and support – thanks to Sarah Armstrong, Hayley Katzen, Emma Ashmere and Amanda Webster. Author Carig Cormick gave detailed feedback and author Katherine Heyman also gave me valuable comments early in the manuscript.

My agent Jo Butler generously read the manuscript more than once and provided feedback.

I am grateful to the Australia Council for the Arts for supporting me with a new work grant to write this novel.

Thanks to all at HarperCollins for their enthusiasm and support – particularly Mary Rennie, Jaki Arthur, Alice Wood, Kate O'Donnell and Emma Dowden.

And, of course, thank you to my beloved partner Andi for her unfailing love and support through it all.